P9-CAF-460

CHURCH OF THE OPEN DOOR
Box 177
HAMPDEN, MAINE 04444

Sarah Anne's Expedient Marriage

Book 3 of the Unshakable Faith Series

Cathy Lynn Bryant
Jessica Marie Dorman

BRYANT & DORMAN
BOOKS†

Copyright © 2014 by Cathy Lynn Bryant & Jessica Marie Dorman
BRYANT DORMAN BOOKS†
Bangor, Maine 04401
bryantdormanbooks.com

Printed in the United States of America

All rights reserved. No part of this publication may be reproduced, stored in a retrieval system, or transmitted in any form or by any means: electronic, mechanical, photocopying, recording, or otherwise, without the prior written permission of the authors.

All Scripture references are from the KJV
Library of Congress Control Number: 2014915848

ISBN 13: 978-0692291566

First Edition: September 2014

Our characters include historical figures intermingled with fictional characters.

Endorsements

The setting of Bryant and Dorman's third book has chronologically moved from the "early settlement" period of the Massachusetts Bay Colony in their first two books, to the early 1700s when social classes began to evolve. It was also a time when unscrupulous men took advantage of wealthy, naïve, young ladies. *Sarah Anne's Expedient Marriage* illustrates how God can turn our plans upside down in totally unexpected ways.

The authors plunge the reader into the utter depravity of man. Although the subject is handled with sensitivity, the reader lives through Sarah, as the gut-wrenching shock of such evil clouds her judgment. In her stubbornness, she makes wrong decisions that bring anguish and heartache to the very people she is trying to protect. Yet, the deep faith of Sarah's friends and the relentless search for her by her husband Alexander allow God to weave miracles out of unspeakable tragedy.

If the reader is not used to period writing, the formal grammar and dialogue will take a while to get used to. Once that happens, the book's storyline captivates the reader and the formality is never given a second thought. The selflessness of Sarah in helping others is a welcome contrast to the self-centered nature of our modern generation. If you read this book, you are in for a treat of immersion into the 18th century culture.

Michael S. Coffman Ph.D.

http://www.americaplundered.com/

Authors Cathy Lynn Bryant and Jessica Marie Dorman have once again captured the hearts of their readers with their newest novel titled, "Sarah Anne's Expedient Marriage." I was immediately captivated with the sweetness of Sarah. The unspoken awkwardness of her innocence swept me away as I ventured back to the year 1730 to a picturesque New England Bay Colony. I was moved to tears several times. By the time I reached the conclusion, I did not want to leave. This is a beautiful story that will leave you believing.

Author, L. A. Muse

Acknowledgements

We would like to thank our husbands, Charles Bryant and Nathaniel Dorman, for their support.

Others on our list of people to whom we are most grateful: Kristie Pelletier, Stephen Harvey, Lynn Harvey, Vicki Doolittle, Susan Coffman, Dr. Michael Coffman, Lori Whitty, Valerie McDougal, and Tara Heffner. They willingly offered their time to a thorough read through of the manuscript offering helpful edits and suggestions. Additionally, Jarad Bryant was our tech guru extraordinaire.

We are also grateful to God for His word and all that it teaches regarding healthy relationships.

Prologue

Early summer, the year 1730,
Amesbury, Massachusetts Bay Colony

Alexander Swyndhurst, a recent widower, had agreed to meet with his father's close friend, Mr. Joseph Goodwin. He had only consented to the meeting to please his father and because his father's friend had not been given long to live. Alexander had been informed that the man was seeking a husband for his daughter; nonetheless, he had felt compelled to go—if merely to inform the gentleman that he was not the man for the job.

It had been a week since the meeting had taken place. Alexander was still unsure how he had been persuaded to take another wife, considering that he had no such wish. He had, in fact, sworn that after losing his beloved Rebecca, he would never marry again. And since remaining in the home he had shared with her had simply been too painful for him, he intended to return to England—the land of his birth. A new wife might foil his firmly set plans.

Recalling the relief he had felt after Mr. Goodwin had explained that he had materially provided for his daughter with the income she was to receive from his holdings—Alexander shook his head; for he soon learned that the concerned father's reasons for wanting his daughter wed had nothing to do with basic necessities;

rather, his concerns were purely for her safety.

As Alexander, again, thought over the old gentleman's chief concern, that one man in particular had been a great deal too persistent—even restraining the young woman in her father's barn on one occasion, he felt certain he had not been presented with a choice. And even though the young woman would be left alone with his servants when he returned to England, much as she would have been at her home in Cambridge upon her father's death, there would at least be someone to notify if any trouble developed. Moreover, she would be removing to Amesbury, out of reach of the man her father feared.

Standing there, glancing out the window, the soon-to-be groom thought about the man who had attempted to force his attentions upon Miss Goodwin. He wondered how any man could do such a thing. He then reflected back to what Mr. Goodwin had said regarding the incident. *Thankfully, her father rescued her before she had come to any real harm.*

Shaking his head as he moved away from the window, Alexander wondered yet again how he had gotten himself caught up in the affairs of a young woman he had never even met.

◊◊◊

Sarah Anne, just one and twenty, had always been a dutiful daughter; consequently, though she had wanted to, she had made no argument over her father's request that she marry. As the man she was to wed had little interest in securing a wife and would, therefore, be returning to

England soon after the wedding, Sarah Anne believed she had little to fear in consenting to the marriage—at least that was what she had been telling herself. But as the day of the wedding approached, she spent many hours praying that God would give her the courage to go through with it.

Chapter 1

The year 1730, Amesbury, Massachusetts Bay Colony

It was now midsummer. It had been a few weeks since the marriage had been arranged between Sarah Anne Goodwin and Alexander Swyndhurst II. The day of the wedding was at hand. Nervously, Sarah Anne approached her groom as he stood in front of the magistrate. Since they had met just prior to this day, they knew very little about each other. Swallowing hard, she pressed on and was soon standing beside the man who, in a matter of minutes, would become her husband.

Alexander observed the young woman as she moved in his direction. Just now, he believed that had his heart not been so injured by the loss of his first wife he might have been able to love the beautiful, trembling creature that was ever so slowly approaching. As he studied her, he again noted how very petite she was, so unlike his first wife, who had been nearly six feet tall. When Miss Goodwin's chin lifted in his direction, he observed that she had the loveliest blue eyes he had ever seen. He wondered, then, how he could have overlooked such magnificent eyes. Thinking back to when his father had taken him to meet his future wife, his conscience stung, for he now realized he had paid the young woman little notice that day.

While he continued to observe her, he remembered one thing from their meeting: though her chestnut colored hair was presently swept up, as appropriate for the occasion, it had reached all the way to her waist. He thought once more about her diminutive size in relation to the situation from which her father had wished to protect her and was now certain he had made the right decision. This tiny woman needed his protection. He even felt a twinge of guilt over the fact that he would soon be leaving for England without her. *The servants will look after her*, he consoled himself. *What is more, she shall be far away from that beast of a man who threatens her safety.*

Now positioned beside the man she was about to marry, Sarah Anne sensed that, as he stood towering over her, his eyes were upon her. Though she had no desire to marry, to her, Mr. Swyndhurst was quite striking with his dark-brown hair, bluish-green eyes, and broad shoulders. It was a bit unsettling for her, however, that the top of her head was not much higher than his lowermost ribs. Yes, she knew she was rather small, at a height of just over five feet; but, she reasoned, he was also a bit out of the ordinary, at just shy of six-and-a-half feet tall. *If he were to remain in Amesbury, I am certain I would not have married him. It is just too frightening a thought.*

With the nuptials over in the space of a few minutes, the pair hastened out the door as husband and wife. The awkwardness they both felt was obvious to all. Before long, Alexander had conveyed the young woman to his estate and introduced her to the servants. Her belongings had preceded her, but she had not, until this day, set foot in her new home. When Sarah Anne and Alexander had met before their wedding day, it had been at her home in Cambridge.

Upon their arrival, the head servant, Martha Fowler, a stout, elderly woman, took her new mistress to her bedchamber, where her things had already been placed. It was located on the upper floor at the far end of a long hall, beyond several unoccupied rooms. Martha's room was adjacent to Sarah Anne's.

To Sarah Anne's dismay, her father had not lived long enough to see her married. With his death occurring just days before her wedding, and not having the benefit of time alone to grieve, she had yet to feel the full pain of the loss. Thus, standing alone in an unfamiliar bedchamber, the distraught young woman finally allowed her tears to flow.

Though the room was quite elegant, Sarah Anne scarcely noticed all that it held, such as the lovely oak bedstead with its intricately carved rose-petal design, the half-dozen lace pillows neatly arranged at the head, and the soft, blue quilt situated at the foot. In addition, on the west side of the room a small settee had been placed a few feet from a little window which overlooked the front yard. It was there that Sarah Anne, still weeping, slumped down and buried her face in its plush seat cushion.

After a few moments, hoping to distract herself from the sorrow, which at the moment was all consuming, she stood up and began inspecting her bedchamber. She immediately noticed an alcove off to one side. As she entered, she observed a maple-wood washstand with a flowery china pitcher and washbasin atop. To the side of the washbasin sat a delicate glass bowl filled with several colorful soaps. Wiping at her tears, she looked up. Just above the washstand hung a brass framed looking glass, which, of course, was hung too high for Sarah's needs. To the left was a wooden cabinet standing about a foot-and-a-half high, in which a chamber pot was placed to keep it out of sight. The lid of the cabinet was sturdy enough to set the chamber pot upon when in use. As she came out of the alcove, she covered her mouth, for though she had tried to stop, her weeping had begun again.

Martha, the head servant, happened to be walking by just then and overheard the mournful cries coming from within Sarah Anne's bedchamber. Her heart broke for her new mistress, for she was aware of the circumstances surrounding the nuptials. Mr. Swyndhurst had informed her that Sarah Anne's father, Mr. Goodwin, had desired for his daughter to come under his protection through an arranged marriage between himself and the young woman. He had assured her that he still intended to follow through with his plans for returning to England, along with his father, and that she would be left to look after the new Mrs. Swyndhurst. Upon hearing the news, the servant had surmised that, had it not been a marriage in name only, her employer would likely not have gone through with it, for his heart still clearly belonged to Rebecca, her former mistress.

Martha had been wondering since Sarah Anne's arrival whether the young woman had been afforded any say in what had taken place, or had her father simply arranged the marriage, leaving her no alternative but to abide by his wishes. As the elderly woman stood there listening at the door, she wondered why, seeing as the poor thing was so distraught, she hadn't simply refused the arrangement. *It would have been easy enough, considering that her father had passed before her wedding day arrived. Perhaps her sorrow has more to do with the loss of her father, rather than her new circumstances. In any case, I shall give her until tomorrow. If she hasn't come out of her bedchamber by then, I shall just have to knock on the door and see for myself that she is well.*

◊◊◊

Though Alexander had desired to bid his new wife farewell before setting off on the long journey to England, she had not come out of her bedchamber since their arrival the night before. Not wanting to linger in Amesbury after the nuptials, Alexander had unexpectedly been able to make arrangements to set sail the day after the wedding.

Presently, however, the new husband was having second thoughts about leaving so soon, for Martha had informed him earlier that morning that Sarah Anne had been crying, almost constantly, from the time they had first arrived. As theirs was not the sort of union that would allow such a personal conversation—had he gone to his new wife—he felt helpless as to what to do for her. Thus, with heavy hearts, the father and son departed, both a little sorrowful for leaving the young woman in such a state.

Martha knocked on Sarah Anne's door late the same day her employer and his father had set off for England. "Mrs. Swyndhurst, you must eat something. Will you not open the door?"

All at once, looking a bit embarrassed, Sarah Anne appeared. "I must apologize, Miss Martha. I should not have been so rude as to stay in my room for so long. It is just that so much has happened of late that I needed to be alone. You see, my father passed not long ago, and now I am to live in a new home away from everything and everyone I have ever known. But I do not mean to complain, for it is clear that God has seen fit to allow me a new friend."

While smiling at Sarah Anne's comment about having a new friend, Martha patted the young woman's shoulder and said, "Mrs. Swyndhurst—"

Breaking in, the new bride said, "No, Miss Martha. Please, do call me Sarah. I have no wish to be addressed so formally, and Father was the only one who ever called me by my full name—Sarah Anne."

"Very well, then, Sarah. But only if you stop addressing me as 'Miss' Martha. To everyone here, I am simply Martha. Now, you must eat. Will you not come down and sit while I fix something for you?"

"All right, M...Martha. I shall be but a moment. This face needs a little tending to," the petite woman replied while forcing a smile.

Within a few minutes, Sarah had joined Martha in the kitchen. The elderly woman soon approached the table with a tray of food. As the two conversed, Sarah picked at her food. After she had eaten all that she desired, Martha gave her a tour of her new home. As they made their way to every room in the house, the older woman introduced her to the rest of the servants. To Sarah's great delight, she found that one of them, Esther Pike, was nearly the same age as she, and within a few days the young women were nearly inseparable.

As the days progressed, Sarah longed to be useful; thus, she often followed after Esther, assisting the young servant with many of her daily chores.

After a time, Sarah had made the acquaintance of many of the townsfolk, particularly those with whom she attended church. Out of her newly formed relationships, the young wife elatedly found herself busier than she had ever thought possible, what with helping the sick and visiting her new friend—a young widow by the name of

Alice Strout and her three children. She had dreaded the move to a new town where she knew not a soul; however, as she found that she was greatly needed, she began to feel as though she belonged in Amesbury.

In the many weeks and months that followed, Martha, Esther, and the rest of the servants had grown very fond of Sarah. In fact, Sarah had endeared herself to everyone she met. For Martha in particular, not having a child of her own, she had quickly grown to love Sarah like a daughter.

Chapter 2

While on his journey to England, Alexander thought a great deal about his new wife. Even though he was still in a bit of shock over how quickly his life had changed—losing one wife and marrying another in less than two years' time—he prayed that God would watch over the wife he had left behind in Amesbury.

Upon the father and son's arrival at the family estate in Bristol, England, they were happily greeted by Robert Hamilton, the head servant. He had been looking forward to the return of the senior Mr. Swyndhurst ever since he had gone away. Unexpectedly for Robert, however, both father and son had arrived together. Knowing how his employer, the elder Mr. Swyndhurst, felt about his son, the servant was overjoyed that the young man had come along with his father. Robert was also aware of the tragic death of his employer's daughter-in-law, Rebecca, for the sorrowful father had sent word that his son's wife had died as a result of smallpox. That was some time ago now. Robert had even begun to wonder whether his employer would ever return.

While maintaining possession of his estate in England, the elder Mr. Swyndhurst had left England to visit his son. When his daughter-in-law suddenly died, he had felt the need to stay on for a time with his grieving son. Then, while tending to some business in Boston, he made the acquaintance of Joseph Goodwin, his new daughter-in-law's father. Given that the two gentlemen had become fast friends, when Mr. Goodwin had shared his troubles concerning his impending death with the elder Mr. Swyndhurst, he readily agreed to assist him in securing protection for his daughter. It didn't take Mr. Swyndhurst long to consider his own son for the task.

As the two downcast men entered the house, the head servant moved to assist them with their belongings. He then directed the cook to prepare the weary travelers something to eat. After some conversation and a bit of nourishment, quite exhausted, the father and son made their way to their individual bedchambers.

Before turning in for the night, the concerned father knelt down beside his bed. He then beseeched the Lord on his son's behalf that one day very soon Alexander would return to Amesbury to live with his wife, Sarah Anne. He had not let on to his son that this was his wish all along. He and his dying friend—the young woman's father—had secretly prayed that their children would one day come together, under one roof, as husband and wife. Since Mr. Swyndhurst, Sr.'s, friend was gone now, it was up to him to daily pray about the matter.

The following day, the two Swyndhurst men were up with the sun. The father arrived in the dining room ahead of his son, whom, after such a long journey, he had not thought to see much before midday. Nonetheless, following the older man's arrival to breakfast, within a few minutes his son appeared. The head servant was also quite astonished to find the two gentlemen up so early. Smiling, he quickly directed the cook to prepare breakfast for them. Later that afternoon while father and son were reclining in the parlor, the elder Mr. Swyndhurst inquired as to how his son was fairing. His son, a man of only thirty, had experienced many changes in his life, and all in a relatively short time.

Still feeling a bit numb over all that had happened, the younger of the Swyndhurst men wasn't exactly sure how to respond. "Father, I believe I have not yet sorted out my feelings. The only thing of which I am sure is that my heart still aches for Rebecca. And yet, in hearing the distraught woman, who is now my wife, crying behind her bedchamber door before we set off on our journey, my heart hurt for her as well. Through no fault of her own, she has also suffered a great loss and had her life completely altered. I shall be praying for her that she overcomes any fears she may be experiencing, relating to her circumstances."

The father felt hope in his heart for the first time concerning his son and daughter-in-law's marriage. To his mind, if Alexander could think beyond his own pain to Sarah Anne's, then perhaps his heart would change with regard to a future with her. Realizing he hadn't indicated that he had heard what his son had said, the older man responded, "How good of you, Alexander. I shall be praying for her as well. From what her father disclosed to me about his relationship with Sarah Anne, with her mother long since passed, they meant everything to each other. She must be heartbroken over his passing. And for one who had always been under her father's protection to now be for all intents and purposes on her own, the young woman must be quite frightened."

Hearing his father's words did little to relieve Alexander's concerns for his young wife; they had in fact had quite the opposite effect. He now felt worse than before. While rubbing his hand across the back of his neck, he responded, "I know, Father. But what was I to do about it? I am in no frame of mind to be a husband to the girl. Besides, Martha and the other servants shall look after her needs. It isn't as though she is living in that house all alone." Then, dropping his head, he fell silent.

Seeing the pain flash across his son's face, Mr. Swyndhurst, Sr., felt that perhaps he had said too much. "I beg your pardon, Alexander. You have done a very good thing in marrying the girl and bringing her into your home in Amesbury. I know it wasn't your wish to remarry and that you only did it for Sarah Anne and her father. Do not think on it any longer. You are correct in saying that it is not as though she is on her own. Furthermore, Martha is sure to send word if the girl is in need of anything."

With his head still low, Alexander nodded. He knew his father had not meant to injure him with his words concerning Sarah Anne and her state of mind. He also sensed that his father was now trying to console him after speaking thus. The last thing Alexander wanted was to cause tension between himself and his father.

Believing his son needed to be alone with his thoughts the elder Mr. Swyndhurst rose to his feet. While passing by Alexander on his way out of the room, the father patted the younger man's shoulder. "I believe I shall leave you to yourself for a while."

Alexander glanced up and said, "Very well, Father." The two men were not together again until the following day. The elder Mr. Swyndhurst decided not to broach the subject of his daughter-in-law again. If his son wished to discuss Sarah Anne, he would have to initiate the conversation. The older man felt that, in handling things in that way, he was less likely to say something he shouldn't.

◊◊◊

A few months had passed when the younger Mr. Swyndhurst received a missive from Martha, his head servant. Anxious to read it, he made his way to his bedchamber.

As with Mr. Swyndhurst, Sr., the compassionate servant had begun to pray that the couple would eventually come together as husband and wife. Even though she had only known Sarah a short time, she felt that without her husband there to look after her, she would continually be at the mercy of those who had been taking advantage of the young woman's kind and charitable nature. And yet she wondered if having Mr. Swyndhurst return would be the right thing, for she was certain Sarah had no wish to be married, at least not in the traditional sense. To Martha, her mistress seemed quite content to be the wife of an absent husband. In the time that the young woman had been there, she had rarely even spoken of him. Martha believed that, to Sarah, it was as if Mr. Swyndhurst didn't really exist.

Sitting by the window in his bedchamber, Alexander opened the missive from his servant-friend. As he read, he found himself hoping there would be news of Sarah Anne. She had been on his mind ever since he had taken leave of Amesbury. As he scanned the missive for word of his wife, his eyes met her name scrawled halfway down the page. Eagerly, he read on. It seemed that without saying as much, Martha was intimating that she had some concerns relating to his wife. As his servant wrote not a word regarding the nature of her concerns, he wasn't exactly certain what it was that had been worrying her. *I wish she would have just come out with it. She must have known that I would wish to be informed if there were any real trouble. I shall simply have to send off a missive of my own to inquire as to the reason for her concern.* Later that day, Alexander did exactly that.

After a few months, the concerned husband received a response—from Martha—to his missive that all was well and that he should not worry. Unbeknownst to him, his head servant had decided it had been unfair of her to burden her employer with something over which, given that he was so far away, he had little control.

Though his servant had thought to ease his mind by her subsequent missive, had she been there when it arrived, she would have seen that it accomplished very little in that regard, for Mr. Swyndhurst still believed that there was something his elderly servant-friend was not telling him.

Chapter 3

1732, Amesbury, Massachusetts Bay Colony

As Sarah had such a kind heart, she had taken on many of the responsibilities of running the estate, including assisting the servants with several of their duties. She had also befriended a couple of the neighbors who had a tendency to lean a bit too heavily upon her. On more than one occasion, Martha had observed that Sarah was working herself to the point of complete exhaustion.

One of the neighbors, Alice Strout, a widow of but eight and twenty, had three youngsters to look after. Sarah had often gone to the Strouts' in order to assist Alice with the children. Mary, the youngest, was just two years of age. The other two—Elizabeth and Samuel—were nine and ten. Mary had begun to think of Sarah much the same as another mother, even more so, at times, than her own mother, given that Alice Strout had not the natural inclinations for the role. The older Strout children also adored Sarah and eagerly looked forward to her visits.

Another of the neighbors upon whom Sarah regularly called was an elderly, blind woman by the name of Addy Johnson. Sarah went two times a week to read to the woman, and while there she always found a chore or two that needed doing. On top of that, Sarah spent a good deal of time with her church family in whatever capacity she was most needed, which often times meant paying a visit to the sick from amongst the flock.

Sarah's busy schedule had been going on for some time when Martha finally decided she needed to have a word with the young woman. Oh, she had tried numerous times to speak with her mistress about her concerns, but since her words always seemed to be ignored, Martha now intended, if necessary, to be harsh with her. A while back, she had attempted to send word to Sarah's husband regarding the situation; however, after receiving word back from the worried man, she had thought better of it. From so far away, he could do little else but worry. She had decided then that it rested with her to see to the young woman's well-being.

Another worrisome fact for Martha was that in the time she had known her, Sarah had never had much of an appetite. In fact, it took great effort on the part of the head servant to get the young woman to eat more than a few bites of food on any given day. And even though Sarah had always been rather thin, lately she appeared, to Martha, to be nothing but skin and bones. Esther, one of the other servants, had also taken notice of her friend's frail condition and had shared her concerns with the head servant, which only served to bolster Martha's resolve to take the matter in hand once and for all. She would not allow Sarah to brush her fears for her aside any longer.

Finding the young woman in the kitchen heating water, Martha said forcefully, "Sarah, you cannot continue on in this way, taking care of everyone from sun up to sun down, and with very little to eat, I might add! You are going to work yourself into an early grave." This was said one evening when Sarah had returned after a long day at the home of Alice Strout. Martha had observed that Sarah's face appeared even more gaunt than it had that morning—indicating that, once again, she had most likely gone all day without food.

"Not to worry, Martha. I am quite all right. I shall try to do better about getting nourishment. It is just that I simply don't think of it whenever I am busy doing other things."

"That is just not natural, Sarah. God has given us hunger pangs for a reason. People do not just simply forget to eat."

"I know. I don't understand it myself. I believe it is just that I simply get distracted. I have to remember that my body requires food. It is only when I begin to feel weak that I remember to eat something; nevertheless, I shall try to do better."

"Proper rest would be of benefit as well. You must allow that Alice Strout woman to learn to take care of her own children. Though she behaves like one, she is not an invalid."

"Now, Martha. You must not think so ill of her. You know as well as I do that, since she was raised by her father, she doesn't know much about such things."

"She might know more if you were not always doing everything for her. Whenever I see her in church, she looks well rested and well fed. It is not a wonder either. She has you making the meals and taking care of her children's every need. Truth be told, you are practically living with that family."

"Martha, you do have a tendency to exaggerate where she is concerned. I am only there a few days a week."

"Maybe so, but you must admit that when you are not playing slave to her, you are either reading to our blind neighbor or visiting any number of the sick from church. All I am trying to say, my girl, is you must learn to restrain your giving nature a bit, or you shall be of no use to anyone when your own health fails."

"I shall try, Martha," she responded with a sigh. Wanting to put the matter to rest, she asked, "May we talk of something else?"

"Very well, but I must know; are you going to stay at home tomorrow? As I have said, you need a rest."

"I shall do that very thing the day after tomorrow." Surreptitiously glancing over at the pinched face now glaring at her, she continued, "I am sorry, Martha, but I have already made plans to be at Alice's tomorrow."

"I might as well talk to that wall over there, for you never hear a word I say!" the frustrated servant said while pointing at the wall.

"Pray forgive me, Martha. I do, really I do, but I cannot leave her to herself tomorrow. I am to take care of the children while she—"

"Yes, while she what? Takes a bath, reads a book, or some other leisurely activity?"

"Well...I...I believe I shall go and take a bath myself," the young woman said with a sheepish grin. "Would you mind asking Peter to carry the hot water into the buttery for me when it is ready?" She had put it on to heat just before Martha had come into the kitchen. "He was good enough to carry in the wooden tub from the laundry for me a little while ago. I do hate to bother him, but he is much stronger than I."

"I can see that you wish to change the subject. I shall allow it as long as you are finally going to do something for yourself. I shall send Peter in to fill the tub as soon as the water has heated."

Sarah thanked Martha and then went to her bedchamber to gather up the things she would need for her bath. Within a short while, she was tucked away, behind a closed door, in the buttery. Taking a bath was a luxury—one of the few in which she often allowed herself to take pleasure. Once the water had cooled to the point that the young woman was becoming a bit chilled, she decided it was time to climb out, dry off, and don her nightdress. Besides, she now felt quite exhausted and thought it best to turn in for the night.

Later, while snuggled in her bed, Sarah gave some thought to what Martha had said. She knew it was true that she had not been taking proper care of herself, but as she thought about it, she didn't much care. Her friends needed her. "I am grateful, Lord, that someone—other than You, of course—cares for me. Bless Martha, Lord. She is such a kind soul. Before she came into my life, I missed Mother so very much. With Martha here with me every day, some of my longing for Mother has diminished."

Chapter 4

1732, Bristol, England

Things had been going on unaltered for the nearly two years the husband and wife had been living apart: Sarah working herself to death—to the chagrin of Martha—and Alexander attempting to recover from the loss of his beloved Rebecca. As time went by, the prayers Alexander had been lifting up on behalf of his new wife had not only been increasing in frequency, they had unexpectedly affected his own heart. Truth be told, he now found himself thinking more often of Sarah Anne than Rebecca, and a desire started growing within him to return to Amesbury.

When he came to his father one day to explain what he had been thinking about, with regard to Sarah Anne, his father had all but cried. It had been his sincere wish all along that his son and daughter-in-law would come together, under one roof, as husband and wife. With his father's blessing, Alexander began making plans to return to Amesbury.

The arrangements had been quickly settled. The days leading up to Alexander's departure hastened on.

With his journey nearly at hand, he wondered again if he had made the right decision about keeping his impending arrival to himself, or if he should have sent word of his coming. He had thought long on it, and decided against informing his servants and wife that he was returning. He wasn't even sure how his wife was going to feel once she learned that he intended to stay on with her at their Amesbury estate. Just now, he felt a little relieved that he had discussed the matter with his father, or his angst about how he was handling things, he believed, would be even more severe.

When he had asked his father's opinion on the matter, his father had agreed that perhaps he should set off without making his plans known. He also worried about his daughter-in-law's reaction, for she had agreed to the marriage under the assumption that it wouldn't be a traditional marriage. Having knowledge of what had happened to the young woman in her former town by a man who had attempted to force his intentions upon her, the elder Mr. Swyndhurst hoped and prayed she would not be fearful at the prospect of having her husband living under the same roof with her.

The day had come for Alexander to set sail for Amesbury. The father and son, through tears, said their goodbyes, not knowing when they would see each other again. Turning to leave, once his son's ship had sailed, Mr. Swyndhurst, Sr., prayed that his son would arrive in

Amesbury safely. He also prayed that Sarah Anne's heart would be prepared for the alteration in her situation.

◊ ◊ ◊

After a few weeks at sea, the husband's excitement at starting a new life with Sarah Anne became difficult to contain. He knew it wasn't going to be easy getting his wife to agree to the change, but he prayed that eventually she would be happy to have him there.

Something occurred to the young husband on one of the final nights of his journey; he realized that his thoughts had been so consumed with Sarah Anne he had given little thought to Rebecca. He was more than a little astonished at himself, for at one time he had believed himself incapable of ever caring for another woman. To his delight, he had been wrong.

At first he had felt a bit guilty for having pushed Rebecca from his mind; however, he soon realized that it was as it should be. Rebecca was safely in the arms of her Lord. Sarah Anne was the one that needed him now. As he thought about it, he knew he needed her, too.

Chapter 5

The morning came, and Sarah, as expected, set off for Alice Strout's home. Martha stood helplessly in the doorway, praying her young mistress would come to her senses and cease from busying herself to such an extent, in the service of others. The elderly servant dearly loved the girl, and continued to be more than a little anxious about her welfare.

It had been twelve weeks since Alexander had set sail for Amesbury. On this day, at around noontime, he arrived at his home in Amesbury. In the two years Mr. Swyndhurst resided in England, his new wife had remained at his estate in Amesbury. Though he wasn't certain what would come of his returning, he knew he had to at least try and make a go of his marriage.

As he entered the parlor, his servant-friend Martha looked up at the sound of someone approaching. Alexander smiled with delight at the sweet woman staring back at him. He had missed his old friend more than he had ever thought possible.

As her employer's face came into focus, the elderly woman was completely stunned. "Mr. Swyndhurst! I...I had no idea you were coming home.

After chuckling at Martha's reaction to his arrival, Alexander responded, "Martha, it is good to see you. As it was late when my ship arrived in Salisbury, I lodged there at the ordinary. I know I was not expected, but I thought I might surprise you, rather than send word of my coming."

"That, you did," she replied with a rather large smile. Martha had earnestly loved Alexander Swyndhurst ever since he was a boy. She had worked for his father when Alexander was very small. Following that, when, as a grown man, Alexander had removed from England to Amesbury, she had come along to continue looking after his needs.

"Is Mrs. Swyndhurst about? I should let her know I am here."

"She isn't here at present. As usual, she is out on one of her missions of mercy. Are you here for a lengthy stay, or shall you soon be returning to England?"

"In truth, Martha, I hope to be here for some time. I believe you are aware of the agreement that Mrs. Swyndhurst and I had made upon entering into our marriage; that is, that we would always live separately."

Eyes wide, she nodded in affirmation, all the while wondering if her prayers had finally been answered. *Has he at last come home to be with Sarah?*

"Well, I am not at all certain that my wife shall be agreeable to my returning here to live, but that is exactly why I have come."

It is as I had hoped. I believe he actually intends to stay on here with Sarah. A bit flustered, she questioned him in order to be sure she had understood him correctly. "Is that your plan—to remain here, in Amesbury?"

"Yes, that is my hope, Martha."

As the elderly woman contemplated a moment about what might be the best approach for her employer to take with Sarah, she suggested, "Maybe you should not tell your wife right away. Give her some time to get used to you being around before letting on that you mean to stay."

"You may be right. For the time being, then, I shall put off telling her."

"Not that I am unhappy to see you, but what brought about this change?"

"After a time, my heart began to heal over the loss of Rebecca. With a clearer mind, I realized that it was not right that I had left my young wife alone. Oh, I know it was the agreement we had made, but maybe she has had a change of heart as well."

"Or you may just scare the poor thing half to death when she comprehends the reason you have come."

"You believe she shall not want me here, then?"

"No...no, she is not at all like that. She is eager to please everyone—too eager, in my opinion. I would not wish for her to go along with your plan unless it is what she desires as well. The difficulty is that we may never know what it is that she wants, as she is not likely to tell us. No matter what, Mr. Swyndhurst, I believe your place is here. But as for a marriage in the traditional sense, my advice is that you not rush the girl."

"As you have suggested, I shall be patient and give her time to get accustomed to me before I divulge that I wish to alter our agreement. Where is she? In her bedchamber?"

"As I have said, Sarah is not here. She is at Alice Strout's house for the day and most likely shall remain until late in the evening," she replied, grimacing.

"Who is Alice Strout, and why are you unhappy about Sarah Anne going to her house?"

"Alice is a young widow with three children. She uses our girl very ill—in my opinion. Your wife goes over to help her several days a week. The woman takes great advantage of Sarah's giving nature. But you must not let on that I said so. Sarah does not share my view on the matter. Mr. Swyndhurst, sit yourself down and I shall tell you all about your young wife."

"Very well, Martha. As Peter is tending to my belongings, I shall remain here with you as long as you like. In truth, I am most grateful to learn whatever I can about Sarah Anne."

"Are you hungry? I could go to the kitchen and prepare you something."

"No need. I breakfasted in Salisbury."

"Some tea, then?"

"No, I am fine, Martha. But I am anxious to hear all about Sarah Anne, so please do go on."

After they each had taken a seat, Martha began, "First, let me say that Sarah wishes to be addressed simply as Sarah, not Sarah Anne, or even Mrs. Swyndhurst."

"Very well. I am obliged to you for telling me. Please continue."

"Certainly. To begin with, Mr. Swyndhurst, your wife is one of the most giving, loving, as well as self-sacrificing people I have ever known—even to a fault."

"How can you find fault with such noble attributes?" Mr. Swyndhurst inquired with a furrowed brow.

"You shall soon see that your wife is so busy caring for everyone else that she takes little interest in seeing to her own needs."

"There are others besides the Strout woman?"

"Indeed there are. A day or two every week she reads to Mrs. Johnson, our elderly blind neighbor. As I have said, three or four days a week she spends much of the day, sometimes late into the evening with the Strout family. Quite often, she visits the sick from church. When she has time, she even helps out the servants here with their chores. Believe me, that was not an exhaustive list. She finds many other things to do as well."

"It sounds as if she does not have a moment to herself. Was this what you were alluding to in the first missive I received from you, after returning to England? I felt then that you were trying to tell me something. It was a little frustrating that you did not come right out and say what was on your mind. Since you never mentioned anything along the same lines again in any of your other missives, I allowed the matter to drop."

"Yes...well...I began to believe it wasn't exactly fair of me to burden you with it, as you were so far away."

"Oh, well, that is understandable, I suppose," Mr. Swyndhurst replied.

"As you are here now, I shall continue to explain what it was that I had been, and still am, concerned about. From what I have just disclosed, you may understand why I believe that Sarah is working herself into an early grave. I cannot get her to alter her schedule one little bit. She does not even take time to eat. You shall see what I mean the moment you lay eyes on her. She is nothing but skin and bones." All at once, a grin came upon Martha's face. Not that she was making light of the situation with her mistress, but she had just had a pleasing thought. "Mr. Swyndhurst, you might be just the one to take her in hand. Lord knows I have tried."

Alexander grew concerned after listening to all that Martha had shared about his young wife. He had already lost one wife; he was not about to lose another. "I am much obliged to you for telling me, Martha. In time, I shall speak with her about all that she is doing. If she doesn't alter her activities, I shall simply insist that she abide by my wishes. I shall dislike having to be forceful about it, but I am not going to allow her to become ill simply because she is working too hard. You can depend on that!" After hearing himself speak concerning his wife, Alexander began to doubt what he might actually say to Sarah if she continued on as she had been before his arrival. *Do I really have the right? It is not as though I have showed her any concern before now. To her, I am little more than a stranger.*

Not aware of her employer's thoughts regarding his right to require anything of his wife, Martha felt as though God had sent him along to take care of Sarah. *That young woman needs direction, and he is just the man to do it. Whenever he admonished Rebecca, he handled her kindly, but firmly. That one was always a bit too full of herself—so unlike Sarah. Any reproving the first Mrs. Swyndhurst had needed was never for being too self-sacrificing. More often than not, it had been for speaking too sharply to one of the servants. I know Mr. Swyndhurst loved Rebecca, but Sarah— she is just such a dear. She shall be easy for him to love.*

Following his conversation with Martha, disappointed that he hadn't yet seen Sarah, Alexander retired to his bedchamber for a rest.

Chapter 6

While her employer napped, Martha remained in the kitchen to await Sarah's return. Late in the evening, looking much the worse for wear, the young woman finally came through the door.

Turning to her mistress, Martha said with a sigh, "You look simply dreadful! What kept you so long?"

With a tired smile, Sarah answered, "Thank you for the compliment. Alice was so exhausted I simply could not get away until now. In fact, I believe she is coming down with something. She was feverish all day. With their mother sick, the children needed someone to put them to bed."

"Sarah, you are a lovely young lady, but when you are this spent, it is not that easy to perceive."

"I am quite all right, Martha. I just need a little rest."

"You say Alice was exhausted, what about you? Could she not see that you are done in as well?"

Mr. Swyndhurst had come down from his bedchamber just as the conversation in the kitchen had commenced. Given that Martha was scolding his wife, he decided it was best to wait a moment before going in. He was also curious to hear what Martha had to say, for he couldn't remember her ever speaking in such a way to Rebecca, and he was quite certain that if she had, Rebecca would not have reacted as calmly as apparently Sarah was now. As things in the kitchen began to calm a bit, he entered. Moving into the room, he glanced down at the back of his wife's head. Not wanting to interrupt, he stood silently behind Sarah and continued to listen.

"Martha, I am sorry that I continually cause you to worry. I really am trying to do better. It is just that the children needed someone to look after them with their mother feeling so poorly. Have some pity for her. After all, she is raising the children all by herself."

By this time, Martha, though distracted by her conversation with Sarah for a moment, had noticed that Mr. Swyndhurst had come into the kitchen. Thinking about how her young friend might react to her husband's arrival, she was now paying little attention to what Sarah was saying. Deciding to break the news, she said softly, "Sarah, your husband has come home."

Stunned, Sarah asked, "When? Where is he now?" All at once, she heard Alexander clear his throat. It startled her so much that she gasped.

Answering her question, he replied, "I arrived last night. As it was very late, I stayed in Salisbury and set off for home after a leisurely meal this morning. It is good to see you, Sarah."

By now, Sarah had turned around to face Alexander. Given the differences in their heights, the petite woman had to tilt her head up to look at him. "I was not aware that you were coming," she said breathlessly. Feeling her face flush, she felt the need to distract herself from the panic that had arisen within her. While fiddling with her hands, nervously, she inquired, "Did you have a smooth journey?"

As Alexander answered Sarah's question, he held out a chair for her. "Indeed, it was a fine journey. I decided to surprise you all rather than send word of my coming."

While Martha bustled about preparing food for the couple to eat, Alexander took a seat at the table next to his wife. Before long, their elderly friend approached them with two trenchers full of summer vegetables, cold chicken, and fresh bread.

Seeing the food, Sarah began to protest. "Martha, you needn't have gone to so much trouble. It is late. You should have been in bed hours ago. Besides, I believe I am much too tired to eat."

Scowling, Martha glanced at Mr. Swyndhurst and then back at Sarah. "Sarah, you must eat something. I highly doubt that you have had anything at all to eat today."

"I...ah...am certain that I have," she responded while looking away from Martha's penetrating gaze. Truth be told, she could not remember whether she had in fact had anything to eat the entire day. As she thought about it, she realized she actually hadn't.

At this point, Mr. Swyndhurst and Martha looked at each other. Martha finally indicated by a nod that he should be the one to speak.

"Sarah, Martha informs me that you tend to pass your days without taking much food. It might be best if you try and eat something. You are looking rather slight."

Upon learning that her elderly friend had shared such a thing with her husband, whom she scarcely knew, Sarah's faced reddened with embarrassment. She didn't know what to say. It would be a lie to say that she had eaten. And even though she wished Martha hadn't made such a fuss, she didn't want to cause her any added concern. "Perhaps you are right. I shall try and eat at least a little, since you have gone to the trouble of fixing this fine meal."

Martha felt relief wash over her as she observed that Sarah had begun to eat. *With her husband here, she might just put on a little weight. Just maybe, she shall leave off from working herself to death as well.*

With his eyes fixed on his wife, Alexander said, "Sarah, I thought we might go for a walk tomorrow. I would be delighted to know more about what you have been doing while I have been away."

Sarah felt a jolt in her stomach as he spoke. *I wonder what this is all about. Why is he even here? I feel ill. How am I to eat now? Martha shall not be happy with me if I do not.* Agitatedly, she responded, "Well...I have plans to go to Alice's tomorrow. You see, she felt feverish today, so I am needed to look after the children. I am planning to remain there until she is well. I only came home tonight to get a few things. Had I known I would be needed, I would have brought along enough changes of clothing to last for a few days. But I think they can get by until tomorrow, when I am to return. Perhaps when I come back, we might take a walk." She knew she was rambling on, but having her husband home set her on edge.

"I shall be leaving in a couple of days. I was truly hoping we might have at least a few moments together tomorrow."

With relief that she had avoided spending time with her husband, Sarah responded, unconvincingly, "I would have enjoyed that. I am sorry that I shall be otherwise occupied." *He is planning to journey back to England so soon. His time shall be so short, I wonder at his reason for even coming. Ah well, no matter—all the better for me. I should not wish to have him questioning my dietary habits any longer.* "Well, I shall be praying for your safe journey back to England." That much was true. She did not wish any harm to befall him.

Seeing that Sarah was clearly relieved by the belief that he would soon be leaving, with a sigh he responded, "No...what I meant to say was that I am taking a short trip to see to some matters of business. I shall be away but a few days."

Supposing this to be the reason he had come—for business purposes—she wondered how long he intended to stay. "Then, you are not leaving for England right away?"

"No...I am not." He decided to follow Martha's

advice and not let on, just yet, that he would not be returning to England. "Perhaps when we both return, we might have a day together."

Whatever can he want? He is so insistent. For two years we have done just fine, going about our own business, not bothering with each other. While glancing down at the table to rein in her thoughts—she finally formed a response, "To be sure. I shall not schedule anything when I return. Well, I must turn in. With Alice feeling poorly, I have a long few days ahead, I imagine. I am much obliged to you, Mar—" Unbeknownst to Sarah, her elderly friend had slipped out of the room to allow the couple time alone.

"She left a few moments ago. I suspect she wanted to give us some privacy. Allow me to escort you to your bedchamber." He then took hold of Sarah's hand to help her to her feet. As his wife stood up, he noticed that she started to sway. Suspecting that she was weak from her ordeal at the Strouts' home, he quickly grabbed hold of her arm to steady her.

"I must be more tired than I thought," she said, with heat rising in her cheeks.

The worried husband glanced down at his wife's ashen face. While forcing himself to smile, he directed her from the room. As they walked, Sarah was keenly aware of his hand resting gently on her back.

The two ascended the stairs together. As Alexander stopped at Sarah's bedchamber, he bid her goodnight. She nodded, and then turned toward the door. While attempting to adjust to the idea that her husband was actually there, she could not make herself move forward into her bedchamber. Turning again, she watched him as he walked away. Then, shaking her head, she turned and entered her room, determined not to think about him any longer. She needed her rest, for she intended to be up with the sun—when she would gather up the few things she would need and then set off for Alice's. Worrying over how she was going to manage having Alexander at home, no matter how briefly, would only rob her of her sleep. She resolved not to allow that to happen. As weak as she felt, just now, she knew she would need every bit of strength she could muster to get through the next few days.

Chapter 7

Early the next morning, just after sunup—with her bundle in hand, Sarah set off for Alice's. Upon her arrival, she found that not only was Alice extremely ill, but two of the children were as well; therefore, she set right to work seeing to her friend and the sick children.

Back at the house, while Martha and Mr. Swyndhurst were breakfasting together, they discussed Sarah. Martha expressed her gratitude that he had spoken up the night before concerning Sarah and her wish to go to bed without taking any nourishment. "Had you not been here, Mr. Swyndhurst, she would have gone to bed, yet again, on an empty stomach."

"As you had said, she is extremely undernourished. If necessary, I shall see that she eats something when she returns. In fact, I think I shall delay my trip for a time. I believe I am needed here more. I shall go in a few weeks, after I have had some time with Sarah. Perhaps we might fatten her up a bit during that time," he said with a wink.

"It is going to be wonderful having you here, Mr. Swyndhurst," responded the faithful servant, who was feeling relieved that someone other than herself would be there to encourage Sarah to take better care of herself.

The two talked for an hour or so before setting off to different areas of the house. Alexander had matters to discuss with Peter, while Martha made her way to check on her underservant, Esther.

When evening came, despite what Sarah had said about not coming back for a few days, Alexander hoped that she might return—but that was not to be. With concern, he questioned Martha. "How long do you suppose Sarah shall be at the Strouts' home?"

"Lord only knows. When it comes to Alice and her children, it might be days."

"You certainly were not exaggerating about how it is with Sarah. Though I have been here but a day, I share your concerns."

◊ ◊ ◊

It had been three days since Sarah had set off for the Strouts' home. She had pressed on with very little sleep the entire time she had been there. Alice and the two older children had been quite ill when she had first arrived. Although they were not completely well as yet, they were finally on the mend. Little Mary, however, had come down with the sickness during the second night that Sarah was there.

On the third evening, after making certain that all of the children were settled in for the night, Sarah went to speak with her friend. "Alice, the children are all in their beds. I believe they shall sleep through till morning. I must go home and get some rest, but I shall return at day break, before the children are even up. Listen for little Mary, won't you?"

"Sarah, I don't know how I would have managed without you. You are such a good friend. Yes, go home for the night and rest. We shall be just fine."

With that, Sarah set off for home. As she dragged herself along, she wondered if she could take yet another step. In the past, Sarah had seen no need to bother one of the servants to convey her to Alice's. As the Strouts' home was not far from the Swyndhurst estate, she had always walked; however, on this night she almost wished she had been a bother. But as she thought about it, there would have been no way to send word that she was ready to return home.

As she continued to walk unsteadily along, she felt as though someone were watching her. While glancing toward the tree line, she caught a glimpse of a tall man standing there in the shadows. Though it was difficult at that distance to make out the man's face, from his silhouette she knew just who it was. It was Matthew Raymond. She had yet to tell anyone that he had apparently followed her from Cambridge to Amesbury, showing up just a few months after her husband had set off for England. Seeing him at church had been unnerving enough, but observing him in the shadows was even more frightening to her. As she hastily moved past, she recalled the incident in the barn and shuddered. When her foot finally touched down on the grass at the Swyndhurst estate, she thanked God that she had made it safely home. As she scurried toward the door, she wondered at his reason for being there, lurking in the shadows. His home was a mile the other direction, beyond the Swyndhurst estate. Then, believing he may possibly have been keeping track of her comings and goings, she began to tremble all over. After shaking her head as if to dislodge the unsettling thought, still trembling, she grasped hold of the door handle.

Upon entering the house, she found that Martha had waited up to see if she might return that evening. Her faithful servant would not allow her to go to bed on an empty stomach, if she had anything to say about it. While attempting to regain her composure before her elderly friend sensed that anything was wrong, Sarah dropped her eyes to the floor.

"Sarah! You look as if you might collapse!" exclaimed Martha as she quickly approached and took hold of the weary woman's bundle. Setting it aside, she grasped Sarah's arm and directed her over to a chair at the table.

While unfastening the pins from the young woman's hair, she inquired, "You have been gone for three days now. What kept you? Surely Alice could not have been sick for so long a time."

Alexander listened from his study just off the kitchen, where he was presently looking over the records his bookkeeper had given him earlier in the day. Following Martha's question, he listened for Sarah's response.

"The older children had come down with the sickness before I arrived three days ago. Since then, little Mary has fallen ill as well. After I tucked the children into their beds tonight, I told Alice that I needed to go home for the night to rest. I assured her that I would return in the morning."

"You shall do no such thing! Alice is surely well enough to take care of the children by now," Martha responded, with her temper rising.

"Martha, she is not quite herself, as yet. Perhaps in a couple of days she shall be able to take over again," Sarah replied in barely a whisper. By now, the young woman had rested her head against the back of her chair. Then, with the intention of taking herself off to bed, looking white as a sheet, she attempted to stand.

While placing her hand on Sarah's shoulder to keep her from rising, Martha blurted out, "Oh, no you don't! I know you are exhausted, but you must eat at least a little something before going to bed."

"Oh, Martha, all I want to do is wash, change my clothes, and climb into bed. I promise to eat something in the morning."

All at once, Alexander appeared. "Good evening, Sarah. Busy time with the Strout family, I see. You look as though you could sleep for a week. Then again, what can another few minutes matter? Why not take a little food before retiring?"

While her employer attempted to persuade Sarah to eat, Martha had placed a trencher full of food and a cup of water in front of the young woman. As thirsty as she was, Sarah drank half the cup before speaking. "Maybe just a bite." She knew there would be an argument if she refused, and as before, it would be two against one.

By this time, Alexander had taken a seat beside Sarah, while Martha sat directly across from her. As they waited to see if the young woman would, indeed, take some nourishment, with concern they peered over at each other. Martha tilted her head in Sarah's direction. Mr. Swyndhurst nodded to indicate he had observed the same; Sarah looked dreadful.

In a short time, with her elbow on the table, Sarah had rested her chin on her upraised palm. Struggling to keep her eyes open, she stopped eating after just a couple of bites. Martha raised her hands in frustration. "Mr. Swyndhurst, I believe she is asleep. No use trying to get her to eat now. Perhaps you should carry her up to her bed. I shall follow to help her into her nightgown."

Alexander rose from his seat and came around to the other side of Sarah's chair. As he gently lifted her, he gazed down at her pale face. Though it was clear she was suffering from a lack of food and sleep, to him, she was still quite lovely. Then, as he left the kitchen with Sarah in his arms, he noticed how slight she truly was; to him, she felt no heavier than a child. *A boney one at that,* he thought.

Martha followed him up the stairs to Sarah's bedchamber. After turning back the bedcovers, she turned to Mr. Swyndhurst. "Just lay her there," she said, pointing. "I shall ready her for bed."

After placing Sarah on her bed, the worried husband, making his way from the room, waited on the other side of the door for Martha to emerge.

Within a few minutes, closing the door behind her, she appeared. "Mr. Swyndhurst, the moment she rises in the morning she is sure to set off for the Strouts' home. I am concerned that, unless something is done to stop her from all she is doing, she shall eventually collapse. I thought she might do just that when she first came home tonight. She looks simply awful."

His countenance falling, Mr. Swyndhurst nodded. "I should have been here, Martha. Had I been, perhaps things would have been different. I would have had some say about her leaving for three days. But to Sarah, I am little more than a stranger. As such, I have no right to speak out where she is concerned."

"So you have said, but I do not agree. You are her husband, after all. Furthermore, Mr. Swyndhurst, you needed your time to grieve. You are here now."

"We must stop her from going back there tomorrow," he stated unwaveringly. *Martha is right. I am her husband, after all. As she seems to shrug off every attempt of Martha's to rein her in, I must at least try and get through to her.*

Glancing up at him, Martha said, "She willingly complied when you asked her to eat something before she went to bed. She might just listen if you express your desire that she remain at home." The elderly servant felt blessed to have Mr. Swyndhurst home and taking her side in these matters. *Things might finally change around here.*

"I fully intend to, Martha, but don't be too hopeful that anything I might say should have any influence over her. We both know that as far as she is concerned—"

Breaking in, Martha said with exasperation, "I know...I know. You are no more than a stranger to your wife." Though she hated to, she had to agree. Sarah had no real connection to her husband. "Nonetheless, you must have a go; otherwise, when she returns to Alice's, I fear the worst. We might lose her."

"I shall do my best, Martha."

With the conversation coming to an end, Mr. Swyndhurst and Martha went to their separate bedchambers. Sleep eluded the young husband as he thought about the conversation he was to have with Sarah the following morning. *Lord, where she is concerned, I have no right to insist on anything; nevertheless, I cannot leave her to make the decision. It is clear that she cares little about herself.*

◊◊◊

Alexander was up with the sun. He immediately went to knock on his wife's door. "Sarah, are you awake?" Not hearing an answer, angry at himself for not rising earlier, he opened the door a crack to peek in. He fully expected to find the room empty, but there was Sarah, sitting on the edge of her bed, looking dazed. "Sarah, are you all right? Did you not hear me knocking?" She made no answer but simply sat there. Alexander then entered the room to ascertain why she had not responded. As he approached, he spoke a bit louder, "Sarah!"

All at once, she glanced up and saw her husband standing in front of her. Weakly, she replied, "Was there something you needed?"

By now, Alexander had surmised that Sarah was ill, and with that glassy look in her eyes, she was most likely feverish. "I have been speaking to you. Did you not hear me?" he said in a softer tone.

"Oh, I did not realize. I need to dress and go to Alice's. Little Mary—"

Alexander had taken a seat on the bed next to her. Upon hearing that she intended to go to the Strouts' home, he interrupted her, "No! You are not going anywhere!" He then gently took hold of her arms and slid her back against her pillow. "Can you not see that you are ill? You need to stay right here and rest."

After he said this he reached over and felt her forehead. He immediately rose from the bed and hurried from the room. Dashing through the house, he found Martha in the kitchen. He then quickly explained that Sarah was quite feverish and that Peter should go for the apothecary, Joseph Brainard, who also served as surgeon.

"I shall send him straightaway, Mr. Swyndhurst. You go and be with Sarah until Mr. Brainard arrives."

He raced back up the stairs to Sarah's bedchamber. As Alexander approached the bed, he explained to his wife that the apothecary-surgeon would soon be there. He then sat down on the edge of the bed.

In great distress, she glanced up at him and said, "But Mary...she needs me. Alice doesn't know how—"

Alexander reached over and placed his fingers over her lips. "Do not concern yourself, Sarah. I shall send Esther in your stead. Mary shall be just fine. At the moment, I am more worried about you."

Comforted by the knowledge that Esther would be tending to Mary, Sarah acquiesced to the wishes of her husband. Then, shivering, she pulled on the covers. In truth, she knew that she really had no choice but to rest, for she was struggling to stay awake.

Alexander breathed a sigh of relief as he watched her body relax at his words. As he observed her, he thought about the selfless woman he had married and how her sweet and giving disposition had served to put her health at risk. And then, with a slight grin he reminded himself that, not only did she have godly character traits, such as selflessness, but she was also very stubborn. Then, growing serious once more as he recalled that her stubbornness was exactly why she was in this predicament, he felt sorry for thinking it a humorous thing. At that thought, he determined that, no matter what, he would not allow her stubbornness to rule any longer. *Not on my watch!*

Chapter 8

Before long, Joseph Brainard, Jr., the son of the late Joseph Brainard, Sr., came into the room. Though he hadn't seen Alexander Swyndhurst in some time, they were very well acquainted. He had been the one to care for the first Mrs. Swyndhurst until the time of her death. There was an epidemic of smallpox the year she passed. Rebecca had contracted the dreaded disease from one of her servants. The apothecary-surgeon, to no avail, had attempted to save her life.

Devoid of a formal education, Joseph Brainard had apprenticed under his father, an apothecary, who had also served as surgeon for the towns of Amesbury and Haverhill. Therefore, as his father before him, he was quite capable of carrying out the duties related to both areas of medicine—one having more to do with dispensing herbal remedies, the other being more hands on, such as suturing wounds and so forth.

As Mr. Brainard approached the bed, Alexander rose and moved out of the way. "How long has Sarah been in this condition?" he asked while feeling her flushed face.

Martha had come in behind him prepared to answer any questions he might have about Sarah. "She appeared quite ill last night. We were unsure, however, whether it was merely exhaustion. You see, she—"

Breaking in, Mr. Brainard responded, "No need to explain Sarah to me, Martha. I am quite aware that she has been nursing the Strout family back to health. I have told her time and time again...well, no need to go into that now."

"Sir, we need to know what you have been telling my wife," responded the worried husband.

Martha spoke up at this point. "We have all been uneasy about Sarah for some time. She is always doing for others at the expense of her own welfare. You may have noticed that she is nothing but skin and bones."

"I am in complete agreement with your assessment of the girl. That is precisely what I have been telling her— that she needs to look after herself. If she goes on this way much longer, I fear the worst for her. In such cases, when an illness grabs hold the person has little strength with which to fight. Sarah has been running about, taking care of the sick in town for far too long."

Turning away, Alexander gripped the back of his neck. He could not bear to lose another wife, especially now that he understood what a treasure he had in Sarah.

While continuing his assessment of the young woman, Joseph Brainard stated, "Alexander, my boy, you need to take this girl in hand, now that you have come home. If you do not...well...I believe you understand my meaning." Joseph Brainard felt sad for the gentleman, for he knew that Alexander had suffered much for his young years.

Looking directly at Alexander now, Mr. Brainard informed him, "Sarah has an extremely high fever. For many years, I have followed the advice of the physicians who believe the best course of action for bringing down a high fever is lukewarm baths, as well as administering cinchona bark at regular intervals. We need to fill a tub with tepid water and place her in it. When the water begins to grow cold, you must remove her from the tub. This is to be repeated whenever you feel that her skin is as hot as it is now. Come over and touch her face," Mr. Brainard then directed the worried husband.

"Yes, I had noticed the fever. That is precisely why I sent for you," Alexander responded as he approached the bed. He then reached down to assess Sarah's fever once more. In understanding of what the apothecary-surgeon had advised, he nodded. Alexander then directed Martha to have one of the servants fetch the wooden tub from the laundry and place it in the buttery.

After Martha had gone, the apothecary turned toward the worried husband, and said, "Alexander, I can assist Sarah if you wish. But as she is your wife, I think it best if you help her with this. Though she is very slight, she is too much for Martha—at Martha's age."

Martha returned shortly after. She informed the two gentlemen that she was heating the water for Sarah's bath and that Peter, as requested, had carried in the tub. "I shall fetch a clean nightgown and some toweling for drying her, and follow you down shortly."

Mr. Brainard thanked Martha before explaining to her that Mr. Swyndhurst would be assisting Sarah. He further directed her to set up a chair in the buttery for her employer, and something with which to dip the water.

"Well, Alexander. I shall take my leave. I have others to see today. This illness has broken out all over town. Keep her as cool as possible. Get her to drink as often as you can manage it, and do not forget to have Martha administer the cinchona bark tincture. I left it over there," he said, indicating the table beside Sarah's bed. "Send for me if you have any trouble getting her fever to come down, but I don't expect that you will. The trouble will be in keeping it down."

With that, the apothecary was gone—leaving Alexander to wonder how he was going to tell Sarah what was about to happen. He disliked causing her any discomfort, for on feverish skin the tepid water would most likely feel like ice.

A short time later, Martha informed her employer that everything was prepared. "I can see that you are bothered by having to be the one to do this. There is nothing at all wrong with you helping her. Remember, though your marriage has been rather unusual up to now, you are her husband. Besides, she can remain in her nightgown. Once you are through, I can come in and help her into dry clothes."

"It is just that having a husband that abandoned you for two years helping you with such a personal matter...well...I am not quite certain how she shall feel about it; however, if I had to guess, I would have to say that once she comprehends what is about to happen, she shall not be very happy."

"I understand, Mr. Swyndhurst, but there isn't a moment to waste. The water shall be too cold if you wait much longer." After saying this, the elderly woman turned to leave.

With trepidation, Alexander approached the bed. As he sat down next to Sarah, he cupped her face with his hands. "Sarah, you must listen. The apothecary says that your fever is dangerously high. To bring it down, he desires for you to be placed in a tepid bath."

With her eyes barely open, she listened. It took the young woman a moment to process what her husband had said. While nodding, she asked, "Where is Martha?"

Feeling bad for his sick wife, he stroked her cheek and said, "Sarah, though you weigh very little, Martha is not strong enough to help you."

Trying to sit up, she replied, "Very well. I shall try to—" Too weak to continue, she fell back against the bed.

"Sarah, you are too ill to do this on your own. Even if you could get yourself into the tub, which is doubtful, if you fainted you might sink under the water. I know that we have not had the sort of marriage that...well...it is just that I shall be the one assisting you."

With her eyes wide, she whispered, "Alexander, I really think I—"

Interrupting her, he replied softly, "Sarah, I am going to help you, and that is all there is to it." He then lifted her into his arms and made his way out of her bedchamber. As they descended the stairs, he observed that she had turned her head away. He was certain that she was so uncomfortable about the whole thing that she couldn't look him in the eye. Feeling her body trembling, he lifted her higher so that he might rest his chin atop her head. He then whispered, "Everything is going to be all right."

As her husband carried her through the kitchen, Sarah stared at Martha—as though pleading with her eyes that she save her from this embarrassing situation. Feeling a bit sick at how ill Sarah looked, Martha turned away.

Behind the closed door of the buttery, Alexander sat Sarah on the chair that Martha had positioned near the tub. He then knelt down in front of her and apologized for what he was about to do—for a tepid bath against feverish skin would be much the same as torture. "Sarah, I am going to lift you now and place you in the tub. Even though the water is slightly warm, it is going to feel extremely cold to you."

Relieved that she would be clothed, she replied, "Very well. I am ready."

After lifting her, he turned toward the tub. He then lowered her into the water. Once she was settled, she rested her head atop her bent knees. Her teeth soon began to chatter. Though he disliked having to do it, Alexander lifted a cup filled with the tepid water and poured it over her head and down her back. With her gown clinging to her skin, he observed just how thin she truly was. He could count every rib. Then, whispering so Sarah wouldn't hear, he prayed, "Lord, what am I to do? I cannot allow her to go on any longer looking after everyone but herself."

Thinking she heard him speak, Sarah inquired, "Did you say something, Alexander? I couldn't quite hear you."

"No...no. It is just that I know you want this over as soon as possible. We have to carry on for a few more minutes." He was relieved she hadn't actually heard his prayer. As stubborn as she had been about continuing on with her life as usual, despite Martha's objections, he believed she would be angry to know that he had no intention of allowing her to keep on as she had been—working herself ragged. With misery for causing her discomfort, he continued to pour the water. As her shivering became uncontrollable, he stopped pouring for a moment. He then came around to where he could see her face. "Are you all right?"

With much effort, she lifted her head and asked, "How much longer?"

"Just a bit longer, and then I shall lift you out of there." Feeling her brow, he nodded with satisfaction at the difference the bath had already made. He was certain her fever had dissipated some.

A few minutes later, as promised, Alexander lifted Sarah out of the water and onto her feet, at which point her knees buckled and she began to fall. The shivering had taken her last bit of energy. Alexander quickly reached out to catch her. He then set her down upon the chair. Calling for Martha, Alexander continued to steady Sarah by stooping beside her and wrapping his strong arms around her.

As Martha opened the door, her employer directed her to grab a drying cloth. Now, toweling in hand, the elderly servant approached Sarah. Alexander kept hold of his wife's shoulders while Martha dried her face, after which she began patting the young woman's hair with the cloth. When Alexander felt certain that Sarah could keep her balance, leaving the women to themselves, he turned and left the room. As he waited on the other side of the door for Martha to call once she had finished helping Sarah into dry clothes, he listened. If Martha needed his assistance, he wanted to be prepared to act quickly.

Before long, the ladies had accomplished the task of removing the wet garment and replacing it with a dry one. Then Martha called to Sarah's husband, whom she was certain had not ventured very far from the buttery. Upon entering, seeing Sarah offering him a weak smile, Alexander sighed at the realization he had been successful at assisting his wife without causing her too much embarrassment. After placing a kiss on the top of her head, he lifted her.

As the relieved husband made his way back through the kitchen, he observed Martha following along behind him, nodding and smiling. It was obvious to him that his elderly servant had also observed that Sarah's fever had come down.

As they made their way up the stairs, the husband and wife each realized that their first time in each other's company, for any length of time, had been rather unusual. Once they were again in Sarah's bedchamber, Alexander placed her back on her bed. After covering her, he sat beside her until she fell asleep, which, as exhausted as she was, didn't take very long.

Chapter 9

That night, Alexander stayed with Sarah, never leaving her side. Though he knew she would be uncomfortable having him on the other side of her bed, he felt he had no choice. He needed to stay close to look after her. When morning came, Sarah's fever had returned—possibly even higher than it had been the day before. Alexander began the process with the tepid bath all over again. As before, he felt terrible for having to bring his wife so much discomfort.

Before long, Sarah—bath completed—was doing a bit better. As the relieved husband carried her back through the kitchen, he informed Martha that, as his bedcoverings were fresh, he would be bringing Sarah to his bedchamber. Martha stated that while Sarah was out of her room she would take the opportunity to launder her bedding.

Though Sarah wanted to protest the arrangement, she was too weak to argue. As the couple mounted the stairs, Alexander reassured Sarah that the only reason he was taking her to his bedchamber was so she could rest comfortably. While keeping his eyes focused on the stairs, he informed her that, owing to her fever, she had soaked her own bed linens. But then, as he glanced down at his wife, he observed that her eyes had closed. His explanation would have to wait.

By the time Alexander had placed Sarah on his bed, she had fallen into a deep sleep. The tepid baths, though they had been necessary, were taking a lot out of her. Shivering for nearly half an hour had burned up what little energy she had. In addition, she hadn't been well enough to take any nourishment since she had come down with the illness, which only added to her weakened state.

By early afternoon, Sarah finally woke. As she looked around, she realized she was not in her own bedchamber. She soon remembered a conversation between Martha and her husband where he mentioned something about bringing her to his room. Glancing about, she observed Alexander resting in a chair. To her, he appeared completely done in. She surmised that he had been taking care of her the entire time she had been ill, and with little sleep. All at once, she remembered a bath—*or was it two?* As she thought about it, her cheeks flushed. She then recalled that it had all been accomplished with her clothed in her nightgown. She was grateful at least for that.

As she watched her husband sleeping, she wondered again why he had come home from England and how long might he stay. Ever since the incident with Matthew Raymond, which had occurred while she was living in Cambridge, she had felt ill at ease in the company of men. As it stood now, she had no choice but to be in close proximity to her husband, considering that he had been the one to look after her. As her gaze settled on him once more, she noticed his eyes flutter and then open.

Once he came fully awake, he realized that Sarah was looking his way. He hastily rose from his chair and approached the bed. "Sarah, how are you feeling? Let me touch your brow." Reaching for her, he placed his hand upon her forehead and smiled. "No fever—that I can detect, at any rate."

"Alexander, why are we in your bedchamber?" she asked shyly. "I remember a conversation between you and Martha, but I cannot recall—"

To set her mind at ease, Alexander broke in with the explanation he had attempted to offer before his wife had fallen asleep. "Your bed linens were soiled from the fever. They were, in fact, completely drenched. I thought you would rest more comfortably in a fresh bed."

"Oh...I see. You look as if you might drop. I think you should be the one in this bed, not me."

"If you are feeling better, per the apothecary's orders, we might get some food and drink in you. I shall let Martha know you are awake and that she should send up something for you."

Sarah really didn't believe she could eat a thing, but she decided not to say as much—not after Alexander had been so kind.

That afternoon, Alexander did his best to get a bit of soft food and some fluids into Sarah. By evening, she was looking much better. The apothecary-surgeon had been to call—leaving orders for her to continue resting. Given that she had already been in a weakened state long before she had come down with this most recent illness, he recommended a month.

Sarah had heard what the gentleman had said; nevertheless, she had instantly reasoned aloud that a month was not at all necessary. Little Mary needed her, as did the others.

Martha had overheard the young woman whispering to herself, so she listened carefully. She later told her employer what Sarah had muttered under her breath when the apothecary had left orders for her confinement. Mr. Swyndhurst simply shook his head and stated that he was a lot bigger than his wife, and if she believed she could simply get out of bed and go to Alice's, she would soon learn differently.

When Alexander was ready to turn in for the night, he went up to his room. Upon entering, he observed Sarah standing by the door—ready to take leave of his bedchamber. He then asked, "Sarah, is there something you need?"

"No...I...ah...well, I thought I would go back to my own bedchamber. I am certain Martha has seen to the bed linens by now."

Taking her by the arm, he gently turned her around and back toward the bed; however, before they had taken a step, he noticed that she had recoiled at his touch. Thinking she was simply angry with him for preventing her from leaving, he said, "Sarah, it is my desire that you remain in here where I can continue looking after you. You are not yet well." *And you would likely slip out early and head off to the Strouts' unless I keep watch over you,* he thought.

Glancing back over her shoulder toward the door, wishing she might escape, Sarah replied, "I believe I am much better now. There is no need for you to lose more sleep over me. I shall just go back to my own room now."

Shaking his head to indicate the answer was no, he explained again. "I know you are feeling much better, but you are not quite yourself. Moreover, you have only been free of a fever for a few hours. If it returned in the night, with you in your own bedchamber, I would have no way of knowing. If you are concerned about having a man in with you, you needn't be. I shan't bother you. Though it has only been a couple of days, I simply have grown accustomed to having you in here with me, where I can see to your needs."

At this point, her stomach was in knots. Hoping this would all soon be over and things could go back to the way they were before her husband arrived—as she made her way back over to the bed—she inquired, "Alexander, when are you planning to return to England?"

To this, he smiled to himself. *I suspect she desires to be rid of me so she might go on doing whatever she wishes— most likely working herself to death.* "Well, that is something I had hoped to discuss with you. You see, Sarah, I have no plans to return to England. In fact, it is my hope that, in time, our marriage will become more conventional."

Eyes wide, and almost breathless, she asked, "Are you saying that you plan on living here?"

"Well, yes. This is my home, is it not?" He sensed that he had thrown her into a panic. "Sarah, I know our agreement was for me to live in England and you were to live here with only the servants, but I no longer wish to be parted from you."

Feeling herself tremble, Sarah glanced at the door. *This was not what we had agreed to. What am I to do now?*

"Sarah, please do not worry about this. I am not going to force a conventional marriage on you before you are ready. What is more, I know you may never be."

Daring a look in his direction, she studied his face. "What if I never wish to have that sort of marriage?" *And I am certain I shall not.* "I had not planned on things changing between us. Father said—"

As he observed her, he realized that, as Martha had advised, he should have waited to tell her. He should have allowed her to first become accustomed to having him around and getting better acquainted. "Sarah, I know this is all very sudden and you are not yet strong enough to process everything I have said, but I hope you will consider allowing me to be a part of your life."

Emotionally as well as physically drained, Sarah hung her head. "Alexander, it isn't that I do not wish for you to stay in Amesbury. It is just that—"

Breaking in, he responded, "I know, Sarah, the idea of having me here scares you. Please do not fret. As I said, I am not going to rush you. The only thing I insist upon is that you remain in my bedchamber. As I have already explained, I have grown accustomed to having you here. I shan't bother you. We shall simply share this room. Whenever you wish to dress for the day or ready yourself for bed, I shall wait on the other side of the door. Does that meet with your approval?"

Sarah was never one to outright argue or insist on getting her own way, other than when Martha tried to rein her in; consequently, she acquiesced. Secretly, however, all she wanted to do, just now, was run out of the room and back to her own bedchamber where she felt safe. After climbing back under the covers, she turned toward the door—away from the other side of the bed, where she was sure Alexander would very soon be.

Alexander felt terrible he had disclosed his plans to Sarah, but he was helpless as to what to do about it now. Glancing over at his wife with the covers tucked up tightly around her neck, he knew that she was terrified at the prospect of remaining in his bedchamber, especially now that she knew he wanted a more conventional marriage and to remain in Amesbury with her.

As he climbed in under the covers on his own side of the bed, he debated whether to say anything else to his young wife. After a few moments of quiet, he decided to ask, "Sarah, are you feeling all right? Is there anything you need?"

"No...no. I am fine," she said in barely a whisper.

"I am sorry that this has all been so alarming to you," he said sincerely. "I truly shall wait as long as it takes. Please, do not feel rushed into anything."

Sarah wondered, at that moment, why he didn't understand that sleeping next to a man, for her, was rushing things—even if he was her husband—the husband she had not planned on living with—*ever*!

Chapter 10

Morning came, and none too soon for Sarah. She had been wide awake most of the night thinking about the change in her situation with Alexander. She had also been reflecting on what had recently occurred with Matthew Raymond, wondering if he had been following her that night when she had seen him standing in the shadows. Suddenly, she heard Alexander yawn behind her. She dared not look over her shoulder.

As Alexander started to rise, he inquired, "Sarah, are you awake?" He thought he had felt her move. Hearing her answer softly in the affirmative, he informed, "I thought I would ask Martha to send up something for you to eat. It would be good for you to remain in bed a few more days. After that you may be strong enough to recline in the parlor, for part of the day anyway. The apothecary does not want you doing too much just yet."

Relieved that he would be out of the room for a few minutes, Sarah answered, "Very well, Alexander. I believe I shall go to my bedchamber to wash and change my clothes."

"If you wish, I shall have Esther bring whatever you need to this room. As I will be downstairs for a while, you shall have more than enough time to wash and change into a fresh nightgown."

"It really is no bother for me to go. I do not wish to trouble Esther. She already has so much to do."

Sighing, he came around to where he could speak to her face to face. "Very well, Sarah. You must try and remember, however, that it is Esther's job to tend to your needs. I know very well that you dislike having others do for you, but you are ill, after all."

As she rose, she responded, "I really do think I am strong enough. It is not very far to my bedchamber."

"Allow me to at least see you there. That way, if you feel weak, I shall be there to assist you." *For one so small, you are one headstrong woman,* Alexander thought to himself.

On her feet now, she nodded to his offer to escort her to her bedchamber. Then, together they moved in that direction. After seeing that Sarah was safely in her room, Alexander went in search of Martha.

Finding her in the kitchen, he stated, "Martha, I believe Sarah is ready to eat something. She is in her bedchamber changing, but she shall be returning to my room directly."

"Should she be up?" inquired the worried servant.

"You know how she can be, Martha. She didn't want to trouble Esther with fetching a clean nightgown for her; however, as much as it worries me that she is up, I am more concerned that she eats something."

"Very well. I have everything prepared. Will you be breakfasting with her?"

"Yes, I believe I shall." A little hesitant to reveal that he had not followed his servant-friend's advice, he said in a muffled voice, "Martha, I told Sarah that I plan to stay on in Amesbury. I also told her of my wish to alter the arrangement we had made when we married."

Brows raised, she glanced over at him. "You did? How did she take the news?"

Sighing, he rubbed his chin. "Not very well, I'm afraid. In fact, I think I frightened her half to death, just as you had said I might."

"What prompted you to tell her so soon?" she asked, surprised that he had not waited until he had been home for a time to inform his wife of his plans.

"Well, for one thing, before we retired last night she attempted to return to her own bedchamber, stating that she believed herself well enough. I told her I wished for her to remain where she was, in my room. I went on to say that I had come home to stay. The rest just came spilling out; that is, about having a conventional marriage. I assured her that I would not rush her. In truth, Martha, just being here with her shall be enough for me; nonetheless, I hope we shall one day, at the very least, have a special friendship."

As Martha listened, she began to understand Mr. Swyndhurst a little better. *He simply wishes to be here with Sarah in whatever capacity she will allow.* "What did she say that made you think you frightened her?" she then asked with concern. Though she knew Mr. Swyndhurst to be an honorable and kind gentleman, she hated to think Sarah was upset by his news.

"It wasn't so much what she said as what she did. After climbing back in bed, she proceeded to pull the bedcover up so only the top of her head was showing. She had also turned away from me, facing the door. I was sure she had comprehended my meaning when I said I would not rush her. In truth, Martha, the chief reason I wanted her in there with me was that I didn't trust her to return to her own bedchamber where she might slip out whenever she likes. And she has only been free of a fever for a short time. What if the fever returns and I am not there with her? I would have no way of knowing."

Looking thoughtful, Martha responded. "Yes, those are legitimate concerns. We cannot be sure the illness has indeed passed. And I share your belief that it would be good to keep an eye on her. I know you assured her that you had no intention of hurrying things, but maybe she didn't quite take your meaning."

"Perhaps you are right; however, without that time together each night, I believe she shall remain distant from me. At least I can count on having her attention every evening to establish some sort of a connection with her. And as I said, after it occurred to me that I could keep a better watch over her comings and goings if she remained in with me, like you, I thought it a good idea. As you know all too well, she runs off quite early many a morning. We may not be able to alter her schedule if we don't know when she rises. Having her with me, if necessary, I shall be right there to stop her from running off to the Strouts' home, or anywhere else for that matter."

In understanding, the elderly servant nodded. Next, she cautioned, "Remember, Mr. Swyndhurst, though you have been married before, Sarah has not; consequently, she has never shared her bed with a man. What is more, she believed she never would. This all feels quite natural to you. It is not the same for her. And did you not tell me that a man in her former hometown had incessantly pursued her—even seizing her one time, in her father's barn?"

Thinking about this, he answered, "Yes, that is true. How could I have forgotten that? It isn't a wonder she seems so fearful of me; however, I was told by her father in confidence, so we must not let on to her that we are aware of what happened. I only alerted you so that you might keep your eyes open, should a stranger come around looking for her."

Martha nodded. "I have never said a word, and I never shall. And not once has Sarah mentioned it. I assumed she had put it behind her."

"I highly doubt it, Martha."

A short time later, the couple had returned to Alexander's bedchamber. While they ate, Sarah asked her husband if he had gone on his business trip while she was away taking care of the Strouts. She thought she remembered him saying something about having delayed his trip for a time.

"No, Sarah. As yet, I have not. I shall go in a few weeks, when you have fully recovered."

"Seeing that my fever has subsided, I believe I am no longer in any danger. I shall be just fine here with Martha and the others if you wish to go," she informed him, hoping he would be gone from the house for a few days, for as soon as he left, she intended to go directly to check on Mary. The next time, however, she planned to be home before dark, for she had no desire to find Matthew Raymond lurking about again.

"Sarah, I am going to stay right here with you until I know for sure that you are well; therefore, it shall be some time before I go," he responded warmly. He suspected it was her desire that he go away either because she was uncomfortable around him, or so she might return to her usual routine. As he thought about it, he suspected it might have a little to do with both reasons.

Just then, Esther knocked on the door. Mr. Swyndhurst called for her to come in. Upon entering, the servant observed her mistress sitting up in bed. The sight caused Esther's face to light up with joy. "You are looking much better, Mrs. Swyndhurst."

In private, Sarah had admonished her friend for her formal address; thus, when they were alone, Mrs. Swyndhurst was "Sarah" to Esther.

"Is there something I may do for you before I go to the Strouts' home?" inquired Esther.

Excited that Esther would be seeing the Strouts, Sarah replied, "No, I am just fine, Esther. Do come and see me when you have returned. I should like to know how you find them today. How were they when last you called upon them?"

"Surely, Mrs. Swyndhurst. I shall come to you the moment I return. As for how they are faring, Mrs. Strout is doing quite well, as are the eldest two, but Mary continues to suffer," Esther explained solemnly.

Upon hearing the servant's report, Alexander became vexed at the young woman for disclosing too much to his sick wife. "That will be all, Esther. Thank you for coming to ask after our needs."

As she glanced over at Alexander, Sarah observed that his face was flushed and he appeared rather angry. Seeing this, she decided it was best to drop the matter and allow Esther to take her leave. Still, she remained more than a little concerned about Mary. *Alice does not know what to do for her, of that I am certain. I pray Esther takes the situation in hand. As soon as I can get away, I shall see to Mary myself.*

Seeing the worry flash across his wife's face troubled Alexander. *This is not going to be easy, getting her to amend her view that she should labor on behalf of others to the point of dropping.*

After Esther had gone, Alexander attempted to put his wife's mind at ease about Mary. He also wanted her to feel comfortable with regard to sharing his bedchamber. Taking her hand, he said, "Sarah, Mary shall be just fine. Esther knows exactly what to do for her."

Peering over at her husband, Sarah nodded. On some level, she knew he was right—Esther was quite capable of handling the situation; however, until she saw little Mary for herself, she knew she wouldn't be able to rest easy.

"Also, I know I made you fearful when I asked you to remain in my bedchamber, but there is truly no need for concern. I simply wish to look after you while you are ill. And I believe we shall become better acquainted if we have more time for conversing each evening before going to sleep. I have recently been reminded that sharing a bed with my wife comes more naturally to me, given that I was married before. I realize it is not the same for you, and therefore must feel quite unfamiliar—or even distressing."

Looking down, so as not to gain eye contact, Sarah simply nodded. She was now no longer hungry. Her meal scarcely touched, she leaned back against her pillow.

Seeing that Sarah had stopped eating, Alexander inquired, "Are you feeling poorly again?"

Not wanting to give her husband any reason to insist that she remain in the house any longer, away from her friends, she quickly responded, "No...no, I am fine. I simply don't seem to have much of an appetite."

From what Martha has said, for you—little lady— that is nothing out of the ordinary, he thought, but what he said was, "Perhaps you should take a rest. I will clear your tray away." After placing everything aside, he sat on the edge of the bed next to her. As he leaned down to kiss her brow, he whispered, "I shall check on you in a little while."

Sarah's eyes followed her husband as he stood to his feet and left the room. After he had gone, she prayed for God to help her make sense out of all that was happening. Having her husband home to stay, as well as the most recent incident with Matthew Raymond, had left her quite unsettled—not to mention her concern for little Mary.

"Lord, I have been managing Matthew Raymond's presence in town on my own. Now that Alexander is here, should I tell him about Matthew and all that has happened in the past, as well as that the dreadful man seemed to have been waiting for me the other night, while standing in the shadows? I am afraid if I mention it, Alexander will say that I cannot walk to Alice's anymore. And, Lord, another concern that I have is that when I married Alexander, we had not planned on living under the same roof. He now desires to have a traditional marriage. Father assured me that Alexander would never wish for that sort of marriage. Now, here he is, in Amesbury, even insisting we share his bedchamber. For me, though, Lord, the most frustrating aspect of all of this is that I have always been able to come and go as I please. That clearly is a thing of the past. I tried to never misuse my freedom. I have always attempted to use it for good. Oh, Lord, so much has changed. How am I to find peace with it all?"

Chapter 11

Sarah had been in bed for the better part of a week. She was beginning to grow restless. Expressing her discontent to her husband had done little to change things. Each time she had attempted to discuss the matter, he simply stated that she needed more time to recuperate before venturing out of bed.

As a child, she had always been obedient; consequently, the feelings of rebellion against her husband's wishes she was presently experiencing were very new to her. She had been left to herself, other than the servants, for two years. Having to answer to someone after all this time, for her, was exasperating.

On this day, however, she was determined to have her own way. She wondered how she would ever make it over to see Alice Strout and her children if everyone continued to look upon her as sickly. She reasoned that if they all noticed that she was up and about, they might see for themselves that she was well. After making her way out of bed, Sarah started for her own bedchamber. She intended to dress and go downstairs for a while. Just as she was approaching the door to her room, Esther appeared.

"We have guests, Mrs. Swy...Sarah. Mr. and Mrs. Bleasdell have arrived," she informed while smiling at her mistress. The young maid was delighted to see the lady of the house looking a little better every day.

As Sarah glanced at her friend, she smiled with pleasure that guests had come to call. Since she had been confined to the house for so long, having visitors sounded wonderful to her. "Very well, Esther. Please let them know that I shall be down directly."

The young woman nodded and replied, "Very well, I shall go this moment." It pleased Esther that things seemed to be returning to normal.

Jonathan and Hannah Bleasdell were both in their early fifties. Given that Mr. Swyndhurst and his first wife had attended church with the couple, they had been counted amongst Alexander's friends for some time. The new Mrs. Swyndhurst had admired Hannah and her sister, Susanna, since they first became acquainted.

While Sarah readied herself, she thought about Hannah and Susanna. Although they were both now up in years—though not exactly elderly, in Sarah's opinion, they were still very lovely. In fact, although Jonathan had a bit of a round middle, to Sarah he, too, had remained rather striking—with very little silver in his mostly dark hair and kind eyes that had always made her feel at ease in his company. The arresting presence of Susanna's husband, William Pressey, then came to Sarah's mind. She thought about how the man towered over most everyone except

Alexander. William, nearly the same height as her husband, didn't look up to many, she supposed.

As she continued to dress, Sarah recalled that the Jameson sisters, as they were formerly called, once told her of Jonathan's father's harrowing journey over from England on the *Angel Gabriel*, the ship on which he and his parents had traveled. She thought she remembered the ladies mentioning that Henry Bleasdell was only three when the ship went down just off New England's coast, and that he and his parents had nearly drowned. Shivering at the thought, she reached for a facecloth. As she studied her image in the looking glass, which had long since been re-hung to suit her tiny stature, she thought again about Ralph and Elizabeth Bleasdell, Henry's parents. Considering that they were Puritans, they had fled England during an extremely turbulent time for those holding to such beliefs, for their views had stood in stark contrast to the Church of England. Having always been captivated by the accounts told by the Presseys and the Bleasdells, Sarah had long believed the stories were book worthy.

Sarah soon realized that her musings had caused her to take longer than she had intended. She quickly finished readying herself, and then made her way to the stairs, which she descended rather swiftly. Arriving in the parlor nearly out of breath, the petite woman smiled as she greeted her guests. Glancing to her left, she caught a glimpse of Alexander, with a strained expression, moving in her direction. Taking her arm, he escorted her over to a seat near their guests.

While studying the couple sitting across from her, Sarah recalled a story Martha had shared concerning Hannah. Hannah was the granddaughter of a woman— Susanna North Martin—who had been hung as a witch. Upon hearing the account, Sarah had been certain that the woman had been no such thing. Looking across at Hannah just now, Sarah's heart ached for what she must have gone through. She then thought about the entire Jameson family, which consisted of six children in all. Though she had only ever set eyes on the other three sisters once or twice, Sarah had also made the acquaintance of Mary, Esther, and Elizabeth, as well as their brother John.

Scarcely hearing the conversation that was taking place around her, Sarah recalled that the most intriguing story she had heard relating to the family was the account of Hannah's sister, Susanna Pressey. Susanna had married William Pressey, the son of John and Mary Pressey, two of Susanna Martin's accusers. A few years after the death of the sisters' grandmother, William's parents had reconciled with their son and daughter-in-law. In Sarah's view, after what William's parents had done, Susanna must have had a very forgiving heart to have allowed them any part in her life.

Like Hannah and Jonathan, Susanna and William had been to the Swyndhursts' home many times while Alexander was away. Sarah had always been too busy helping others to do much entertaining and was often not at home when any visitors had come to call; therefore, though she knew much about the families from the few times she had been in their company—as well as from what information Martha had shared—she was only somewhat acquainted with them, or any of her husband's friends, for that matter.

An hour had passed when Jonathan and Hannah Bleasdell, glancing at each other, rose to their feet. They had each sensed that Sarah was growing weary. "It was wonderful to see you looking so well, Mrs. Swyndhurst," smiled Mr. Bleasdell.

"Sarah, if you please, Mr. Bleasdell," she responded with a smile. Though she had, on a previous occasion or two, asked him to call her Sarah, he seemed to have trouble on his subsequent visits remembering to do so. Sarah wondered, then, if the familiarity was difficult for him, considering that they were so little acquainted.

"Very well, then. But you must do me the courtesy of addressing me as Jonathan."

Smiling in his direction, she surmised that she had been wrong about not being familiar enough for using one another's Christian names; otherwise, the gentleman would not have suggested that she call him Jonathan. *Perhaps he has asked the same of me in the past, and I have forgotten as well. As I am almost always off somewhere when they have come, I certainly have not made it easy for us to become better acquainted.* At that thought, she determined to be more accessible to the Bleasdells in the future.

Just then, Hannah took hold of Sarah's hand and gave it a squeeze. Though Sarah had stood to see them out, Hannah was attempting to say their farewells in the parlor. She had no wish for the young woman to be on her feet any longer than necessary. Within a few moments, Alexander and Sarah were alone. "Sarah, I didn't want to say anything in front of our guests, but are you sure you should be out of bed?"

Attempting to appear completely at ease with the question, Sarah answered. "I am much better today. And I simply cannot tolerate another day in bed. I shall not overdo, Alexander." If he insisted she return to their room, she knew she would be miserable.

Taking her by the hand, he led her back to the settee. After turning her so that her feet were up and her back was against a pillow—placing a quilt over her lap—he nodded and left the room. As she reclined there, Sarah felt as though she were a bird let out of its cage. After a time, Martha approached with some tea and cake for her young friend.

While setting her offerings down on the little table beside Sarah, Martha smiled and said, "Well now, you are looking much better. You gave us quite a scare, young lady."

"I am sorry, Martha. As you see, I am just fine now." Sarah wanted to convince her protective friend that she was her normal self again. If she could persuade Martha, perhaps Alexander might believe it as well. *I simply have to get over to see Alice and the children.* Thinking about the Strout children brought tears to her eyes. She had never before been separated from them for so long. She dearly loved Alice, but she knew that, as a mother, the young woman was deficient in more ways than one. That Alice's youngest had survived her illness with only her mother there to look after her, to Sarah, seemed a miracle. She then remembered that Alice had not been left to herself. Alexander had sent Esther along to help.

"I must admit, that was truly good of Alexander," she said, a little too loudly.

Having observed that Sarah seemed a bit distracted, Martha had decided to leave her to herself. The elderly servant was just leaving when her employer re-entered the parlor. While nodding to him, she called back over her shoulder to Sarah, "Try and eat, won't you?"

Sarah started at the sound of Martha's voice. For a moment, she had forgotten anyone else was in the room. Glancing toward the doorway, Sarah called to Martha, "I shall, Martha."

Seeing her husband approaching with a grin on his face, Sarah's cheeks flushed at the thought that she had been talking to herself, and he had obviously heard.

As he made his way over to her, Alexander inquired, "Were you speaking to me? I thought I heard my name."

Flustered, Sarah responded, "No...no. I was just thinking out loud."

"Anything you wish to share?" he asked, still grinning.

Watching him as he took a seat, Sarah explained what she had been thinking about. "It is just that I am grateful to you for sending Esther to help Alice with the children."

Surveying his wife, Alexander realized the Strout children, as usual, had not been far from her mind. With that thought, he wondered how long it would be before she insisted on going to see them. *Allowing her to see them is one thing, but she is not going to return to her old way of doing things.* Not wanting to upset her with his plan for altering her hitherto busy schedule, he merely replied, "I was happy to do it. And Esther assures me everyone is well."

"Yes, so she has said." Though Sarah hated to admit it, she was beginning to grow tired.

Alexander noticed the fatigue showing on her face but forced himself to allow her time to decide on her own to return to her bed. While rising to her feet, his wife explained that she was heading back up the stairs. Alexander stood and came to her. "Shall I escort you?"

"If you wish, but I am sure I can make it on my own," Sarah answered while keeping her eyes focused frontward. She didn't want him to know that she had suddenly felt weak. She was certain that if he knew, he would insist she return to her bed for a few more days.

Taking her hand, he slid it through his bent arm, and they then moved in the direction of his bedchamber. Once there, he helped her back into bed. Before turning to go, he kissed her on the brow and said, "You rest a while. I shall return a little later, and perhaps at that time I shall read to you."

Once he left the room, she heaved a heavy sigh. "Lord, all I want is to be out of this bed and back to my normal life. I can see that Alexander intends for me to stay here for the remainder of the day, or else he wouldn't have offered to read to me. I do so appreciate all that he has done, especially in sending Esther to care for the Strouts, but...oh, please forgive my impatient heart. I am grateful for the people in my life, even if I grumble against them at times. Besides Alexander, Esther has also been an angel, taking care of the Strouts for me. Without her, Alice's children may not have fared so well."

Before very long, Sarah had fallen asleep. The activities of the day had been too much. Alexander had checked on her once or twice, in case she wished for him to read to her. But that was not to be, for she never even stirred until he came to bed that night.

The following morning, to Sarah's chagrin, she felt too shaky to rise from her bed. It was the next day before she was well enough to attempt being out of bed again.

Chapter 12

M r. Brainard paid the Swyndhursts another visit. After checking on his favorite patient, he went in search of Alexander. "Well, young man, it seems your wife is doing much better. But do not let her fool you—she still has a long way to go before she is well. In fact, I would like to see her keep to her bed a little while longer. I have said as much to her, but I got the distinct impression she wanted to argue the point. Not that she did, but I am certain she wanted to."

Amused that the gentleman had correctly diagnosed just what he had been dealing with, Alexander responded, "You picked up on that, did you? My wife does a pretty fair job of feigning that she is well so that she might be out of her bed."

Smiling, the apothecary nodded. "Though your wife is the sweetest woman I have ever known, she can, at times, be quite stubborn. Alexander, I am quite serious. She is not to return to her usual schedule for some time yet. Eventually, she shall be able to do some of what she desires, such as helping out with the Strout children, but she is never to do it to the extent that she did before."

"I quite agree. Now, convincing her of that is another matter altogether. I have no desire to thrust my demands upon her. I had hoped she would come to understand the need for a change without my having to say it."

"I understand, Alexander. If she doesn't come around to our way of thinking, however, you shall simply have to insist that she bend to your wishes in this."

While indicating his agreement with a nod, Alexander walked the gentleman out. Following that, he went to check on Sarah. As soon as he entered the room, he noticed the stubborn look upon her face. Surmising the reason, he slowly approached the bed. He didn't want to have an argument, but he sensed that one was looming.

Looking up at her husband, Sarah scowled. "How long does he think he can keep me in this bed?"

Trying not to show his amusement at her ill temper, Alexander kept his gaze directed elsewhere. "Just long enough to get you well, I would imagine." Aware that he had not given her the answer she was hoping for, he changed the subject. "Would you like for me to read to you?"

Tucking her chin in, she crossed her arms over her chest and responded, "I am sure you have better things to do than read to me."

"Actually, I have nothing too pressing at the moment. I believe I shall crawl over there beside you. If you do not wish for me to read to you, how about we talk for a while?"

Feeling a bit childish for her behavior, Sarah stole a peek in her husband's direction. Seeing his eyes on her, she began to grin. "I am sorry, Alexander. I seem to be in bad humor today. It is just that I was so hoping the apothecary would allow me to return to my regular routine."

Smiling back at his contrite wife, Alexander replied, "That is understandable. Even so, you must know that your schedule can never go back to what it was before. You need to take some time to prioritize. There shall be no more running hither and thither every day. Do you understand?"

The bad humor for which Sarah had been remorseful only a moment ago had returned and was now directed at her husband. *Who does he think he is, telling me what to do? I got along just fine without him here.* But as she thought about it, she knew that was not exactly true. "May we talk of something else?" she asked, attempting to change the subject while she bridled her emotions.

Endeavoring, once again, to hide a grin, Alexander acquiesced. "Certainly. Let us discuss what you would like to do once you are allowed out of bed. I was thinking perhaps a ride out to the Presseys' home, or over to see Jonathan and Hannah."

Diverted for a moment from her sullen mood, Sarah smiled at her husband. To her, a ride sounded heavenly. Though she knew them but a little, she truly liked the Presseys as well as the Bleasdells; thus, she believed that visiting with any of them would be great fun. Furthermore, she had already determined after the Bleasdells' last visit that she wished to become better acquainted with them. Her excitement faded a little, however, when she remembered that it would not happen right away, as the apothecary had just given orders for her continued convalescence.

Alexander, as he had suggested, read to Sarah for the better part of an hour before glancing over to find her asleep. Smiling at his wife as she lay there sleeping, Alexander couldn't help but wonder what would have happened had he remained in England. To his mind, there was a real possibility that his young wife would have died. Deciding to stay where he was, next to Sarah on the bed, Alexander took a moment to pray. He thanked God for His mercy in sparing his wife.

The following morning, while Sarah was still asleep, Alexander set off to see the pastor of the Amesbury church. He hadn't seen the man since returning from England. Upon his arrival, Reverend Edmund March greeted him warmly. He then ushered Alexander over to a seat. It was just after the reverend had settled in as minister of the First Church of Amesbury that Alexander had removed to England. The reverend had always felt bad for the poor man, given that he was so young to have lost his first wife. He had also observed that Alexander's grief over his wife's death had caused him to miss out on getting to know his new wife, Sarah. He was delighted the man had finally returned and hoped that he intended to remain in Amesbury.

Since becoming acquainted with Mrs. Swyndhurst, Reverend March, though not in any unwholesome sort of way, had grown to admire her immensely. It was simply that he knew her to be the most selfless person with whom he had ever been acquainted. As he observed Mr. Swyndhurst sitting there, he whispered a silent prayer, thanking God that the man had finally returned.

"Mr. Swyndhurst, first allow me to say how delighted I am to see you. Is this to be a short visit, or shall you be staying on?"

Smiling at the kind reverend, Alexander responded, "It is my desire to remain in Amesbury. In truth, I should never have gone away in the first place. But I have to say, I was not thinking clearly at the time. The loss of my first wife had left me in somewhat of a state of confusion. I only remarried to honor my father's wishes, and to offer some protection for Sarah. I have only been home a few days, and already I find myself wondering how I could have ever left such a wonderful woman."

"I am glad to hear it. As for your reason for having left, it was, and is, completely understandable. Your heart was broken and needed time to mend; still, I am very happy to hear that you have had a change of heart. You are quite right in saying that Sarah is a wonderful woman. I have never known anyone like her. She is as selfless as they come. In the short time I have known her, she has been constant in her care of others."

Alexander was not surprised to hear the reverend's assessment of Sarah. "Reverend, my wife is presently recuperating from an illness. The apothecary explained to us that her case was rendered more serious because of her selflessness. While caring for others, she neglected to take care of herself. It is my wish that, when she is well, we not allow her to return to things as usual."

"I am certainly glad to hear it! Perhaps you may have more of an influence over her than I. You see, I have thought for some time that she was wearing herself out. But whenever I brought up the matter, she insisted she was fine."

"That sounds about right," smiled Alexander while shaking his head. "Nevertheless, I am here now. I intend to put a stop to most of her activities, even against her wishes if that is what it takes."

With relief, the reverend assured the concerned husband that he would abide by his wishes. "I take it that she shall not be in attendance for a while."

"Quite so. Mr. Brainard, the apothecary, has said it shall be weeks before she shall recover completely. Be that as it may, I may slip out of a Sunday and join you—that is, whenever I believe my wife is behaving herself enough for me to leave her in the care of the servants," he said with a chuckle.

Reverend March decided to take this opportunity to speak with the gentleman about another concern relating to his wife. "Mr. Swyndhurst, while you are here, there is another matter I wish to discuss with you." Seeing that he had the man's attention, he continued. "While you were away, I noticed that Sarah seemed oblivious to the attentions of other men. Each time a new man in town came to church, he would inevitably be drawn to your wife. I saw it happen time and time again. I always took care of it by explaining to the young men that Sarah was married. Given her disposition, I never mentioned anything to her, for I was quite certain to disclose such information would have made her uncomfortable. In addition, Martha usually accompanies her, but not having her husband attending with her—" The reverend cut off midsentence. He didn't want to make the man feel any worse for having left the young woman vulnerable.

Alexander remained silent as he listened. Though he was feeling uneasy at the direction of the conversation, he wanted to hear all that the reverend had to say.

"Mr. Swyndhurst, there is a man who would not heed my advice about staying away from your wife. As far as I know, they have not spoken, but from my vantage point at the front of the church, I have observed that he sits as close as possible—never taking his eyes off your wife. As I have said, Sarah seemed oblivious to the others; however, it is different with this man. She always appears ill at ease in his presence, even moving away from him whenever he has attempted to approach her. There is just something in the man's eyes that concerns me. As I said, I have asked that he keep his distance from her, but my words seemed to have fallen on deaf ears."

Alexander was once again glad he had come home. *Sarah doesn't need another scoundrel bothering her. By leaving Cambridge where the last man had attempted to force himself on her, her father hoped she would be free from this sort of thing.* "I am much obliged to you for telling me. I shall make a point of making my presence known. If I may ask, what is the man's name?"

"Matthew Raymond. You should keep watch for a rather tall man, approaching forty years of age, with dark, piercing eyes and brown hair streaked with silver. Whether or not there is actually anything about which to worry, I thought it best to mention it. Well, let us hope that having you here shall put an end to it."

Alexander nodded, wishing then that Sarah's father had disclosed the name of the man from Cambridge. *Or perhaps he did. I was in such a state, I simply cannot recall. But it couldn't possibly be the same man.* Shaking his head, he decided to dismiss the idea.

After the two men parted company, Alexander remained thoughtful for the rest of the day. He was thankful his wife had remained safe during his absence. He was also grateful that if things continued on as they had been, with Sarah resting a good deal of the time, she would soon be well.

Chapter 13

The following Sunday, Alexander went to church alone. Sarah was still too ill to attend. When everyone was seated, with a twofold purpose, Reverend March welcomed Mr. Swyndhurst. He hoped to make the man feel at home, but he also wished for all of the single men to know that Sarah's husband had returned. As he glanced in Matthew Raymond's direction, the reverend observed a hostile look upon the man's face. He hoped that in the future, though the man was clearly upset that Sarah's husband had come home, he would now keep his distance.

Matthew Raymond glared at the tall gentleman seated on the right side of the bench in front of him. *Who does he think he is, coming back here after leaving his wife alone for two years? She shall never be his! I shall see to that!*

Following the service, William Pressey and his wife, Susanna, approached Alexander. They had been staying in town for a few days with their grandchildren while the children's parents were away. The Presseys typically attended services at the Haverhill church. In fact, for many years Susanna had avoided the Amesbury church altogether. Some of its members had been the very ones who had accused her grandmother, Susanna Martin, of being a witch, which ultimately led to her death. On this particular day, the Presseys had been looking forward to seeing Alexander Swyndhurst. Susanna's sister, Hannah, had mentioned to them that Alexander had returned from England.

"Well, Alexander, it is wonderful to see you," smiled William Pressey, with Susanna standing close by. "Hannah told us of your return. How is Sarah? We heard that she has been ill."

"I am delighted to see you both," responded Alexander. "Yes, Sarah had been quite ill. Though she is not completely well as yet, she has improved a great deal. Jonathan and Hannah came to call recently. Sarah mentioned that you have all been attentive to her whilst I was away. I am much obliged to you for befriending her."

Susanna Pressey spoke up at this point. "Well, in truth, Alexander, Sarah has been so busy we have had very little time with her."

"Yes, I have heard, as well as seen for myself, just how hard-working she is. I hope to change all of that now that I have come home."

William grinned at the young husband. Just then, he was remembering a time when he had attempted to prevent Susanna from doing too much during her recovery from a fall. It happened before they were married. Susanna and a friend had gone out riding. Susanna's horse had spooked and reared up, sending her tumbling. She had injured her head in the fall. After thinking about it a moment, William decided to share the story.

"Well, Alexander, allow me to give you a bit of advice. Proceed with caution. I recall just such a time with Susanna before we were married. She had been injured from falling off of her horse. As I recall, she was somewhat ill-tempered during her recovery, and my reminding her to take it easy didn't go over very well." While glancing at his wife, he laughed at the look upon her face.

Susanna roared with laughter after listening to her husband. "I know all too well how irritable one can be from being ordered about. Our poor, dear Madeline Osgood bore the brunt of my bad humor, since I was staying with her at the time."

With an innocent look upon his face, William gave his version of the story to Alexander. "It wasn't so much that I ordered her about. I believe I simply suggested that she follow the apothecary's orders. As for Madeline Osgood, in view of the fact that she also had a bit of a spirited side, she was greatly amused at seeing Susanna so cross."

All three adults were laughing at this point, and as the young husband observed his friends, he was grateful to have two such wonderful people in his life.

"You have both spoken of this Madeline Osgood so often over the years, it is quite clear that you truly loved her," Alexander said with a smile, for he felt much the same about Susanna and William.

"Yes, she was one of a kind. And if it had not been for her, Susanna and I would most likely never have met," William responded as he looked devotedly at his wife.

As he observed the affection the couple had for one another, Alexander hoped that someday he and Sarah might share a similar kind of relationship. "Well, I hope you come to the house for a visit. Sarah is very fond of company, and I am certain the distraction would be much appreciated."

"But of course," smiled William. "We would be delighted to pay you both a visit."

The Presseys left after that, with a promise to call very soon at the Swyndhurst estate. Alexander then made his way out of the church. As he passed by a gentleman fitting the description the reverend had given him of a man who had been paying his wife a little too much attention, he observed that the man was glaring at him. If he had any doubt about whether this was the man about whom they had spoken, after observing his expression he believed he must indeed be Mr. Raymond. *Yes, I would describe his eyes as piercing. He appears none too happy to see me. He couldn't possibly have thought that Sarah was pleased by his attentions.* As Alexander approached his wagon to leave, missing Sarah, he was eager to get home.

A short time later, Alexander stabled his horses. After entering the house, he went in search of Sarah. Finding her in the parlor reading her Bible, he went over to inquire as to how she was feeling.

Looking a little downcast, she responded, "I am fine, Alexander. I just wish I could have gone with you."

With compassion, he replied, "I am certain that in a few weeks you shall be able to come along with me. The Presseys send their regards. They are staying with their son's children while he and his wife are away."

"Oh, how nice. The Presseys are such lovely people. So kind."

"They are indeed. They intend to visit in the near future. They want to see for themselves how you are getting along. In fact, William shared a story with me about a time when Susanna had been injured and had to convalesce for a time. It seems she didn't take it very well."

Smiling, Sarah inquired, "Did his account remind you of anyone in particular?"

Shaking his head, he answered, "If I am not careful how I answer that question, I might find myself in hot water."

The couple had a good laugh over this. Martha happened to be passing by the parlor just then. Hearing the laughter, she stopped to listen. The elderly woman was delighted to hear the two young people getting on so well. Looking up, she beseeched, "Lord, I pray for the Swyndhursts. Let them grow to love each other as a husband and wife ought."

Later that night, Alexander and Sarah were, once again, in Alexander's bedchamber. Sarah, though not completely comfortable with the idea, was becoming accustomed to sharing her husband's room. She was, however, grateful he never pressured her for anything more than conversation. Truth be told, she was beginning to enjoy their private times together. Being in her husband's company, at first, had been a good distraction from what would have otherwise been unvarying days of rest. Now, spending time with him was quickly becoming the highlight of her days. To her, he always seemed so attentive and kind. He also told many interesting stories relating to his childhood. Still, she had a troubling feeling her marriage was moving in a direction she wasn't yet ready for. Although she felt unprepared for such a change, she couldn't help but be drawn to her husband a little more every day. Nonetheless, had she known how difficult it had been for her husband to behave like a gentleman with a beautiful woman in his bed every night, she may have been hesitant about continuing to share his bedchamber.

Alexander had also been enjoying their time together. He hoped that Sarah might be growing fond of him, for he had already—in so short a time—grown to love her more than he had ever thought possible.

Chapter 14

It had been nearly four weeks since Sarah had fallen ill. After observing his wife growing stronger with every passing day, Alexander was beginning to worry less about her. Furthermore, as he had hoped and prayed, he sensed that she was more at ease around him, perhaps even appreciated his company.

As for Sarah, she was surprised to find that she was now happy to have Alexander home from England. At the start she was quite distressed about the idea, but he had been such a great source of comfort and strength since his arrival that she now felt quite differently. She also knew that if not for him, she would have been very lonesome during her recovery. Even so, there was one area, having to do with her husband, which still bothered her. In her opinion, Alexander had insisted she take it easy much longer than necessary. Left to herself, she knew she would most certainly have returned to her regular routine long ago.

On this particular morning, Alexander had been thinking about his business trip. It had been delayed due to his wife's illness. He knew the time had come for him to go. Sarah was in considerably better health. As he would only be away a few days, to go at this time he didn't believe would be a problem.

Deciding it was time to discuss the matter with Sarah, he went in the direction of the parlor. As expected, he found his wife sitting on one of the settees reading. "Sarah, would you care for a walk?"

Taking every opportunity to get out of the house, she responded happily, "Certainly! I would be delighted!"

While smiling at his wife's eagerness, Alexander escorted her out the back door to the yard. As they strolled around the grounds, he stated, "Sarah, there is something I must discuss with you."

Looking up at him, she responded, "Of course, Alexander. What is it?"

He then directed her over to the bench under a shade tree. Once she had taken a seat, Alexander took hold of her hand. "Sarah, I believe you are well enough for me to consider setting off on the business trip about which I had spoken."

Not long ago, Sarah would have welcomed the news that she would be left to herself for a few days—out from under the watchful eye of her husband. At present, however, she felt a little sad at the prospect of her husband going away, albeit for only a few days. Not wanting him to feel that he couldn't proceed with the trip he had been putting off for her sake, she replied, "Quite right...I am well now. There is no reason to delay any longer."

Alexander heard the hesitation in her voice. He hoped it meant that she would miss him. He then grew concerned that in his absence his wife might not continue to convalesce. "You must promise me that you will rest and not overexert yourself whilst I am away. Even though you are feeling better, you have not fully recovered."

At first, Sarah avoided a direct reply by changing the subject a few times. As this strategy was altogether unsuccessful, given that Alexander persisted in directing the conversation back, she reluctantly promised her husband she would continue to get plenty of rest. Nevertheless, getting rest to her meant something entirely different than it did to Alexander. She reasoned to herself that if she went with her definition of the matter, she could make such a promise. As she observed him, she felt that he needed further assurance, so she continued, "And, I shall *try* not to go beyond my limits, Alexander."

"That is not acceptable, Sarah. I would like your *promise* that you shall continue on as you have been these past few weeks; that is, not overdoing it."

"Oh...very well." *Is it not enough that I promised to rest and "try" not to do more than I ought?* "I promise," she thought about her words carefully, "to take it slow." Taking it slow, to her, was not the same as promising she would not go back to doing some of the things she had before. She was already formulating a plan for slipping away, without Martha's notice, to see the Strout family once Alexander had gone.

Alexander smiled to show his satisfaction that she had yielded. Taking her by the arm, he assisted her to her feet and then guided her back to the house.

Later that night, after Sarah had fallen asleep, Alexander searched for Martha. Finding her in the kitchen, he said, "Martha, I am to be away for a few days. I shall be leaving Monday next. Even though Sarah has vastly improved, she is not to return to her usual routine whilst I am gone."

"I am in complete agreement. As she isn't likely to listen to me, what would you have me do if she attempts to do more than she ought?"

"I am going to explain to her that, during the time I am away, she is to listen to you regarding her health. If you have any trouble with her, you might explain that I have left instructions for you to call for the apothecary with any concerns."

With a twinkle in her eye, Martha responded, "Oh...I see. If I tell her that she shall have to answer to the apothecary, she may just listen."

"Precisely!" With a wink, Alexander turned and left the room.

Upon his return to his bedchamber, as he climbed into bed Sarah stirred. "Oh, Alexander, are you having trouble sleeping?"

Having no desire to explain where he had been—speaking to Martha about her—he let his wife assume that he had been there all along. "No, I am fine. Go back to sleep."

Before he had even finished answering, he heard Sarah breathing heavily, as was often the case when she was in a sound sleep. Grateful she had not inquired further, he settled in for the night.

Over the next few days, Alexander and Sarah spent nearly every moment together. They had even had a meal together out of doors—on a quilt, where they might be alone, away from the servants. As Alexander was still reluctant to allow Sarah to venture too far from home, the meal had been on their property.

The time arrived for Alexander to set off on his trip. Although they had still not come together as husband and wife—in the traditional sense—the couple had grown very close. Alexander felt blessed to have his adorable Sarah, and Sarah was beginning to believe that having a husband was not so very bad after all.

Chapter 15

Alexander was out of bed earlier than usual to make preparations for leaving after breakfasting with his wife. As the couple conversed over their meal, they discussed Alexander's trip and all he hoped to accomplish with regard to his holdings in Boston. Besides owning a few properties in that town, he had shares in a shipbuilding company. As he had been away a long time, he intended to establish, personally, that things were going as all communications to England had implied.

As soon as Alexander had loaded up his wagon, he came to his wife, who had been waiting by the door to the house. As she observed her husband approaching, for a second time she felt a sense of sadness at his leaving. As before, she was surprised that she had grown such a deep affection for him.

Lifting her chin so that he might see her face, Alexander whispered, "I am going to miss you." He then bent his head and placed a kiss upon her brow. Just now, he wished more than anything to pull her into a full husbandly embrace, where he might feel her lips pressing against his. But alas, as close as they had become, he still felt that it wasn't yet time to demonstrate the full force of his feelings for her. He had no desire to scare her away just as she had begun to show signs that she was happy he had returned from England.

For a quick moment, Sarah leaned into his chest and answered, "I shall miss you as well. Do take care."

"I shall. No need to worry."

As Alexander turned to go, Sarah felt heaviness in her heart. She then prayed that God would keep him safe on his journey.

Alexander rode off praying for his wife that he would find her well upon his return.

Unbeknownst to Sarah and Alexander—since Matthew Raymond had been keeping a close eye on the Swyndhurst estate, after having heard that Mr. Swyndhurst was planning a trip—he had observed Sarah's husband as he was leaving.

In the weeks that Sarah has been ill, she hasn't been in church. I hope she has recovered enough to be out and about on her usual strolls while her husband is away. If I am ever going to have her, now is the time to put my plan into action. Her husband won't be here keeping watch over her. I have to act now, or I may never be presented with another opportunity! Matthew Raymond told himself.

A few days later, when her maid entered her bedchamber, Sarah was dressing. Glancing over at her, she said, "Esther, there is something I must ask you to do for me."

"What is it?" the servant inquired with curiosity, for Sarah rarely asked anything of her. Her mistress then explained that, as it had been some time since she had been to call on the Strout family, she planned to slip away to see them. Though Esther was concerned for her friend's health, she quietly listened to Sarah's plan.

"You see, I may need you to distract Martha while I make my way out of doors. I have no wish to deceive her, but I fear she would try and stop me." Once Esther had agreed to the arrangement, Sarah explained that once she had gone, should Martha inquire, the maid was at liberty to answer truthfully any questions as to her whereabouts.

Having sent Esther down first to distract Martha, Sarah quietly made her way out the front door. Once she was on her way, she breathed a sigh of relief. As she ambled along, she recalled the night she had seen Matthew Raymond hiding in the shadows. That thought caused her to pick up her pace. She also made a mental note to return home before dark. She soon spotted the Strouts' home, and all thoughts of Mr. Raymond flew out of her head. She was so excited at the prospect of seeing the children again that she nearly sprinted up to the front door. While grinning from ear to ear, she knocked, loudly.

After peeking out the window to see who was banging so forcefully, with surprise, Alice rushed over to the door and thrust it wide open. "Sarah! I had not thought to see you for some time yet. I was told at church that you suffered greatly. I felt dreadful when I heard the news, for your sickness was probably on account of your caring for us when we were ill. Nevertheless, here you are! But are you quite certain you should be out and about? Surely, your husband was not agreeable to the idea."

While hugging Alice, Sarah contested the notion that the Strouts were in any way responsible for her illness. "And as for my coming to call so soon, my departure went unnoticed. You see, my husband is away on business; otherwise, as you supposed, he would not have allowed me to come. Martha was too preoccupied to take any notice." Sarah chuckled as she offered her explanation of how she had successfully crept away. She was so happy that, at that moment, she little cared what anyone else thought about her coming to call on the Strouts.

Though she was grateful for Sarah's reassurance that her illness had nothing to do with her, or her children, Alice didn't quite believe it. And as she was a little hesitant over the news that her friend had slipped away from home to come and see them, she wanted to inquire further as to her friend's health. She didn't like the idea that Sarah may not be well enough to be out visiting; however, she remained silent while she continued to study the young woman. Looking into Sarah's happy face, she wondered how things were going at her home now that Mr. Swyndhurst, her friend's long lost husband, had returned. Sarah had never spoken much of him, thus Alice was surprised when she learned that he was back in Amesbury.

In truth, she was glad that Sarah had come, regardless of how she had managed it, for Alice had so much she wanted to know.

As Sarah studied Alice, she noticed that she appeared troubled, for unbeknownst to Sarah, her friend had many questions to ask her. To set Alice's mind at ease, Sarah assured her, "Oh, I can see by your expression that I have not convinced you. I am fine. Truly I am, Alice." Sarah then took a seat, scooped up little Mary, and placed her on her lap. When Samuel and Elizabeth approached, she pulled them into an embrace as well. Young Mrs. Swyndhurst felt so content, she never wanted to leave.

Sarah was yet unaware that Matthew Raymond had been keeping an eye out for her and had seen her out walking, on her way to the Strouts' home. While he waited for her to pass by again on her way home, he decided to stand in a different location than he had previously, for he was certain Sarah had seen him the last time he had secretly waited and watched for her. Before, all he was prepared to do was watch her. This time, however, he intended to act. He didn't want her catching a glimpse of him and making her escape.

Sarah remained for most of the day. In fact, to her dismay, when she was finally prepared to set off for home, it was growing dark.

Back at the Swyndhurst estate, Martha had just become aware of Sarah's absence. She had been too preoccupied with taking an inventory of the food stores to notice her mistress had gone out for the day. She had also assumed Esther, as she had been directed, was looking after Sarah.

"You say she has been gone all day?"

"Yes, M...Martha. She assured me that she would be gone but a short time," Esther, answered with a downcast look. She knew it wasn't in Sarah's best interest to be out as yet, but as her employer's friend, she had been reluctant to make her feelings known. Moreover, she was all too aware of Sarah's love for the Strout children, and that she had been unable to see them for weeks. She also didn't think Sarah would be gone long enough for any real harm to come to her. In fact, she thought it might just set her friend's mind at ease if she were to see the children.

"Send for Peter straight away. I wish for him to go and fetch Mrs. Swyndhurst this instant!" spat Martha, angry that she had allowed such a thing to happen. After Esther had gone, Martha continued to mull over what had occurred. *What will Mr. Swyndhurst say when he learns of this? Sarah is not yet strong enough to be out visiting. Such a thing might have an ill effect on her health. Knowing her as I do, I should not have been so irresponsible. I ought to have checked on her hours ago.*

◊◊◊

Just as Sarah was passing by the place where Matthew Raymond—hidden from view behind some shrubbery—was waiting for her to reemerge, he reached out and snatched the young woman. Covering her mouth to

118

hide her cries, he dragged her down the road toward his house. She fought him the entire way, but she was just too small. No matter how much she thrashed about, she simply could not break free. To her utter dismay, she noticed that they were almost at his front door. As soon as they had entered, he carried her in the direction of his bedchamber. As they mounted the stairs, her heart was beating so fast, she thought it might fly out of her chest. Her mind raced with how she could get herself out of the horrifying situation, but by this point, she was completely exhausted from the struggle. Her legs were also shaking to such an extent that she wasn't certain she could even stand if she tried.

"I have waited for you, little miss, for a very long time. You have never even glanced my way at church. And whenever you have passed by my home on your way to that blind woman's house and I have called out to you, you scarcely answered a word. For quite some time now, I have attempted to gain your attention! Did you think that by leaving Cambridge you would be rid of me?"

Trembling from head to toe, Sarah answered in no more than a whisper, "I do not understand. Why have you brought me here?"

"Because you are mine! Do you hear? That husband of yours had no right to return. I knew you first. What is more, he abandoned you for nearly two years. In all of that time, I have patiently waited for you to understand that my love for you is vastly different. Did I not demonstrate my deep affection for you by following you to Amesbury? And I would never have gone away and left you. I had hoped you would come to me willingly. Had that been the case, we might have remained in Amesbury. As it is now, we shall have to go away from here."

As Sarah attempted to gain control of her emotions, though she knew his name, she couldn't address him properly. All she could squeak out was, "Mr....ah—"

Angered by the belief that the young woman, who had long been the object of his affections, did not even remember his name, the enraged man pulled Sarah over to the bed. He planned to show her right then that she belonged to him; after that, he would follow through with his plan to take her away. He had waited so long to have Sarah for himself, he little cared that he would be leaving his home, and everything he owned behind.

After what seemed an eternity to Sarah, the man appeared to have relaxed his hold, affording her the opportunity to slip from his grasp. Pulling her clothes down over herself, while shaking uncontrollably, she darted from the room. After nearly falling down the stairs, she stumbled out the door before Mr. Raymond could retrieve his own clothing and go after her.

Once out of doors, she hastily made her way along the shrubbery, attempting to conceal her location should the man follow after her, which she was certain he would do. When she was almost home, while pausing to be sure the horrible man was nowhere to be seen, she observed an elderly gentleman approaching whom she knew to be Joseph Hoyt from church. Before her most recent illness, which had caused her to be absent on several Sundays, she had been introduced to the kind gentleman. Just now, he was strolling by and noticed her hiding in the shadows, crying.

Recognizing her, he asked with great concern, "My dear, what has happened? May I be of some assistance?" Nearly fainting, she fell into his arms. It did not take long for him to figure out what had transpired. Watching for her attacker, he stood guard over her as he helped her along. Some distance behind them, Matthew Raymond spotted the pair. While cursing himself for allowing Sarah to escape, he returned home, hoping for another opportunity to present itself, and that Sarah, as he had warned, would not reveal what had happened.

As soon as she felt they were at a safe distance from her attacker, since she was now in front of her own home, Sarah felt that she had no choice but to disclose the entirety of what had happened to the elderly gentleman. While explaining, she came to the realization that she must flee from Amesbury, for it was her belief that her husband would surely not want her now, and to remain might put her in further jeopardy. She knew the man who had injured her would do just as he had disclosed—hold her captive in some other town where no one would find her—if he captured her again.

After explaining everything to the gentleman, Sarah believed he would agree with her plan to leave town. She also secretly hoped he might assist her in escaping.

Having understood the young woman's wish to get away, given that she believed her husband would no longer want her and that she feared her attacker, Mr. Hoyt promised to help her. He quickly came up with a plan, though he did not disclose the whole of it to Sarah. He explained that he had a daughter in Boston who would surely take her in. His intention was to convey her there, and then send word to her husband of her whereabouts. He little believed the young woman was correct in her assumption that her husband would discard her after what had happened. In his mind, the young woman was just too distraught to be thinking clearly.

Having readily agreed to the kind man's offer of assistance and stating that she would be ready when he returned, Sarah quietly entered her home and made her way to her bedchamber to gather up a few of her belongings. Martha was so distracted by the fact that Peter had been so slow in departing for the Strouts' home that she had taken little notice of anything else. Esther, on the other hand, had seen her mistress making her way up the stairs, thus she followed after her.

Upon entering Sarah's bedchamber, Esther quickly noticed the torn garments and specks of blood on her friend's face and clothes. She also thought, when looking at Sarah's profile, she detected a bruise emerging just below her eye, and a swollen lip. "What happened? Did you take a fall?"

As her mistress turned toward her, it became obvious to the maidservant that Sarah—appearing utterly terrified—had been crying. Quickly approaching her mistress, she grabbed ahold of her shoulders.

"Tell me what has happened to you?"

Sarah finally spoke. Through her tears, she divulged almost all that had taken place as well as her plan to go away. Without revealing his name, she explained about the elderly gentleman who had assisted her. She went on to say that he would be returning for her to take her away where she would be safe. After pulling off her torn, stained garments, she went over to her washbasin to clean herself.

While in shock over what she had just been told, Esther quietly watched as her young mistress all but washed herself raw. In hearing Sarah sob as she scrubbed herself, Esther's heart nearly broke. Not knowing what to do, she just stood there. Finally, she spoke, "Are you quite certain that this is the best course of action? Surely, there is no need to go away. Your husband will protect you from that awful man."

Glancing over at Esther, she replied, "I have to go, Esther. Please understand. Alexander isn't going to want me after—" Turning her head to conceal her emotions, she continued. "Esther, I have no choice! Can you not see that?"

Then, gaining strength for what she must do, Sarah swiftly dressed. Following that, she hastily threw some of her belongings into a sack. After placing her soiled garments into her friend's hands, she asked her to keep them out of sight and at the first opportunity to discard them. As she approached the door to take her leave, she made Esther promise to keep her secret.

Weeping, Esther nodded her head. After Sarah had gone from the room, Esther prayed for her friend. She then prayed that God would help her to honor Sarah's wish that she keep her secret. She knew it would be no little task, as she would most certainly be questioned.

Chapter 16

Martha was beside herself with worry by the time Peter returned. Her underservant sensed, by her strained expression, that she was eager for news; thus, he quickly explained that Mrs. Swyndhurst had left the Strouts' home earlier that evening. Thinking a moment about what to do next, Martha decided to send the young man on to some of the other neighbors' homes to learn whether Sarah had made more than one visit that evening.

A short time later, Peter arrived back at the estate. He told Martha that with the exception of Alice Strout, Mrs. Swyndhurst had not been seen by anyone else that evening.

Having moved from anger to despair at having no word of Sarah's whereabouts, Martha sat sobbing at the kitchen table. Esther remained out of sight, for she was certain she would soon be asked if she knew the whereabouts of her mistress. What she didn't know was Martha was so consumed with worry that she had not even thought to inquire further of her.

The following afternoon, upon his arrival, Alexander Swyndhurst came sauntering into the house, in the direction of the kitchen. He had finished his business much earlier than he had thought possible, and was delighted to be returning home to Sarah so soon. He wished he had not had to make the trip at all, but he had seen no way around it. Upon entering the kitchen, he found a despondent Martha sitting at the table.

Considering the fact that she had gone, herself, that very morning to call on all of the neighbors Sarah frequently visited, the elderly woman was at a loss as to what to do next. As she looked up at Mr. Swyndhurst with red, swollen eyes, she scarcely could find her voice. "Mr. Swyndhurst, something has happened to Sarah."

Alarmed by her words, he swiftly moved toward the doorway with the intention of going directly to his wife. Martha called him back over to the table. Taking a seat beside her, he grabbed hold of her hand and inquired, "What has happened? Has the apothecary been here?"

"No, Mr. Swyndhurst, it isn't that. I don't know how to tell you this except to come right out with it. Sarah is...missing." With her head hanging low from worry and exhaustion, Martha explained that Sarah had slipped out to call on Alice Strout and her children. She went on to say, "I was so preoccupied that I never noticed until it was growing dark that I had not seen Sarah about all day. Not finding her anywhere, I sent for Esther to inquire what she knew, if anything, of Sarah's whereabouts. She informed me that your wife had gone to the Strouts' home. So, as you see, the fault is mine. I should have been looking after her myself, rather than expecting Esther to see to her."

"Martha, I am not concerned with whose fault it is. Have you sent anyone there to fetch her?" the husband asked with growing concern. "Perhaps she has simply been delayed. It isn't unheard of for her to stay the night in order to look after Alice's children."

Nodding, Martha responded, "As soon as Esther told me where Sarah had gone, I sent Peter after her. She had taken leave of the place before Peter arrived. I then sent Peter to check with all of the neighbors that Sarah regularly visits. She was nowhere to be found. Just this morning, I went myself to all of her usual places, but to no avail."

With fear rising up in Alexander's heart, he insisted that Martha assemble the servants in the parlor. Before long, they were all gathered for their employer to question them. With Martha at his side, Mr. Swyndhurst, in turn, looked each of his servants in the eye to inquire if they had any information regarding his wife's whereabouts. He was hoping that one of them knew something that would explain Sarah's absence.

Esther was greatly troubled as she stood before Mr. Swyndhurst and his head servant. She watched intently as the worried husband made his way down the line of servants. When he finally approached her, she dropped her eyes to the floor. She believed that in order to keep Sarah's secret she must not look up, for the distress she had observed on her employer's face as he spoke with each of the other servants was almost more than she could bear.

Martha had been observing Esther all the while Mr. Swyndhurst questioned the others. She suspected that Esther knew something; thus, she was anxious for it to be the young woman's turn to be questioned. Martha felt some relief at the thought that the maidservant might know Sarah's whereabouts. *Perhaps it is nothing more than Sarah, up to her usual practices, not wanting anyone to stop her from going off to the aid of some unfortunate soul. Sarah has most likely sworn the young woman to secrecy; otherwise, why would she be behaving so strangely?* But as soon as Martha gave herself a moment to consider upon this line of thought, she dismissed her suspicions. They had checked all of Sarah's usual places. *What is it, then? She surely seems to be hiding something.*

"Esther, look at me!" Mr. Swyndhurst demanded. He had also sensed that Esther was concealing something.

As Esther glanced up, she began to cry. "She made me promise not to tell."

"What did she make you promise not to tell?" the master of the house impatiently inquired.

"What am I to do? She shouldn't have made me promise. She was hurt and—"

Fear flashed across the worried husband's face at the thought that Sarah had been injured in some way. Angry that the young woman would not reveal what she knew, he glared at her. By now, Esther was beginning to believe that divulging what she knew of the situation might just be the right thing to do.

Wanting to address Esther privately, Mr. Swyndhurst sent the other servants out of the room and then escorted her over to a seat. He attempted to calm himself before inquiring further of the distraught young woman. "Esther, what happened? What did you mean when you said that Sarah had been hurt?"

"Please believe me; I meant no harm. She asked me not to tell, and then convinced me it was the right thing to do—keeping quiet, I mean."

"Yes, yes, Esther. Now out with it!" He was, once again, losing his temper with the young woman.

Sobbing, Esther began, "Sarah was attacked on her way home last night. When I came upon her in her bedchamber, she was shaking violently. As I approached her, I noticed her gown was torn and bloodstained." Taking a deep breath, she continued. "When I inquired about her appearance, through her tears she explained that a man had taken her against her will. As she was terrified of him coming after her, since he had said he planned to take her away somewhere, she felt the need to escape." Not wanting to say more, especially that Sarah had thought her husband would no longer want her, Esther turned her head away.

Upon hearing Esther's account, Mr. Swyndhurst was left speechless. He wanted to find out all he could, but no words would come. His heart hurt for Sarah too much to speak.

Though she was feeling ill at the thought that Sarah had been attacked, Martha spoke up, for besides observing the state her employer was in, at that moment she sensed there was more to the story. "Esther, there is more, is there not? You best tell us everything you know."

Looking at her lap, Esther continued, "Mr. Swyndhurst, Sarah believed you would no longer want her now that another man has—" She couldn't even bring herself to say it. What had happened to Sarah was simply too dreadful to be spoken aloud. Glancing at Mr. Swyndhurst, Esther sighed, for to look at him now, she knew Sarah had been wrong about her husband not wanting her. As Esther had suspected when Sarah had revealed her fear of being rejected, it just could never be true. Mr. Swyndhurst loved her friend too much to toss her aside because of what had happened.

As she continued to survey her employer, she wished she hadn't had to burden him, along with everything else, with what Sarah had thought about how he would react to the situation. But given that she wasn't practiced at concealing things, as evidenced by the fact that Martha and Mr. Swyndhurst had already called her out, she felt she had no choice but to tell all.

With tears in his eyes, the distressed husband persisted in questioning his maidservant, "You say her garments...were torn and covered...with blood?"

Esther nodded in the affirmative. "Not that much blood," she clarified in an attempt to reassure the devastated husband that his wife would be all right. "It must have been from where the man struck her in the face, and—" While clamping her hand over her mouth, Esther's eyes grew wide, for she knew she was only making things worse by sharing too many details with her troubled employer.

Wincing at the thought of someone striking his tiny wife, Mr. Swyndhurst asked, "How do you know she was struck in the face, Esther? Did she tell you she was?"

As she shook her head no, wishing all the while she had just kept her mouth shut, reluctantly she responded, "Her lip was swollen, and there was a bruise beginning to show on her cheek. I think she was injured in other ways as well, from the way she carried herself."

Then, with heavy hearts the three went up to Sarah's bedchamber. Esther had cleaned the washbasin but had not had time to remove Sarah's ruined garments from the room. After retrieving them from the floor in the corner of the room, Esther handed the garments to her employer and backed away. Alexander sobbed at the sight of the torn, blood-stained clothing. He then rolled Sarah's things up in a ball. There was no doubt in his mind now—his wife had been violated.

"Esther, what do you know of her means of escape?" Martha inquired since Mr. Swyndhurst was still too upset to formulate very many questions of her own.

"She told me that an elderly gentleman—though she would not reveal his name—had come to her rescue after she had broken away from her captor. She stated that the gentleman had said he would take her someplace where she would be safe."

Gaining control of his emotions, her employer asked, "Is that all she said?" He was hoping for more information.

"That is all. I know of nothing more." With sadness in her eyes for Mr. Swyndhurst, sobbing, Esther stood there wishing she hadn't had to add to his misery. Soon, Martha dismissed her. Alexander and his elderly friend remained in the room to discuss all that Esther had disclosed.

Chapter 17

An hour later, having remembered what the minister had said about the man who had been much too interested in his wife, Alexander set off for Reverend Edmund March's house. Upon his arrival, he quickly informed the reverend of all that had taken place. He then requested that the reverend accompany him to Matthew Raymond's home. He intended to question the man about Sarah's whereabouts. Alexander didn't expect an honest answer—or that the man even knew where Sarah went—but he hoped to ascertain, by the man's demeanor, whether he had been involved in what had happened to her.

Matthew Raymond, passing by his front window, caught a glimpse of two men approaching. As he looked closer, recognizing Mr. Swyndhurst and the reverend, he grew angry. He had planned to be long gone by now. To his utter amazement, the tiny woman had escaped him. He had run after her, but by the time he had dressed and gained the out of doors, she was nowhere to be seen. As he had continued to look for her, he had spotted her down the road with another person, not far from her home. He had, therefore, been forced to give up the chase, or risk revealing his identity to whomever was with her.

While making his way to the door, Matthew Raymond wondered if he should have fled. He didn't think he was in any real danger of being discovered, for he was aware that Sarah had been missing since she had escaped him. Two different servants from the Swyndhurst estate, a young man and, later, an elderly woman, had come to inquire whether he had seen Mrs. Swyndhurst, and they hadn't seemed to suspect him in the least. To him, it appeared as though she had secretly taken leave of the town. Besides, he reasoned, if the men had come because Sarah had revealed what he had done to her, they would likely have been accompanied by the constable. Therefore, as calmly as possible he opened the door to the two men and ushered them in. As they questioned him, he feigned sympathy for the husband's plight. Though they justified their reasons for having questioned him—that he lived close by—their facial expressions indicated otherwise. They suspected him, all right, and he knew it.

Once they had gone, he breathed a sigh of relief. Though he believed that Sarah would have been too fearful of what he might do to her if she had told, he hadn't been all that certain she would remain silent. Just now, however, he grasped that the visit with the men would have gone drastically different if she had in fact informed on him. He reasoned that he may have even been hauled off to jail;

however, that she was missing, the despicable man knew was an unforeseen advantage for him.

As he hadn't been completely certain that Sarah had not eventually returned to her home, this visit with the reverend and Mr. Swyndhurst had confirmed for the treacherous man that Sarah was still missing. *She must have been too ashamed or too scared to remain. I shall have to keep an eye on Mr. Swyndhurst's comings and goings if I am to learn where Sarah has gone.*

Even though they both truly felt that Mr. Raymond was somehow involved, Alexander and Reverend March spent the rest of the day calling upon many of the people with whom they attended church. They hoped that one of them might have seen something.

Just as Alexander was getting ready to take his leave—after bringing the reverend home—he had a question, "Reverend, what do you know about Matthew Raymond? I don't believe he was residing in Amesbury prior to my leaving for England."

"Well...no, no I do not think he was. If I remember correctly, he came along shortly after you left. Why do you ask?"

Looking thoughtful, Alexander replied, "What I am thinking is just too unbelievable to be true."

"What is?"

"Well, there was a man in Sarah's home town who had incessantly pursued her. In fact, that was the chief reason her father, aware that he was dying, wanted her to come under my protection. Do you think it possible that Matthew Raymond and the man from Cambridge are one and the same?"

"Anything is possible. As I said before, though she little noticed the attentions of other men, she did seem to shy away from Mr. Raymond whenever he came near. If it is the same man, I wonder at her not telling you about him."

Hanging his head, the guilt-ridden husband responded, "Why would she? It is not as though I have been available to her. I have only just returned from England."

The reverend wished he hadn't asked. He could see the worried husband didn't need anything else about which to feel at fault. "One would think she would have at least told Martha, if, in fact, it is true—that he is the man from Cambridge. But it surely would seem to fit with what your maid-servant told you happened to Sarah."

Alexander nodded in agreement. "That was my thinking—what has happened is just too similar to what occurred in Cambridge. And as for Sarah's reasons for not telling at least Martha, she never was one to worry others, especially Martha. No, I am certain; if Matthew Raymond and the man from Cambridge are one and the same, Sarah would not have told Martha. Furthermore, whether he is or he isn't the one who...it is not as though he would know where Sarah is now." Glancing at the reverend, Alexander sensed that he had thought the same—Matthew Raymond was of no use in their search for Sarah. "I better be going. I am much obliged to you for coming along with me today."

"Think nothing of it. Sarah is very dear to all of us. We shall pray that you find her, and soon."

With that, the two men parted company. It was quite late when the troubled and exhausted husband finally returned home. Coming into the kitchen, he found that his servant-friend had been awaiting his return. As soon as she noticed the expression upon her employer's face, she knew he hadn't been successful at finding his wife. The pair remained at the table until the wee hours, deciding what to do next.

A couple of days later, Alexander made arrangements with a gentleman by the name of James Haddon to seek out all possibilities for where Sarah might have gone. The hired man was also to see what he could learn of the older gentleman with whom she had gone away.

Similarly, Alexander had devised a schedule for himself to visit the surrounding towns. He hoped to learn whether Sarah had passed through or might yet be in one of the towns he planned to visit.

Martha and the other servants were beside themselves with worry over their beloved mistress. Esther had been especially troubled by the fact that she might have prevented Sarah from leaving, had she just informed Martha. Mr. Swyndhurst had attempted to reassure her that he did not hold her responsible, but Esther could not help but blame herself for her employer's misery.

Alexander's heart ached for his poor wife. He knew that what had happened to her had to have been most devastating, and as it was now, he could not be there to comfort her. The thing that troubled him most was that she could possibly think he no longer wanted her. He would never have held her responsible for what had happened. In reality, if he was holding anyone responsible, other than her assailant, it was himself for not having been there for her since they were wed. Oh, he knew he had been back for a while now, hoping to make it up to her, but it was too late. He had left his poor wife unprotected for far too long.

And then there was Martha. She had also been blaming herself for not keeping a better watch over Sarah. From the time the young woman had vanished, she was all the elderly servant could think about, wondering where she might have gone. They had to locate her, and soon. Martha feared that the longer it took, the less likely it would be that they would ever find her.

Just then, there was a knock at the door. Martha hastily opened it, hoping there might be news. Who she found was the constable, standing there on the threshold. She ushered him into the parlor to wait while she went in search of Mr. Swyndhurst. Finding him in his bedchamber, she informed him that the constable was waiting in the parlor to speak with him. After following his servant-friend down the stairs, Mr. Swyndhurst went to find out what had brought the constable to his house.

As Alexander entered the room, he greeted the gentleman. He had been to see Charles Caldwell, the constable, the morning after Sarah had been attacked. At that time he had disclosed his suspicions about Matthew Raymond to Mr. Caldwell. Following that, the constable had made inquiries of his own with the man in question, but to no benefit. In spite of this, after having met with Matthew Raymond, the constable shared Alexander's concerns—there was something not quite right about Mr. Raymond.

At this moment, Alexander hoped there had been news of Sarah. Once the constable had explained that he had no further information concerning Mrs. Swyndhurst's whereabouts, the two men spoke about what to do next to find her. Alexander enlightened him to the fact that he had a man going from town to town to see what he could learn—if anything. Alexander then informed the constable that he himself would also be making visits to as many towns as possible in the days to come. Mr. Caldwell agreed with Mr. Swyndhurst's plan, and then offered to send missives on his behalf to the constables in the surrounding towns.

Once that bit of business was settled, the constable reluctantly explained the real purpose for his visit. He had some information as to the possible identity of the elderly gentleman who had helped Sarah. He knew the concerned husband deserved to know any information he had uncovered, but he disliked getting the man's hopes up. "It seems that Mr. Joseph Hoyt took leave of the town around the same time as Sarah. Though Mr. Hoyt is rather new to Amesbury, he has made the acquaintance of many of the people in town—each of whom, when asked, spoke well of him. One in particular disclosed that he believed Mr. Hoyt might have gone to see his daughter. The problem being that no one seems to know the whereabouts of the gentleman's daughter—only that he had mentioned his intentions of paying her a visit in the near future."

Given all of this, the constable and Mr. Swyndhurst surmised that Mr. Hoyt must have indeed set off to see his daughter—possibly taking Sarah along.

Upon hearing this bit of information, and that the constable, like himself, believed it plausible that Sarah was with Mr. Hoyt, Alexander felt hope for the first time since Sarah had gone missing. The constable assured Alexander that he would keep digging until he came up with more information with regard to where Sarah had gone. As he observed Mr. Swyndhurst, he realized that, though he hadn't wanted to raise his hopes, the man obviously needed some bit of promising information. He was glad he had decided to share what he knew.

Once Mr. Caldwell had gone, Alexander relayed to Martha all that had been said. Just as he had, she felt hopeful that the new information might eventually lead them to Sarah.

Chapter 18

Sarah had hidden herself under a blanket in Mr. Hoyt's wagon as they made their way out of town. She did not want to be seen by Matthew Raymond or anyone else. Still in shock over what had taken place, as well as what had transpired since—that she was leaving town with Mr. Hoyt—Sarah, now that she had come out from under the blanket, sat staring straight ahead.

Late the second day, after having stayed the night at an inn in one of the towns through which they had passed, Sarah inquired as to where they were going. If the elderly gentleman had mentioned their destination, she could not remember. Mr. Hoyt, knowing he had already informed his young friend that he was taking her to Boston, assured her that where they were going, she would be quite safe. He was sure she just wanted to be certain she would be out of danger. He further informed her that it was to the home of his daughter and son-in-law, Joanna and Daniel Thompson, who were both about ten years older than she. Mr. Hoyt felt certain she would feel at home there, and said as much to her.

The elderly man had already been intending a visit to his daughter's home; therefore, that they were doing so now was not that much of an inconvenience. Given that his son-in-law was a physician, Mr. Hoyt was doubly glad that he was taking Sarah there. He hoped that Daniel would have a look at his young friend, for he felt that, if her bruised face and slow movements were any indication, she might have been seriously injured in the attack. As she had communicated little since they had set off, he was convinced that, had she indeed been hurt beyond what was visible, she would not have let on. This worried him exceedingly.

As there were no opportunities for university training in the discipline of medicine within the colonies, Joanna, Mr. Hoyt's daughter, and Daniel, his son-in-law, had removed to England for a time where Daniel could receive university instruction, for it was his wish to be a physician rather than an apothecary or surgeon. He had now been practicing in Boston for five years.

As it was nearly forty miles from Amesbury to Boston, Sarah and Mr. Hoyt had traveled for two-and-a-half days, stopping off each night along the way. The elderly gentleman had taken it slow, not wanting to further injure his traveling companion.

As they journeyed, Sarah kept an eye out for her husband. She was sure he would be passing along the same road on his way home to Amesbury. If need be, to escape his notice, she had every intention of scurrying beneath the blanket again.

As Mr. Hoyt pointed toward his daughter's house, Sarah, though a little surprised at not seeing him, was relieved they had arrived without coming upon her husband along the way. She presumed that either he had been delayed in Boston longer than he had intended or when she and Mr. Hoyt had stopped off each night, they had simply not been on the road at the same point in time.

As they approached Mr. Hoyt's daughter's home, more than a little nervous, Sarah felt a knot in the pit of her stomach; however, as Joanna Thompson came hastening out the door with a large smile on her face, Sarah's nerves began to calm. Still observing Mrs. Thompson as she made her way over to them, Sarah noted how lovely she was. From where she sat, the woman appeared rather tall, with long, shiny brown hair, which was presently pinned back at the sides of her head.

Stopping at the side of the wagon, Joanna, still smiling, looked up. "Father, I am so delighted to see you. You sent word that you might pay us a visit, but I had no idea you would come so soon."

After climbing down, Mr. Hoyt embraced his daughter. "Yes...I came a bit earlier than I had originally intended. I hope my arriving at this time is acceptable."

"Of course, Father. Now, who do we have here?" Joanna inquired as she observed Sarah. She quickly detected that the taut face staring back at her appeared quite bruised.

"This is my young friend, Sarah Swyndhurst. She shall be staying as well." Mr. Hoyt knew his daughter well. She would never turn anyone away.

"That is simply wonderful!" Joanna replied so as to put her guest at ease, for she had surmised that the young woman must have suffered some terrible ordeal to be so black and blue. Talking directly to Sarah now, Joanna said, "Sarah, you are quite welcome here."

Not completely believing that her unexpected presence was truly satisfactory to Mr. Hoyt's daughter— while grasping Mr. Hoyt's hand as he assisted her down from the wagon—she responded, "I hope this is not too much of an imposition."

"Not at all. Just leave your things. I shall send Daniel or one of the boys out to collect them." Daniel and Joanna had two sons: Daniel, Jr., age ten, and Joseph, two years his brother's junior. With their shiny brown hair, both boys resembled their mother.

Sarah and Mr. Hoyt followed Joanna to the house. Sarah would typically have taken in her surroundings, especially since they were so charming, what with Joanna's lovely flower garden and large, well-maintained house. But with such a heavy heart, she scarcely noticed a thing. Soon they were seated in the parlor with tea and cookies. "I shall show you both to your rooms after you sit a while. We will be having our evening meal in a couple of hours. If you feel the need to rest beforehand, do not hesitate."

Before long, Sarah was shown to one of the guest bedchambers, where her belongings had preceded her. After her hostess had gone, Sarah slumped down on the bed. As when they had first arrived, she barely noticed her surroundings. Had she been interested, she might have observed the white lace pillows and brightly colored patchwork quilt upon the bed. It was a spacious room with its own little settee against the west wall. The view from the window, had she been looking, might have brightened her mood a bit, as it overlooked an expansive backyard with a glistening stream in the distance. She may also have detected the decorative bench situated under a lovely shade tree from which one might observe the sparkling water.

As it was, Sarah could scarcely keep her eyes open long enough to pull off her shoes and rest her head against one of the pillows. As she slept, her mind went to the terrible man who had harmed her. She tossed and turned from the torturous images.

In the parlor, Mr. Hoyt gave a brief synopsis of what had happened to the young woman he had brought along on his visit. After cautioning her sons not to mention Sarah's bruised face, which her husband hadn't yet seen, Joanna had sent the boys out before their grandfather had begun his explanation concerning Sarah. Though they wanted to know more about the bruises on their guest's face, the boys had acquiesced to their mother's wishes. Just now, with eyes wide, husband and wife were listening intently to the family patriarch.

"Daniel, I am not certain but that Sarah might have been injured—beyond what can be seen, that is. I do not believe she would have let on if she had been. Additionally, she hadn't been to church in weeks because of an illness. For both of these reasons, do you suppose we might find a way to convince her to allow you to have a look at her?"

With understanding for Joseph's concerns, Daniel responded, "Well, with what she has been through, she might be reluctant to allow any man near her, but I shall certainly try. I am concerned as well about the bruises you mentioned."

Joanna had tears in her eyes as she thought about what Sarah had suffered. She wanted to help her in any way that she could. "Perhaps I might persuade her to allow Daniel to see to her."

Soon, the three sitting in the parlor heard noises coming from the direction of Sarah's bedchamber. To them, it sounded like someone was crying. Realizing it was Sarah, Joanna hastened to her.

As she entered the bedchamber in which her guest was currently resting, Joanna noted that her suspicions regarding the noise had been correct. She quickly went to the young woman. Gently taking hold of Sarah's shoulders while whispering her name, Joanna attempted to wake her.

After opening her eyes, Sarah glanced around the room and then at the person sitting beside her. She soon remembered where she was. As she observed a woman with large brown eyes looking so intently at her—recalling her name, she asked, "Is there something wrong, Joanna? Have I slept too long?"

"No...no. It is just that you sounded as though you were having a nightmare. We heard you cry out."

With embarrassment, Sarah dropped her eyes. "Oh, I am sorry, Joanna. Please forgive me. I did not mean to disturb anyone."

Feeling bad for the young woman that she would think she had been a bother, Joanna assured her, "Sarah, you didn't disturb anyone. We were simply concerned for you. Are you all right?"

By now, a tear had slipped down Sarah's cheek. "I really do not know how to answer that."

Without saying a word, Joanna leaned forward and pulled Sarah into her arms. The two women then spent the next few minutes weeping.

After a while, Sarah, completely unaware of how her face appeared, pulled back to look at Joanna's face. "Did your father tell you what happened?"

A bit hesitant to answer, in case Sarah might not have wanted what had happened to her to become known, Joanna finally answered, "Yes, Sarah, he did. But...he need not have said anything for us to know that something had happened. My dear, have you not seen your poor injured face?"

Reaching up to where her face had been throbbing, Sarah responded, "Oh, I should have known. It has been aching some."

"I thought as much—you have not had a look at it, then."

Sarah shook her head no, and then dropped her eyes. "I hope it shall not upset your boys to see me like this."

Touched by the fact that the young woman worried more about the boys than she seemed to care about her own injured face, Joanna answered, "Do not concern yourself over them. They have had plenty of bruises and shall most likely think you were hurt by taking part in some out of doors amusement. In fact, if anyone questions you about it, we shall simply allow them to assume just that. Not that we shall lie about it, but we shall merely avoid a direct answer."

Sarah smiled then and found herself believing she was going to like this woman.

"Furthermore, you need not worry that Daniel and I have been made aware of what happened; we shan't tell anyone. My father just wanted us to be informed, should you need anything. In fact, Sarah, my husband is a physician. We discussed that it might be best if you allowed him to have a look at you—what with all that has happened and as Father explained, you have not been unwell of late."

With a flushed face at the thought of having a man come near her, Sarah quickly responded, "No! I am quite all right! My illness was weeks ago, and I am only a little bruised—nothing more. There really is no need. In fact, I think I should be going." Without thinking through where she would actually go if she were to leave, Sarah attempted to push past Joanna.

Joanna placed her hands against Sarah's shoulders to stop her. As she was a good deal larger, she had little difficulty in preventing the young woman from rising. "Sarah, I am not going to force you to allow Daniel to examine you. Please, do not worry. As for your leaving, I shall not hear of it. You are to stay as long as you wish. Truth be told, I could use another woman around here. Those boys of mine are too high-spirited much of the time for my liking."

Sarah's racing heart began to calm as she comprehended that she would not be forced into an examination. The last man to have touched her nearly destroyed any sense of safety she had previously had. Thinking a moment about being useful to Joanna with her sons, she decided if they truly needed her, she would stay. She had always been comfortable around children. Truth be told, she had known no greater joy than being with Alice Strout's children. Moreover, she knew she didn't have anywhere else to go.

"Very well, Joanna. If I can be of any use to you with the children, I would be delighted to stay. I must apologize for my outburst. Can you ever forgive me?"

"Of course. Besides, there is no need to apologize. We shall not speak of it again. Now let us go and prepare dinner."

With Joanna backing down, the matter of allowing the physician to see to Sarah was dropped for the time being; however, when Sarah was finally introduced to Mr. Thompson, just the thought of him coming near her—to see that she was well—made her shudder. Though he had kind, light blue eyes, she was glad that he would not be examining her.

Chapter 19

The following morning, Joanna suggested a walk to Sarah. Though Sarah truly enjoyed the out of doors, given what had happened to her while she was walking home from Alice's, she was reluctant to agree.

Surmising it was fear that held the young woman back, Joanna decided to try another tactic. "It is simply that I wish to call on one of our elderly neighbors, Elizabeth Brown. She lives alone and has not been well lately. Whenever I am able, I have been dropping by to assist her with her daily chores."

Joanna had been informed by her father that Sarah had been attacked while returning home from a visit with one of her neighbors. Although Sarah had said very little on their journey about what had happened or anything else to Joanna's father, he had gleaned that much the night of the attack. Armed with this knowledge, Joanna believed that helping a neighbor might just induce her new friend to accompany her. She was concerned that if Sarah didn't face her fears, she might remain indoors, indefinitely.

Sarah, though she was ill at ease about the idea, yielded. Before long, the two ladies were on their way to call upon the Thompsons' neighbor, leaving Mr. Hoyt in charge of the boys.

Within a short time, they arrived. After making the introductions, with Sarah's assistance Joanna went right to work preparing a meal. The woman was grateful the ladies had come to help. At one point, while Sarah was out of doors hanging laundry, Joanna's neighbor inquired about Sarah's bruises. Believing the information being requested to be Sarah's private affair, Joanna evaded the question. Sensing that the topic was off limits, the neighbor, Elizabeth, allowed the matter to drop.

While Sarah worked at helping with the laundry, she had all but forgotten her fears with regard to venturing away from her hosts' home. And after a few hours, Sarah and Joanna were on their way back home. As they strolled along, Sarah's anxiety about being out of doors returned. By the time they arrived, Sarah was covered with perspiration. Joanna had observed the fear upon Sarah's face while they were yet on their way. As the ladies entered the house, Joanna ushered Sarah into the parlor to rest. She then went to find her husband and father.

Discovering them out in the yard with her sons, Joanna quietly explained what she had witnessed with Sarah. Not wanting the boys to overhear, she spoke softly. As they were not at all certain that it was merely fear that had caused the reaction in Sarah, they all thought it best if Daniel had a look at her.

After his wife informed him of where to find the young woman—in the parlor—Daniel insisted Joanna and his father-in-law remain where they were while he went in alone to speak with Sarah. He had no desire to overwhelm her by the presence of all three of them; however, upon entering the parlor, the tiny woman was nowhere to be seen. He surmised, correctly, that she had gone to her bedchamber. Since he would not be able to speak with her at this time, he returned to the backyard.

As she observed her husband approaching, Joanna sent her sons off to play. She then inquired, "Why have you returned so soon? You couldn't have had enough time to see to Sarah."

"She wasn't in the parlor. She is most likely resting in her bedchamber. I shall speak with her later. What is to be done, Joseph? Her family must be beside themselves with worry. You haven't exactly said why it was that she left her home."

Nodding in understanding for his son-in-law's concern, the elderly gentleman responded, "I may not have made myself clear when I attempted to explain the situation, for I was more concerned with your knowing what had happened than her reasons for taking leave of her home. Like you, Daniel, I have been thinking about the worry her absence is undoubtedly causing for her family, but I do not believe we should act just yet. Sarah is in no way prepared to see her husband. And if I have not already explained, she believes her husband will be disgusted at the sight of her after what has happened. Perhaps even turn her out."

Stunned by news that the young woman could believe such a thing, Daniel inquired, "What do you know of the man? Could this be true? Would he indeed abandon her because of this?"

"In truth, as I have not been a resident of Amesbury for long, I know very little of the man. And from what I understand, he has been away in England for the past two years. He has only recently returned to Amesbury. I am not even sure it was to be on a permanent basis. The whole thing seems rather odd—that he would live in England while his wife resides in Amesbury. Though I have heard that he is an honorable man in business matters, perhaps Sarah knows best about what he is like as a husband. Let us wait a while before we decide what is to be done. I dislike leaving the gentleman in the dark regarding his wife, but I would also hate to see her injured any further if he were to reject her while she is in such a fragile state."

"I cannot fathom anyone leaving his wife alone for two years. Perhaps you are right. We should leave it up to Sarah for now," replied Daniel with a sigh. Turning to his wife, he pulled her into an embrace and whispered, "I could never be parted from you."

Feeling much the same, Joanna smiled at her husband. "Nor could I."

Later that night, Sarah finally emerged from her bedchamber. As she entered the parlor, she observed the family relaxing together. To make the young woman feel welcome, Joanna stood and ushered her to the settee on which she herself had been sitting. After Joanna had reclaimed her place, with Sarah now seated beside her, the two sat companionably for the remainder of the evening. And as Sarah appeared to be doing well, the plan to have Daniel take a look at her was forsaken for the time being.

Over the next few days, Sarah began to adjust to her new surroundings. Furthermore, the fear she had been experiencing at being out of doors was beginning to subside, for she had been forcing herself to walk about the yard several times a day. Not knowing what she would have done if not for Mr. Hoyt and the Thompsons, Sarah was most grateful the elderly man had been there the night of the attack, as well as having brought her along on his visit with his family.

◊◊◊

Joanna learned in the short time Sarah had been there just what a help she could be. She often found the young woman preparing meals or assisting the boys in whatever they were doing. She had even observed Sarah helping the servants with their duties. To say that Mrs. Swyndhurst was as selfless a person as she had ever known, in her estimation, was not an overstatement. Unbeknownst to Joanna, everyone with whom Sarah had ever come into contact thought much the same thing about her.

At times, when Sarah was out of earshot, the Thompsons and Mr. Hoyt discussed her state of mind. They had begun to believe she had not suffered any serious or long-term bodily injuries; however, they were not convinced that her mind would mend so easily. Still unsure whether it would be a good idea to send word to Mr. Swyndhurst as to his wife's whereabouts, they had all rejected the notion for the time being.

Chapter 20

Back at the Swyndhurst estate, Alexander was beginning to believe he may never find his wife. To no avail, he and his hired man had searched several of the surrounding towns.

In all this time, Matthew Raymond had been anxiously keeping watch over Mr. Swyndhurst's activities. He hoped to discover the moment the man learned of his wife's whereabouts. He had been contemplating whether to follow Mr. Swyndhurst and attempt to seize Sarah yet again, or take leave of town in the case that, should she be found, she divulge what he had done to her.

Martha and Esther's hearts were still breaking over the hurt their mistress had suffered. They tried to carry on as usual, but Sarah had been so much a part of everything that went on at the estate that to go on as before proved almost impossible.

On this particular day, Jonathan and Hannah Bleasdell paid Alexander a visit. They hoped to be of some comfort to their friend. Alexander had not been to church since his wife's disappearance for them to learn firsthand what had happened, but given that Jonathan Bleasdell was a close acquaintance of the reverend's, he had informed them of the details concerning Sarah.

Upon the Bleasdells' arrival, Martha shepherded them into the parlor. Finding Alexander there, Jonathan greeted the distressed husband. "Alexander, how are you, my boy?" Just to look at his young friend, he knew the answer; for Alexander's eyes were surrounded by dark shadows and his countenance was one of a man with a heavy weight on his shoulders.

After motioning for them to be seated, Alexander responded, "Not well, I'm afraid. It seems Sarah has simply disappeared." Alexander knew that Jonathan and the reverend had spoken, for he had given his consent to his pastor to speak with the Bleasdells and the Presseys. "We have searched in all of the surrounding towns. My hired man is now venturing farther."

Hannah had remained quiet while her husband attempted to console their young friend. When there was a lull in the conversation, she spoke reassuringly, "Alexander, with all of us praying, she is sure to be found. Have you any clue as to the identity of the man who attacked her?"

Hesitant to besmirch the character of the man he suspected, Alexander simply shook his head as an indication that he did not—which was in fact true; he hadn't any proof concerning his suspicions.

"I dislike disagreeing with you, Alexander, but it seems you know more than you are letting on," insisted

Jonathan. "I have known you a long time; thus, it is useless to try and conceal anything from me."

Alexander looked intently at his friend before answering. "Jonathan, I do have my suspicions; however, I am reluctant to taint someone's reputation without any real evidence against him."

"Usually, I would agree with you, but with Sarah missing, I am of the opinion that any information—even if it turns out to be incorrect—may be beneficial. You must know that Hannah and I shall surely keep anything you say to ourselves. What if you are right and we might have been able to learn something by keeping our eyes and ears open around the man, whoever he is?"

"You may be right." Taking a deep breath, he began, "You see, when I returned from England, Reverend March informed me of a man who had been paying a little too much attention to Sarah. He also informed me that Sarah was quite uneasy whenever the man was in close proximity to her. We even questioned the man the day after Sarah disappeared."

This time, Hannah spoke up. "Who is the man, Alexander?" She was certain she knew, as she had observed much the same as Reverend March.

"Matthew Raymond. As I said, I am uncomfortable with mentioning his name in case he is actually innocent," responded Alexander.

"No need to worry. Your suspicions regarding whom you believe to be the culprit shall not leave this room," assured Jonathan. "I am fairly certain that Hannah shall agree with what I am about to say: had you not revealed the man's name, we could have guessed. We had also observed his interest in your wife. Sarah little noticed when men gave her undue attention; nevertheless, when it came to Mr. Raymond, as the reverend stated, Sarah always seemed discomfited in his company."

Once again, a sense of guilt swept over Alexander for having left his wife alone for so long. Hanging his head, he muttered, "This is not the first time a man has forced his attentions on Sarah; however, her father was there to stop the other man from bringing her any real harm. This time, it is entirely my fault for having left her alone. Had I been here, the man would not have felt that she was unprotected." Alexander had no desire to make known, at this time, what his other suspicions were concerning Matthew Raymond.

"You are here now, doing your very best to find her," smiled Hannah. "Now I understand why Sarah seemed content with the sort of marriage the two of you had entered into. The incident from which her father had saved her was sure to have had an impact on her. I do not think Sarah would have ever agreed to marry you if your marriage had not been one of convenience. While you were away, besides Jonathan's desire to be certain that everything was running smoothly in your absence, we often came just to check on Sarah. On such visits, as Sarah was frequently not at home, Martha and I chatted. And from what she tells me, as well as what you have just disclosed, Sarah wasn't looking for a husband. I believe she was simply honoring her father's wishes. So, you see, you cannot blame yourself. You both went into the marriage with no real desire to be married."

"I did so appreciate your willingness to look after things in my absence, Jonathan. And, Hannah, I am grateful to you for reminding me that Sarah was no more prepared for marriage than I." Sitting there listening to Hannah, Alexander had to admit that what she had said was true. Sarah would never have married him if he had planned to remain in Amesbury. *She only consented because she believed the marriage would be in name only. And yet, I still feel responsible for what has happened.*

The couple remained but a little while longer. Alexander then spent some time thanking the Lord for his faithful friends and again praying that he would find Sarah.

Later that evening, Alexander's hired man, James Haddon, returned with the latest information he had uncovered. Alexander escorted him into his private study where they might be alone. James then explained that he had been unable to discover much regarding Mr. Hoyt's daughter, other than that the man did indeed have a daughter. He went on to say that in view of the fact that Mr. Hoyt was so little acquainted with the town's inhabitants, as he had only been in residence a short time, no one had any helpful information to share. Though he hated to admit it to the distraught husband, it now appeared that they were at a dead end with regard to the elderly gentleman. "This is so frustrating! I am certain Mr. Hoyt is the man with whom Sarah left town. Even though it seems there is no more to learn about the man's family—keep digging. There must be someone who knows where Mr. Hoyt's daughter lives."

After Mr. Haddon had gone, Alexander decided to map out where he would travel next in his search for Sarah. He couldn't leave it all on the hired man's shoulders, and with two of them looking, they were more likely to learn something.

Chapter 21

It had been approximately five months since Sarah arrived with Mr. Hoyt at his daughter's home in Boston. Winter was nearly over. Daniel Thompson had been observing Sarah each morning for the past several weeks. After breakfasting with his family, she had often felt poorly and would need to rest a while. And with as little as she was eating, her midriff, though she had been attempting to conceal it by keeping her cape draped about her, appeared to be expanding. If his suspicions were correct, the young woman was with child. Given that she had yet to share the news, he wondered what was going through her mind.

Having expressed his concern to his wife regarding their guest, he believed the time had come to speak with Sarah directly. When he had discussed the matter with Joanna, she had agreed and shared that she had suspected the same but hadn't wanted to address the issue until Sarah was ready to speak about it. Thus, while his boys were out of earshot, Daniel knocked on Sarah's door. When she saw that it was Daniel at the door, her heart felt as though it might fly out of her chest. Not that she feared him any longer, as she had early on, but it was only that she knew what was coming; he had figured it out. It had taken a few months for her to accept that she was with child, but she had resigned herself to the fact for some time now. She hadn't wished to discuss the matter with anyone until she came to terms with it herself, for accepting it and knowing what to do about it were two vastly different things. As a result, besides trying to wish it away, she had been attempting to keep it a secret.

Sarah's biggest obstacle in allowing herself to believe that she was indeed with child was that Alexander couldn't possibly be the father. What that meant horrified her: the baby had to be Matthew Raymond's. Whenever she thought about that fact, it made her want to go on fooling herself that nothing had changed, that she wasn't really going to birth a child. But if Daniel had comprehended her predicament, then there was no use in trying to pretend it away any longer. For this reason—that the physician would confirm the worst—she hesitated to allow him entry.

Even though Daniel could see that Sarah was ill at ease and most likely knew what was coming, he directed her from her bedchamber toward the room in which he conducted his examinations. Once there, he ushered her over to a chair.

"Sarah, I realize the last thing you wish to do right now is address the situation in which you have found yourself, but denying it will not make it go away. I think we both know that you are with child. I have observed you for many weeks feeling poorly, especially after breaking the fast each morning. Additionally, though you have attempted to cover your midriff by wearing your cape even indoors, I have caught glimpses of your expanding middle."

Hanging her head with embarrassment, Sarah nodded. "I simply did not wish to believe it was true. In spite of this, when the baby moves within me, there is no denying its existence. What am I to do? That man has already ruined my life, and now I am carrying his child!"

Placing his hand on the young woman's arm, Daniel gently responded, "Is there no possibility that the baby is your husband's?"

Turning her head away, Sarah answered. "Daniel, my husband and I have never been together in that way. The baby could not possibly be his." She did not elaborate any further.

Nodding his head but not really understanding a husband and wife having such an arrangement, Daniel reassured her that everything would be all right. He had, of course, heard of such marriages, but he had never actually met anyone who had been in one. While taking a moment to process what Sarah had just revealed, he remembered something about her husband having been away for two years; that is, until just before she took leave of Amesbury. Directing his thoughts back to the young woman sitting before him, he said, "We shall have to take a look at you to be certain that you and the baby are well."

Alarmed by what was about to happen, Sarah felt that if one could die of embarrassment, she surely would.

That she was with child had been difficult enough to bear. Now she would also have to undergo regular examinations.

After calling to his wife to come and assist him, the physician examined Sarah. He knew she would be fearful at the prospect, but having Joanna present he hoped would be calming for his young friend. Once he had finished, he attempted to put Sarah's mind at rest. "Sarah, none of what has happened is of your making. Moreover, the life you carry within you is completely innocent as well. For now, just try and focus on looking after the two of you by taking proper care of yourself."

Nodding, eyes lowered, she said softly, "I believe it is time for me to contact the man here in Boston who handles my holdings in the *Spaulding Hat Company*. I inherited my father's shares in the company, and they usually send my income to Amesbury. I was hesitant before now to contact them, as it opens the way for my husband to learn of my whereabouts, should he inquire as to where the earnings are being sent—though he probably never would. Lest he should, however, I could go directly to speak with the man, as it is not so very far away. You and your wife have been too kind, but I must see to providing for my child and myself."

"Would it truly be so dreadful if your husband were to learn where you are? None of us has broached the subject with you as yet, but I must know, do you fear your husband for some reason?" Joanna inquired with some hesitation. She did not wish to alarm the young woman, for none of them would go against her wishes if she truly didn't want her husband to know where she was.

By now, Sarah had risen and made her way over to look out the window. As she stood staring off in the distance, she whispered, "Joanna, my husband had just returned from England after being away for two years when all of this happened. He left soon after we were married. It was, for both of us, merely a marriage of convenience. He had lost his first wife and had no desire to have another. But when his father had asked him to marry me, on behalf my father, he had agreed. As for me, I was simply following my dying father's wishes. He did not want me to be left alone when he died."

She glanced over at the couple to ascertain whether they had understood. Believing she had explained well enough, as they seemed to have grasped the situation, she continued. "I was surprised when he came home from England and disclosed to me that he now wished to have a marriage in the traditional sense. In fact, I was reluctant at first, but I was beginning to accept the idea shortly before...well, you are aware of what happened. Everything was ruined that night when—"

Not wanting to upset the young woman, Joanna and Daniel quietly listened. Having discussed the matter many times, they each wished they felt at liberty to suggest that any man worth his salt would not have wanted her to go away. After doing their best to demonstrate that they had understood what she had divulged to them, their young friend left them to themselves.

Once Sarah was no longer present, the kind physician prayed with his wife that God's will would be done—whatever it turned out to be—and that Sarah would be willing to obey His will even if it meant returning to her husband.

"Daniel, I am astonished that she even allowed you to examine her. However did you get her to agree?"

"I simply didn't offer her any other option, so she must have felt that she had to comply. I didn't wish to force her, but I felt I had no choice. We needed to be certain she and the baby were well. If left up to her, in my opinion, she would never have allowed an examination. In fact, had we not revealed that we were aware of the baby, as ludicrous as it sounds, I believe she would have gone on, indefinitely, attempting to conceal the fact that she is with child, perhaps even up to the time of her delivery."

"Indeed, she may have," Joanna responded. After sitting there a moment to mull the whole thing over, she continued. "You know...there is something we didn't consider. As much as she loves children, she may have realized it would be putting the baby at risk to refuse the examination."

"You may be right. I hadn't thought of that. It did seem a little too easy, getting her to follow me in here." Smiling, he turned to face his wife. "Is that not just like her, putting others above herself? In this case, her selfless actions were for her own child—a child fathered by her attacker."

"She is an amazing woman," sighed Joanna.

"That, she is, though I often forget that she is, in fact, a grown woman. Not that she acts like a child—but you have to admit, she closely resembles one. Not at all like you, my love. You are definitely a grown woman."

Raising her eyebrows at her husband's comment, Joanna poked him in the ribs. "Do not let her hear you saying such a thing. She is already ill at ease concerning her size."

"How do you know that?" Daniel inquired while feigning pain from the poke.

"Oh, just from some of the comments she has made about how nice it would be to be as tall as I am. But I think she is just lovely the way she is."

When the full impact hit him of how Sarah's size had most likely played a role in her inability to protect herself, lowering his head, the doctor responded, "I should not have said that about Sarah resembling a child. It is not a joke, for had she been larger, she may have been able to fend off her attacker, and may not even be in this predicament. Not that I wish the baby away, mind you."

"Of course you don't. Nor does Sarah, really, I am sure," Joanna replied while hugging her softhearted husband. "Let us not think about how she came to be with child. Sarah needs to feel that the baby is welcome, that we are looking forward to meeting her little one when he or she arrives."

"Yes, let us be as encouraging as we possibly can. They both are going to need us."

The husband and wife embraced, at that point, determined to make the arrival of Sarah's baby a joyful occasion.

Chapter 22

After a restless night, Sarah awoke the following morning with dread. The time had come for her to speak to her solicitor about her quarterly income. As she had indicated to the Thompsons, she now had need of the income from her shares in the hat company in which her father had invested. She could not go on indefinitely accepting help from her hosts. She needed to procure a home for herself and her child.

Her greatest fear in making contact with the man handling her affairs was that her husband would learn of it. Alexander also frequented the town for business purposes having to do with his partnership in a shipbuilding company as well as his many properties. She little expected that he would actually have come looking for her—for she believed that Esther surely would have, by now, been compelled to reveal what had happened—but she disliked taking the risk.

Perhaps, as I had mentioned to the Thompsons, it would be best if I went directly to call upon my solicitor rather than send word, thought Sarah. *I best go and speak with Joanna.*

As Mr. Hoyt's young friend approached him and his daughter in the kitchen, he observed the pensive expression upon her face. "You look as though you have something on your mind. Is there anything Joanna and I can do to be of assistance?"

Knowing that Joanna and Daniel probably had shared her predicament with her elderly friend, Sarah sat down at the table and sighed. "Mr. Hoyt, no doubt Daniel and Joanna have informed you that I am with child."

Before answering, the elderly gentleman took a seat beside Sarah. "Sarah, they did not have to say a word. I recognized the signs, as I have been through this twice before with Joanna's mother. With all that you have already been through, this must be most difficult for you."

With tears welling up in her eyes, burying her face in her hands, she began to sob. "It is just another reminder that I shall never be able to go home. What husband would want a wife who is carrying another man's child? It was bad enough that another man had forced himself upon me before my husband and I had—"

Joanna came up on Sarah's other side and sat down. While placing her arm around the young woman's shoulder, she said softly, "Sarah, can you be sure that your husband would feel thus? For myself, I cannot believe him so cruel as to turn you out for something over which you had no control."

"I cannot take the chance, Joanna. In addition, even if Alexander allowed me to stay with him at the house in

Amesbury, what kind of life would that be for either of us? I would be bringing along another man's child. I couldn't bear to have him merely tolerating my presence out of some sort of obligation. Furthermore, the man who attacked me still lives in Amesbury. I could not stomach being near him, and I would be too afraid to ever venture away from my home where he might take hold of me again."

Joanna listened intently as Sarah expressed her fears. "Sarah, if you were to make known what that man did to you, he would most certainly be put in jail."

"It would be my word against his. I could not take the risk that he might remain free. If that were to happen, as we live in the same town and attend the same church, there would be no way of avoiding him. As I have said, I would be no less than a prisoner in my own home for fear of seeing him. And as it is now, Alexander need never know about the baby, or anything else—that is, if Esther hasn't revealed my secret. Even if she has, she doesn't know about the baby. If I return to my home, he shall surely know all."

As she was having little success at convincing Sarah to return home to her husband, Joanna decided to approach the subject from another direction. "Sarah, what must your husband be thinking? He most likely believes his wife has simply run off and left him. If that be the case, he is probably blaming himself for making you unhappy enough to leave."

Glancing over at Joanna, Sarah sighed. "I have thought of that. It breaks my heart that he might blame himself, but it cannot be helped. Besides, if Esther, my maid, has indeed told him the truth regarding what happened, he is probably hoping that I never return. And if she has not, I would rather he believe that I have simply run off than know the truth." Taking a breath, she continued. "Joanna, I know you are just trying to help, but you must see that I am right. As there is no way to change what has happened, I must make plans to visit my solicitor today. Do you know where I might hire a driver?"

As she rose from the table, Joanna responded, "Nonsense! If you are sure this is what you must do, Daniel or Father shall take you. I would feel better if someone accompanied you when you speak with your solicitor. Women are often taken advantage of in such matters. Having a man along might dissuade your solicitor from doing anything underhanded."

"I am most obliged to you, Joanna. I shall never be able to repay you and Daniel for your kindness. You have taken me in as though I were family."

Joanna smiled. "I have so enjoyed having you with us, Sarah. I hope you are here a long while yet. And as it has been some time since there was a baby in the house, I am so looking forward to having yours here with us."

Sarah was warmed by Joanna's words. It delighted her to hear her baby spoken of in such a way—like he or she was actually wanted. Still, as she thought again about what she must do, visit the hat company to procure her income, her countenance fell; for even though she wasn't planning to reveal where she was currently residing, just making it known that she was somewhere in Boston, to her, felt risky.

Mr. Hoyt patted Sarah's shoulder so as to console her, for he sensed the turmoil within the young woman. *If we could just be certain she is in error regarding her husband, we could send word to him that he might come and fetch her. But if she is correct in her belief that he would not want anything to do with her now, then it is best to allow things to remain as they are, with Sarah's whereabouts kept secret. I do not think she could bear that kind of rejection.*

Sarah smiled at Mr. Hoyt, and then rose to her feet. As she turned to go, she thanked her friends for understanding her wishes with regard to her husband.

Later that afternoon, Mr. Hoyt drove Sarah to the *Spaulding Hat Company* to meet with her solicitor, who also managed the other shareholders' affairs. As manager, the man held a position on the board of directors; thus, his office was on the premises of the hat company.

Daniel had offered to take Sarah, but had thought better of it. If Sarah wanted her whereabouts to remain confidential, having the town's physician along would not have been a good idea. Even if he had never met the gentleman with whom Sarah intended to converse, the man most certainly would have heard his name in connection with his position in the town. For this reason, it was decided that Mr. Hoyt would accompany Sarah.

Upon their arrival, they were shuffled into Mr. Harvey's office. Closing the door behind his visitors, the man motioned for Sarah and Mr. Hoyt to be seated. "It is good to see you, Mrs. Swyndhurst." It had been some time since he had set eyes on the young woman. The last time she had been to the hat company had been with her father before he died. On that visit, the ailing man had made arrangements for his holdings to pass to his daughter upon his death.

Mr. Hoyt introduced himself to Mr. Harvey, and then, seeing that Sarah seemed a little hesitant to speak, he explained the reason for their visit—that Sarah would be in town for a few months and would therefore be coming in person to collect her income, rather than have it sent on to Amesbury—as had been the case from the time of her father's death.

Unbeknownst to Sarah, her husband and his hired man had been to see Mr. Harvey. He was, therefore, aware of what had happened to Sarah. Just now, he hoped to learn something of where she was presently residing. He had promised the moment he learned anything that he would inform James Haddon, who would be regularly checking in. "Perhaps if you told me where I might send the money, I could save you the trouble of coming in person to collect it."

As nervous as she was, Sarah responded a bit too abruptly, "No! It shall not be any trouble for me to come in person."

Allowing the question of what manner the money might be presented to Sarah to drop, Mr. Harvey began, "You must have heard by now that Parliament has recently enacted the 'Hat Act' in order to have more control over the hat industry in the Colonies." Seeing blank stares upon the faces of the man and woman sitting before him, he continued. "By enacting the Hat Act, they have significantly cut into the profits of our shareholders, which, I am sorry to say, includes you, Mrs. Swyndhurst."

At this point, Mr. Hoyt responded to the man, "In truth, Mr. Harvey, as I am not familiar with the hat trade, I have heard very little of this 'Hat Act' before today. And as Mrs. Swyndhurst has been vacationing with my dau…my family for a few months now, I am quite certain she has also not heard tell of it. Would you be good enough to explain just how it shall affect Mrs. Swyndhurst?"

Sarah wondered what Mr. Harvey thought about the fact that she had been "vacationing" with Mr. Hoyt's family. She was sure that he would find it curious, and as a result he might question her about it.

With a sigh, Mr. Harvey began. "You see, Parliament has forbidden the export of beaver felt hats made in the colonies. They have also limited the number of apprentices our company, and others in the trade, may employ. There is a bit more to it, but suffice it to say—the 'Hat Act' has greatly cut into our profits."

After hearing this, Sarah wondered if she would receive any income in the future. "What are you saying, exactly?"

Understanding her concern, he responded, "Do not mistake my meaning. You shall continue to receive an income, but it shall be considerably less."

After hearing what the man had to say, Joseph pinned him down on what amount his young friend might expect to receive. Once everything had been explained and Sarah had insisted, once again, that she would be coming in person to pick up her share of the profits, the two departed.

After taking leave of the hat company, Mr. Hoyt assured Sarah she would be able to get by on the modest income. He then insisted she not rush into anything, explaining that as far as his daughter and Daniel were concerned, she could remain with them for as long as she wished.

Sarah, with embarrassment for feeling the need to question, inquired of the elderly gentleman whether he thought it was obvious that she was with child, for she disliked the idea of her solicitor knowing—all the more risk that her husband would find out. Joseph reassured her that, with her cape draped about her, he doubted the man had noticed.

Upon their arrival at home, after sharing with the Thompsons what had happened at the meeting, Mr. Hoyt wished again that the young woman would return to her husband, where she would be provided for. He worried that the burden of caring for herself and her child might be too much for his young friend, and now it would all be accomplished with even less on which to live. He also disliked the idea of Sarah being alone with only the baby for companionship. If she didn't return to Amesbury, he hoped she would remain with the Thompsons for a long while yet. Having Daniel watching out for Sarah had been some comfort for the elderly gentleman.

Mr. Hoyt had been thinking over the matter ever since the ride back to his daughter's house, following the visit with Sarah's solicitor. With all of this on his mind, he had been unable to fully engage in the conversation from the time they had arrived at home.

Glancing over at his young friend, Mr. Hoyt couldn't leave the matter alone. He was just too concerned. "Sarah, in a few more weeks I shall be returning to Amesbury. Perhaps by then you may wish to come along. I am not trying to force you, child. It is simply that I wonder if you might not be better off with your husband and in the care of your servants. If you were to live on your own, it sounds as though you shall not be able to afford servants, and shall therefore be quite alone."

"Mr. Hoyt, I know you mean well and that you are simply concerned for my welfare, but allow me to set the record straight once and for all. I shall not be returning to Amesbury! It is simply out of the question!" Just the thought of seeing Alexander again after everything that had happened—not to mention setting eyes upon the man she most feared—caused Sarah to tremble.

The three adults glanced back and forth at each other after hearing the tiny woman speaking so adamantly. They had not noticed that she was trembling, nor were they privy to her thoughts regarding her attacker; consequently, though their hearts were breaking for her situation, to them it was a bit humorous to see such an angelic face attempting to appear so fierce. They knew she wanted them to understand how serious she was by her demeanor, but she was just so adorable at that moment that they couldn't help but be a little amused.

Fortunately, Sarah did not notice the exchange of half hidden grins upon her friends' faces. Before she broke down and cried in front of the Thompsons and Mr. Hoyt, she turned and left the parlor. Then, to distract herself, she went in search of the boys. Spending time with them had always resulted in lifting her spirits, much the same as when she had been with the Strout children, whom she greatly missed.

Once Sarah had gone, the three who remained in the parlor spoke in hushed tones concerning the young woman. After having a chuckle over what had just transpired, the mood in the room became somber.

"We should not have laughed at her. She was clearly upset at the prospect of going home, thus her forceful words were spoken out of fear," insisted Joanna, feeling guilty for the way she had reacted to Sarah's ire.

Joseph spoke up first concerning Sarah's wish to remain in Boston. "I hope we are doing the right thing in keeping Sarah's whereabouts from her husband. If he cares about her, and how could he not, he must be out of his mind with worry."

In understanding, Joanna and Daniel nodded. Then Daniel reminded his father-in-law that the decision had to be Sarah's. "We should continue to pray about the situation, as well as Sarah's heart, that God would move her to do what He desires—not what we think is best."

"It is just so difficult watching her suffer," responded Joanna. "I believe, from what she has said, she and her husband do love each other, even though theirs has been an unconventional sort of marriage."

"Yes," Daniel responded to his wife. "From what she has explained, they had just begun a more traditional marriage before she was harmed by that scoundrel."

"Well, as Daniel has suggested, let us continue praying for the Swyndhursts," stated the family patriarch.

When the conversation with her husband and father had ended, Joanna went in search of Sarah. Finding her with the boys, Joanna thought about the day that would inevitably come when Sarah would no longer reside with them. As she observed her young friend, she knew that it would be a sad day indeed.

Glancing over at Joanna, Sarah's thoughts were much the same. She knew she would greatly miss Joanna when the time came for her to live on her own.

Chapter 23

Alexander Swyndhurst had been searching for his wife for months. With the colder weather and snow constantly hindering his travel, the worried husband had had to leave the matter of his wife's whereabouts in God's hands for the time being; that is, at least until the weather changed.

Alexander had been home for a few weeks when Alice Strout came to call at the Swyndhurst estate. Without Sarah around to assist her with the children, she had come to understand just how much her friend had been doing for her. Besides adding to their food supply each week, Sarah had also kept the children clean and Alice's home well maintained. In fact, without Sarah, the young widow no longer felt as though she could manage all of her responsibilities.

As she was ushered into the parlor, Alice felt a knot in her stomach at what she was about to request. She felt simply awful that it had come to this, but she didn't know what else to do.

When Mr. Swyndhurst learned that Alice Strout had come to call, he quickly went to inquire as to the reason for her visit. His first thought was that something had happened to one of her children.

While taking a seat, Mr. Swyndhurst addressed his wife's friend. "Good day, Mrs. Strout. And how are you and the children faring?"

Looking a bit nervous, Alice responded, "We are not doing very well, Mr. Swyndhurst. I had no idea just how much Sarah, while on her visits, had accomplished for me and the children. She made it all look so easy. She supplemented our provisions each week, even doing much of the cooking herself. She had also done so much for the children that I am at a loss as to how to go on caring for them without her help." She didn't want to let on that the little money left to her by her husband was also running out.

With a bewildered look, he hesitated a moment. He then questioned, "Is there anything I can do to be of assistance, Mrs. Strout? I know it would break Sarah's heart if she were to learn that the children were in want."

Dropping her eyes to her lap, she replied, "Mr. Swyndhurst, I have heard that Sarah has not been at home for some time. Would you mind telling me when you expect her to return?"

"In truth, I have been searching for her for months. I am not at all sure of her ever returning." All at once, Alexander felt a strong sense of anger towards the woman, for if Sarah had not gone to her home that dreadful day, she would still be safe at home; however, just as quickly as his anger flared, it subsided. He knew it was wrong to blame Alice Strout for something for which she was not responsible.

Not knowing why Sarah had gone off without notifying her husband as to her whereabouts, Alice didn't know how to respond. And hearing Mr. Swyndhurst's comments regarding Sarah only added to her uncertainty about whether she should state the reason for her visit. After a few moments of indecision, Alice chose to explain why she had come. "You see, Mr. Swyndhurst, I had hoped to ask Sarah...well...I thought she might...take my children in. I know that she loves them as much as I do, considering that she has always taken care of their needs much better than I. Do not mistake me, Mr. Swyndhurst. I love my children, dearly. That is why I would even think to make such a request. It is just that I believe it is in their best interest for Sarah to raise them." Just then, Alice's eyes filled with tears. "I hate to admit it, but I am completely inadequate as a mother."

Utterly speechless, Mr. Swyndhurst simply sat there, staring at the woman.

Wiping her eyes, she asked, "You are stunned by what I have said, are you not, Mr. Swyndhurst?" She really didn't need for him to respond to know the answer, for the man's mouth was hanging open and his eyes had grown quite large.

Scratching his head, he wondered if he could have heard the woman correctly. After a long pause to process that she had actually requested that he take her children in, he replied, "You are right in thinking Sarah would wish to take the children in. Without her here to help with the decision, however, I am not quite certain how best to respond. I have servants enough for the task, of that I am sure. But how shall you bear it—being away from the children, I mean?"

"I was hoping I would be permitted to visit on occasion. I hope to remove to Ipswich to be with my sister, which is not so very far away."

"To be sure. If we were to take the children, of course we would wish for them to see their mother. Your sister—is she unable to assist you with the children?"

"No, as she has five of her own and lives in a rather small home."

Nodding, he stated, "You must allow me time to think this over. Without the benefit of Sarah's input, I must be sure that providing accommodations for your children is the best decision for all concerned." Alexander knew exactly how Sarah would have answered, but was that truly what was best? *My wife always worried so over Alice's children. Having them here where the servants might be of assistance with their care would be in Sarah's best interest as well as the children's. She worked herself sick by going to their house and doing everything by herself. This might just be the solution to that conundrum,* he reasoned. *That is, if she returns; otherwise, I shall be raising them alone. Am I really prepared for that, should it indeed turn out that way?*

I must not even think in those terms. Sarah shall return. She must!

The man had fallen silent, so Alice Strout spoke up, agreeing to allow him time to think over the matter. Her friend's husband nodded his head, and then assured her that he would speak with her again in a few days. With that knowledge, she took herself off home.

Once he was alone, Alexander—while pacing around the parlor—prayed about the situation. "Is she really prepared to give up her children, Lord? What if Sarah never returns? What then? Shall I raise the children myself? I want to believe the best—that Sarah shall indeed return—but what if she doesn't?" After conversing with the Lord about what had been on his mind when Alice Strout was there, Alexander went to inquire as to Martha's thoughts about having the children come to live at the estate.

Finding her in the kitchen, he went in and made his way over to the window. As he looked out through the windowpane, with his back to Martha, he explained the reason Alice Strout had come. Without turning, he waited for her to respond.

Sitting in quiet contemplation, though her employer wasn't looking in her direction, Martha began nodding her head. "You know, that may just be for the best. When Sarah returns, she shall be so happy at finding the children here. What is more, I shall be here to see that she doesn't exceed her limits. There will be no more days and nights away from the house for her if the children are right here under this very roof."

Turning his head far enough to offer his servant-friend a warm smile, he said with a sigh, "It does my heart good to hear you talk as if Sarah shall actually come home." Then, turning once more to gaze out the window, he whispered, "As for myself, I am beginning to doubt that I shall ever see her again."

Feeling bad for the young man she had helped raise, Martha approached. Reaching up, she placed her hand on his shoulder. "We shall simply continue praying for her to return until we see her sweet face coming through the door."

"The following morning, James Haddon—Mr. Swyndhurst's hired man—came to call with news. After taking him into his private study, Alexander, impatient to hear what the man had to say, hastily motioned for him to be seated.

"What is it? What have you learned?"

Studying his friend a moment, he realized, not for the first time, that if he didn't find Sarah soon, his friend's health would be in peril. Alexander was looking so careworn that Mr. Haddon could scarcely look at him. Finally, he forced himself to give their discussion his full attention. "I have had word from Boston. Sarah has been to the *Spaulding Hat Company* to request her income. In the missive I received, Mr. Harvey explained that he is unsure of her exact whereabouts, but he believes her to be in the vicinity. If you are wondering why the man contacted me rather than you, Mr. Swyndhurst, it is just that after our visit with Mr. Harvey, the one in which we had explained the situation, he took me aside to convey his wish that any communications regarding the matter be handled between the two of us instead of with you. He stated that, in his opinion, if he were to learn anything that might lead to Sarah's whereabouts, I am in a better position to act upon the information to see if it leads anywhere before alerting you."

"That is understandable. But this is good news, is it not?" the excited husband inquired.

"That is just what he was hoping to avoid—namely, getting your hopes up. Even so, I felt it best to inform you of this latest development before checking into it. Perhaps I should have waited. I, too, have no desire to give you false hope," responded the hired man with sincerity. "Yes, we know she is well, but we may never learn her whereabouts."

"Not to worry, James. I shall be fine, regardless. That she is all right does more for me than you will ever know. I am delighted we took Mr. Harvey into our confidence. I hated to tell the man such personal things about my wife, concerning what had happened to her, but I felt that if he knew, he would be more likely to contact us if she came around."

"The road to Boston is now somewhat clear of snow, what with all of the melting, owing to the warmer weather. There may yet be time before another storm arrives for me to travel there to see what I might learn," suggested James. "As I am in a position to stay as long as it takes, and you would not want to be seen in town, it might be best if I went alone."

"Perhaps you are right, James. And as winter shall soon be over, we may not be hindered by severe weather any longer. I trust you to send word the moment you learn anything. Do be discreet, won't you? I should not wish for Sarah to hear that I am looking for her. In order to avoid being found, she might remove from there to another location."

"I shall do my best to see that she doesn't find out that I have come to town searching for her," replied James. "I will be on my way, then. The moment I find out anything, anything at all, I shall send word right away." With that, he went home to pack for his trip.

For the first time in many weeks, the husband felt hope rising up within him. He took himself up to his bedchamber to pray that James would be successful in finding his wife. He also thanked the Lord that Sarah appeared well when she had visited the hat company.

Chapter 24

When James Haddon arrived at the *Spaulding Hat Company*, Mr. Harvey shepherded him towards the room in which he conducted business. Once there, the two men spoke of Mrs. Swyndhurst's visit. Mr. Harvey explained that after having been introduced to Mr. Hoyt, the man who had accompanied Sarah, he had asked around if anyone knew the elderly gentleman. One of the men with whom he had spoken had heard of Mr. Hoyt in connection with the town's physician, Daniel Thompson.

"The man disclosed to me that he believed Mr. Hoyt may even be the physician's father-in-law. You see, he has been seen in town with Daniel Thompson's sons. I was not privy to the information about one of my visitor's connection to the town physician until long after the meeting had taken place; thus, while Mr. Hoyt and Sarah were still here, I attempted to discover the location of Mr. Hoyt's family's residence, where Sarah is presently staying. I told them the reason I had asked was so that I might send the income directly to her. To my dismay, she insisted on coming here in person to collect her earnings. In truth, I was only asking that I might gain the information you had requested. But once I learned of Mrs. Swyndhurst's possible connection to Daniel Thompson, the town's physician, I knew just where she was staying, if in fact Mr. Hoyt is the physician's father-in-law."

James Haddon was delighted that he now had the information he had been hoping for. With the name of the town's physician, Daniel Thompson, to present to the town's residents for information regarding Sarah's whereabouts, Mr. Haddon felt certain he would finally track down the young woman, and said as much to Mr. Harvey.

Mr. Harvey chuckled, "Did you not hear what I said? I know where the physician lives. If the supposed connection between Mr. Hoyt and Mr. Thompson turns out to be accurate, then Mrs. Swyndhurst is certain to be there. I am happy to direct you there."

"I was just so overjoyed by your news that it didn't occur to me that you meant you knew the location of Daniel Thompson's residence. But if I go there and present myself and she is indeed there, she may run away again at the sight of me. We are acquainted, you see. She is fully aware that I work for her husband. And if she were to see me, in the time it takes for Mr. Swyndhurst to come to Boston, she might flee. I must speak with this Daniel Thompson to be certain that she is definitely residing with his family, but I have to go about it cautiously. If I could but arrange a meeting with the gentleman away from his home, I could explain the situation."

"Yes, that might be best; otherwise, the Thompsons and Mr. Hoyt may be reluctant to reveal any information about Sarah, not knowing the circumstances surrounding her departure from Amesbury. For all we know, she may not have even revealed the reason she came away."

"Well, I best be on my way. I am much obliged to you for contacting me, Mr. Harvey."

"No need for thanks. I pray that it all works out for the best and that this is not merely a wild goose chase, sending you to speak with Daniel Thompson. As I said, I am not certain that he is indeed connected to the man who accompanied Mrs. Swyndhurst. It does seem likely, though."

◊◊◊

Following his meeting with Mr. Harvey, James went directly to the town ordinary, where he had stayed on previous occasions. That he was yet unmarried made it easy for him to travel about for his employer, which he had done many times before; although, in the past it had been for business purposes, not for personal reasons.

The next morning, James went to many of the local businesses to inquire whether anyone could tell him where Daniel Thompson frequented when he was in town. If he could but speak with the man away from his home, Sarah might not learn that he had come on behalf of her husband. But thus far, everyone with whom he had spoken was reluctant to reveal the information he sought. He assumed it was because he was a stranger and they were unsure of his reasons for searching for the physician. Because he couldn't elaborate, he was unable to gain anyone's confidence. As he thought about it, if he had been willing to lie—by suggesting he needed the physician for an illness or some sort of injury—he may have garnered the information he needed.

Frustrated, he returned to the ordinary that night, determined to find a way to speak with Mr. Thompson somewhere other than his home. However, just as he was about to set off the next morning, he stepped out onto a patch of ice and slipped—landing hard on his leg. Though winter was nearly over, ice was still often present in the early mornings, before the sun had warmed the ground. When James attempted to stand, he found he had injured himself. Two men from within the ordinary caught a glimpse out the window of the mishap. As they hastened out to assist the injured man, one of them called for someone to send for the physician. After hearing the directive, James felt as if he had just been blessed with the answer to his dilemma. *This might just afford me the opportunity for which I have been hoping. All I have to do now is to wait for help to arrive,* he reasoned.

Having been helped back to his room in the ordinary, James reclined on his bed while he awaited the man he was most eager to see. Although his leg throbbed, he took little notice of it. His mind was presently occupied with how he might speak with the man about Sarah without alarming him. If the physician didn't trust that Mr.

Swyndhurst only wanted his wife safely home, he may alert the young woman. If that happened, given her history, she would likely flee. He could not allow that to take place.

Within a couple of hours, Daniel Thompson stood rapping on the injured man's door. One of the men, who had accompanied him to Mr. Haddon's room, suggested that he simply open the door and go in, as the injured man was likely incapable of coming to the door.

As Daniel entered, he addressed the injured man. "Well, let us have a look at you. I am Mr. Thompson, the town's physician."

James looked intently at the rather tall gentleman moving in his direction. "I am much obliged to you for coming. I am James Haddon. I suppose I should have been more careful."

Smiling, Daniel responded, "As I have just seen the melting icy patch where the unfortunate incident occurred, I would have to say that it is not entirely your fault. Anyone might have done the same, and may yet if someone does not see to sprinkling a bit of sand upon the spot. It is sure to ice back over after dark, making tomorrow morning treacherous once again for anyone stepping there."

While the physician examined Mr. Haddon's leg, the injured man wondered how he might obtain the information he required. Presently, he felt the direct approach should not be attempted, not yet anyway. But he had to know if Sarah was indeed staying with the gentleman and his family, so he decided to ask a question that might lead to the answer he sought. "As you made it here in so short a time, your residence must be close by."

While looking over at the injured man, Daniel chuckled, "I am delighted that you consider nearly two hours a short wait. I was suturing a wound when someone came for me, stating that you required my assistance. Are you from the area? I have not seen you about. Or perhaps it is simply that you have been of sound body up to this point."

James smiled at the gentleman. He sensed that the doctor was endeavoring to put him at ease. "Yes, I am usually more careful, and am rarely ill." He hoped the medical man might leave it at that. He had no desire to give away his reason for being in town.

Daniel again questioned where the injured man was from. "As you are staying at the ordinary, I assume that you are either new to the town and have not as yet moved into a more permanent dwelling, or you are just passing through. Which is it?"

Seeing that the physician persisted in gaining more information about him, James answered, "Well, perhaps a little of both." Which was true; he had considered moving to Boston. "I believe if I found just the right place, I should like living in this town. Just now, though, I am here on business. And you—have you lived in Boston long?"

Not wanting to pry, Daniel allowed the matter of why the injured man was in town to drop and simply answered the man's question. "For some time now, yes."

"A gentleman of your age must have a wife and children. Does your family care for the town as well? It is just that I hope to settle down at some point. I wouldn't want to move somewhere that any future wife and children, I may have, disliked." James hoped to keep the man talking that he might spill information concerning Sarah.

Feeling a little uncomfortable at this point, and not exactly sure why, Daniel evaded the question. "Umm-hmm...well, I best be off. I shall check back with you from time to time to see how the leg is faring. I do not believe anything is broken. Just a bit strained and bruised. You should stay off your feet as much as possible for a fortnight at least. You must allow the leg time to heal."

After Mr. Thompson had finished instructing James on how best to care for his wounded leg and James had paid the fee, the physician took his leave. James, a little frustrated with his predicament, decided to send off a missive to his employer to inform him of what had occurred. He had to let Mr. Swyndhurst know that it would be a couple of weeks before he could pursue the matter of finding Mrs. Swyndhurst any further; nonetheless, he felt certain he would soon verify his employer's wife's whereabouts. When he had finished writing the missive, he decided that, for the time being, there was nothing more to be done.

Daniel returned home, a bit concerned that the injured man may have come looking for Sarah. He had no real reason to suspect him, but suspect him he did. Not wanting to upset his guest, he took his father-in-law off to where they might speak privately. "Joseph, have you ever heard tell of a man by the name of James Haddon?"

After thinking a moment, his father-in-law responded, "Yes, I may have heard the name, but I cannot be certain. Why do you ask?"

"That is the name of the injured man I have just been to see. He is staying at the ordinary. He inquired as to how far I live from the ordinary, amongst other fairly personal things. They may have been innocent questions, but what if they weren't? What if he is in town looking for Sarah? I couldn't even get the man to say why he was actually here, in town."

"I am not sure you can assume such a thing just because the man asked you some pointed questions and avoided some of yours," replied the elderly gentleman.

"It isn't only that; it is also a feeling I have about the man. I shall be checking in on him from time to time, so I may have an opportunity to learn more. As I said, he wouldn't exactly say why he is even in Boston. All I could get out of him was that he was here on business, but his response was vague. I wonder just what business brought him here."

"We may be getting ahead of ourselves, but let us keep our eyes and ears open. Then again, if the injured man is indeed here to find Sarah on her husband's behalf, it may just be for the best. Still, it is more likely he has a good reason, other than Sarah, for being in town."

"You are probably right. I may be reading too much into the situation. It is just that I dislike the idea of upsetting Sarah, if the man has in fact come searching for her. She has been through so much already."

The two men agreed to keep watch over Sarah until Daniel could find out more about the new man in town.

Chapter 25

Two days later, Daniel Thompson called for a second time upon the injured man. This time, however, the man was more persistent with his questions about Daniel's family and home. Daniel avoided the queries as much as possible by directing the conversation back to the man and his reasons for coming to Boston. As they were at a standstill, neither gaining the information they desired— even more uneasy than he had been before—Daniel excused himself with a promise to return before the end of the week.

Back in Amesbury, Alexander received the missive from James concerning what he had learned of Sarah's whereabouts. With excitement, he sent word that he would come as soon as James had confirmed that Sarah was with the physician's family. If he went running off before they were certain, he knew that he may disrupt the search, should anyone learn that he was in town. Neither man wanted the name of "Mr. Swyndhurst" to be heard in Boston before they had located Sarah.

Being this close to finding Sarah and not setting off for Boston straight away was going to be a test of Alexander's patience. As it was, his hired man was injured and would not be able to learn anything more until his leg had mended—that is, unless the physician was willing to reveal what he knew of Sarah and whether she was staying at his home.

Alexander had also come to a decision about the Strout children. He would allow them to live at the Swyndhurst estate; therefore, he desired to see the children settled before setting off for Boston. Having to wait might just have been in God's plan, he had reasoned.

Needing to speak with Martha—after searching the house—Alexander found her in the kitchen. "Martha, I have come to a decision. I have resolved to permit Alice Strout's children to live with us; consequently, I wish for you to send Peter, straight away, to collect Alice that I might speak with her. She has been awaiting my response. I feel no need to keep her in suspense any longer."

Smiling, Martha assured him that Peter would be sent immediately. Within the half hour, the young man had returned with the woman. She had left the two younger children at home in the care of their older sibling. She didn't want to bring them along where they might hear what she was considering. If Mr. Swyndhurst agreed to her proposal, she would then reveal her plan to them. If, however, he turned her down, she didn't want to distress them unnecessarily.

Martha escorted Alice into the parlor. While she was on her way to tell Mr. Swyndhurst that Alice had arrived, she prayed about her attitude toward the young woman. As far as she could see, the woman was shirking her responsibilities, yet again, only this time it was Mr. Swyndhurst who would bear the burden. She then remembered how pleased Sarah would be to learn that the children had come there to live. Martha also thought once more about how it would be with Sarah and the children under one roof. Sarah would never again have to work herself sick, for she would have the servants at her disposal. *If only my sweet girl would come home,* the elderly servant thought, with tears welling up in her eyes.

While knocking on the door to Mr. Swyndhurst's study, Martha sighed. She hoped he wouldn't detect that she was a bit weepy. Alexander stuck his head out to see what the elderly woman wanted. As he suspected, Alice Strout had arrived. He followed Martha to the parlor.

Before long, all was settled. The children would come with all of their belongings within a couple of days. Alexander was glad he had remained at home, allowing James to handle things for the time being. As soon as he was sure of his wife's whereabouts, however, nothing would stand in his way—not even the children.

That night, while Martha and Mr. Swyndhurst were having tea in the kitchen, Martha made a suggestion. "Mr. Swyndhurst, should you find Sarah, she is likely to be distraught and in need of solace. I was thinking, you might ask the Bleasdells to look after the children in the time leading up to Sarah's arrival, and well after. I am not saying that they should stay with the Bleasdells forever, just until Sarah has had time to recover and settle in."

"That is a wise suggestion, Martha. I shall go early tomorrow morning to speak with Jonathan. That way, if James does verify Sarah's whereabouts, the children may be sent at once. I know Jonathan and Hannah would be happy to keep them for as long as necessary. In fact, having the children for a while might be good for them. It has only been a few years since they lost their beloved Henry. Little Mary is not much younger than he was at the time of his death, and as they have had eleven children in all, they are also quite experienced."

Martha agreed. She had also felt the Bleasdells might benefit from the children's company.

"Should Sarah return, I shall rely upon you to advise me as to when I should tell her about the children—that is to say, when you believe she has recovered enough to have them home again." Alexander had always had faith in Martha's opinions. Besides the fact that he knew her to be full of wisdom, she had demonstrated her selflessness by always putting his and Sarah's interests above her own.

"Listen to us. I believe our faith—that she shall come home—is growing with this new bit of information from James."

Smiling, Mr. Swyndhurst responded, "I believe you are right. I have more hope than I have had in some time."

Early the next morning, Alexander set off for the Bleasdells'. Unbeknownst to him, however, Matthew

Raymond had been keeping a close eye on his comings and goings. Watching out the window as Mr. Swyndhurst passed by, Matthew Raymond noted that the man was on horseback, and it did not look as though he had packed for a trip; thus, the impatient man did not follow after him.

Additionally, Mr. Raymond had seen a man a few months back arriving at the Swyndhurst estate. At the time, he had assumed that Mr. Swyndhurst had hired the man to find Sarah. This was confirmed when he heard around town that someone had been seeking information regarding an elderly gentleman. He assumed it was thought that Sarah had left with the elderly man. He would have asked a few questions of his own, though surreptitiously so as not to draw attention to himself, but the townspeople had made it known that there wasn't much to tell. No one seemed to know where the elderly gentleman had gone. Matthew was also a bit anxious to learn who the man was, for he believed he was, in all probability, the person he had seen up ahead on the road with Sarah the night she had escaped him.

To Matthew Raymond's mind, it appeared as though Sarah's husband and his hired man had not had any success in finding her, but he felt certain they eventually would. Thus, as soon as Mr. Swyndhurst took leave of Amesbury, Matthew planned to follow. It was crucial that he reach Sarah first, for he believed that as soon as the elderly gentleman told Mr. Swyndhurst what had happened to his wife, he would certainly be captured and imprisoned. But if he could get his hands on the young woman, she would finally be his, and no one could ever make him pay for what he had done, once they were hidden away. He merely needed to bide his time until he could put his plan in motion.

When Alexander arrived at the Bleasdells' home, as always, Jonathan and Hannah were delighted to see him. The Bleasdells were like family to Alexander, and he to them; thus, he enjoyed spending time in their company. After Alexander had explained that he would be taking in Alice Strout's children, he inquired as to whether—should Sarah return—they might be of a mind to look after the children for a time, to which they quickly responded in the affirmative.

They then asked whether Alexander had heard from Sarah. He happily disclosed the latest news his hired man had uncovered in Boston. The Bleasdells assured that they would continue to keep the situation in prayer. As he had on many an occasion prior to his marriage to Sarah, Alexander remained for a few hours, taking his evening meal with his dear friends before starting for home.

◊ ◊ ◊

As the servants at the Swyndhurst estate awaited the arrival of the children, they bustled about preparing their rooms. Little Mary's room was to be adjacent to Esther's, as she would be in charge of her care. For the time being, in order for Mary to feel comfortable in her new home, Elizabeth would share her youngest sibling's room.

Samuel was to have his own bedchamber a couple of doors down from his sisters. Some of the servants resided within the walls of the Swyndhurst estate, while others, such as Peter who lived with his parents, dwelt close by. After he arrived at work each morning, the plan was for Peter to escort the two older children to the schoolhouse and fetch them in the afternoon prior to going home for the day.

Mr. Swyndhurst was pleased to see the preparations for the arrival of the children were well underway. As distracted as he had been while awaiting word from James, he was little help in the endeavor. In addition, he had always trusted Martha's handling of the household affairs and felt no need to alter the arrangement now.

◊◊◊

After a tearful farewell, Alice Strout departed— leaving her children behind with Mr. Swyndhurst and his servants. Though Samuel and Elizabeth tried to hide their pain at being parted from their mother, Martha and Mr. Swyndhurst had sensed it just the same.

The children were soon escorted to their rooms while Martha prepared a meal a bit earlier than usual. If she guessed right, the children hadn't had much to eat that day and were probably famished.

When they were seated at the table a short time later, as she suspected, they dug right in as if they were half-starved. She had prepared a tray of meat, some potatoes, a winter squash, and fresh bread for their first meal together. The children seemed quite pleased with the spread put before them.

During the meal, Mr. Swyndhurst and Martha glanced at each other multiple times. They were both thinking they had done the right thing; these children needed looking after. Martha felt a twinge of guilt for having berated Sarah so many times for giving so much care to Alice Strout's children, for she could now see why it had come about. There was no doubt in the elderly servant's mind that the children's mother was incapable of looking after them, as evidenced by their bone thin bodies and disheveled hair and clothes. As the softhearted servant glanced at the youngest Strout, she felt the little girl, with her pale face and raspy cough, appeared the most frightening of the children. And all three were clad in filthy clothes. *This was never the case when Sarah was around,* thought Martha. *She had seen to it that they were well fed and clean. How much has changed,* the elderly servant thought.

Later that night, with the children tucked in their beds, Martha and Mr. Swyndhurst had tea together in the parlor. Speaking in hushed tones, they talked of Sarah and how delighted she would be if she knew the children were there with them. Having a better understanding of the burden Sarah had felt for Alice Strout's children, Mr. Swyndhurst and Martha vowed that they would look after them with as much care as Sarah had. They then prayed that Sarah would soon return for her own sake as well as the children's. As the evening moved forward, both Martha and Mr. Swyndhurst realized what a tiring day it had been, getting the children settled and all. For this reason, they each turned in a little earlier than usual.

Chapter 26

J ames Haddon's leg was mending well; consequently, Daniel Thompson's visits were becoming less frequent. James felt certain that, by now, he would have learned whether the man had a houseguest, but Mr. Thompson had successfully evaded the questions pertaining to his home and family every time James had inquired.

On this particular day, Mr. Thompson intended to tell Mr. Haddon that as his leg was nearly as good as new, he no longer required his services. When he arrived at the ordinary, he found Mr. Haddon sitting at a table near the entrance to the establishment.

As the physician approached the man he had come to see, he suggested, "Mr. Haddon, why don't we go to your room so that I might have one last look at your leg?"

Rising from his chair, James replied, "Very well." As he made his way along, he felt a little panicked that this was his last opportunity to learn whether Sarah had indeed been staying at the physician's home. Not only had he been hoping to verify Sarah's whereabouts, he also wished to seek Mr. Thompson's assistance in keeping the news of his being in town, on behalf of Sarah's husband, quiet.

Daniel observed that James had little trouble making his way to the room. This only confirmed to him that the man was no longer in need of his care. He felt relief at knowing this would be the last time he would see the gentleman.

While sliding his back against the headboard of his bed to stretch out his leg, James cleared his throat. "I believe my leg has mended quite nicely. I am much obliged to you for tending to me, Mr. Thompson."

Agreeing with the man's assessment of his leg, after taking one last look, the physician responded, "Yes, you are correct in saying that your leg has healed. As I suspected before arriving today, this shall be my last visit. You may now come and go as you please."

Seeing no way around coming right out with it, Mr. Swyndhurst's hired man stated, "Mr. Thompson, there is something about which I need to speak with you."

As he observed the man, who was now moving into a sitting position, Daniel was unsure whether he should make his excuses and hastily take his leave or stay and listen to what Mr. Haddon had to say. As before, he suspected the man might have come to town to find Sarah. But as he thought about it, he would much rather know the man's intentions than be left in the dark. That way, if it became necessary, he could protect Sarah. Having finished his exam of the man's leg, he sat up against the back of his chair. "Yes, go on."

Rubbing his chin while he determined how best to begin, James finally said, "I suspect you have guessed that I have come to town with a purpose—to find my employer's wife, Sarah Swyndhurst. Her solicitor over at the hat company informed me that she had been to see him. He also mentioned your name in connection with the man who had accompanied her." Hesitant that he had been so direct, he studied the doctor's face for a reaction.

Feeling like he had allowed a door to open that he may not be able to shut, Daniel responded, "As you say, I suspected as much. It was just that you inquired so often about personal things pertaining to my family. Will you tell me why Sarah's husband is looking for her? It might seem obvious, as any man would search for his missing wife, but I must be certain of his motives."

Seeing that the physician remained cautious where Mrs. Swyndhurst was concerned, James felt he had no other option but to disclose all. "Sir, Mr. Swyndhurst has been in great distress ever since his wife went away without a word to anyone where she was going. Has she apprised you of what happened to her the night she left town?"

Daniel was beginning to think this might have been a good idea after all—the two men finally being honest with one another. "Yes, I am aware that she was attacked. My father-in-law assisted her in her escape."

"We were not certain that Sarah had actually left town with Mr. Hoyt, but we thought it a real possibility.

Before Mr. Harvey contacted me regarding Sarah's visit to the hat company, all inquiries relating to Mr. Hoyt's daughter's whereabouts were unsuccessful, as not a soul even knew her name—only that Mr. Hoyt had a daughter. Thus, once I learned your name in connection with his, I believed if I could just speak privately with you, I could be certain Sarah was at your home. I couldn't send for her husband until I was sure.

"The poor man has been beside himself with worry. When I injured my leg, I felt that God had given me the answer to my dilemma. I had been asking around where you frequented the most, other than your home, of course, but not knowing why I was looking for you, no one in town would give me a direct answer. I couldn't just come to your home. Sarah might have seen me. She knows that I work for her husband. She ran away once, I couldn't let it happen again." Hoping he had stated the situation well enough to gain Mr. Thompson's confidence, James then waited for the man to speak.

Nodding his head, Daniel responded, "Yes, the people in this town are quite loyal. They would have been more forthcoming had you needed my services, which, as it turns out, you eventually did. It does seem that God had a hand in us coming together. That makes what I have to disclose easier somehow, or else I would not have been certain it was the right thing for Sarah—telling you where she is."

James spoke up then. "That is understandable, Mr. Thompson. While you are not acquainted with Mr. Swyndhurst, for all you knew it might not have been in Sarah's best interest for them to be reunited."

"Just so, Mr. Haddon. Well, now that I feel it is 'in her best interest' for you and I to get this thing figured out, I shall explain what I know of the situation. You see, my wife, Joanna, and I have been looking after Sarah. My father-in-law thought she would be quite safe in our care. As she was frightened of her attacker and she felt her husband would no longer want her, we insisted that she remain with us for as long as she needed. At first we considered sending word to her husband, but it was her wish that her whereabouts remain a secret. Knowing little of the situation between them, we felt we should comply with her wishes."

His countenance one of relief that Sarah had been well cared for, James explained further. "I fully understand your reasons for going along with her wishes; however, to believe that her husband no longer wanted her...well...nothing could have been further from the truth. Mr. Swyndhurst was heartbroken when he learned what had happened to her in his absence. He was out of town at the time it occurred. He loves his wife very much, and after what happened to her, he has been desperately searching for her to bring her home again."

"I little believed a man would turn his wife away for such a thing. Moreover, the man would have to be daft to turn his back on someone like Sarah. She is such a treasure." Daniel was unsure whether he should reveal Sarah's condition.

"Precisely right! He would not. Not only has he employed me to find her, he himself has traveled to numerous towns in hopes of finding her. The Amesbury constable has been apprised of Mr. Swyndhurst's suspicions about who he believes attacked his wife. If it can only be confirmed by Mrs. Swyndhurst, the man shall immediately be thrown in jail. When that happens, she shall be quite safe."

"Yes, well, Sarah has not divulged the man's name. Though we wanted him cast into jail as well, we felt it best not to press her about it."

Mr. Haddon nodded. "With all that she has been through, talking about it may have been too difficult for her. Let me say again, you can be certain that Sarah will be quite safe if she returns home to Mr. Swyndhurst."

As Daniel continued to hear the details concerning Sarah's husband and his quest to find his wife, he began to believe he ought to reveal what he had been holding back. "There is more, Mr. Haddon. Owing to the attack…Sarah is with child—which only served to strengthen her belief that her husband would not want her home again."

Stunned, James simply stared at Mr. Thompson. He then suggested, "Perhaps the child is her husband's."

Daniel shook his head to indicate that it was not. "You will have to take my word for it. The child could not possibly be his."

After a few moments, James responded with a sigh, "The poor woman! Mr. Swyndhurst is an honorable man. That she is with child would not deter him from desiring to have her safely back at home where she belongs."

"Well, Mr. Haddon. I am not sure what to do. If I tell Sarah that you have come looking for her on behalf of her husband, I believe you are correct—she would almost certainly run away again. She hoped he would never learn what happened. I have explained that she owns no part of it, and that I believe her husband would see it the same way; nonetheless, she little believes her husband would accept her back now. And if I do not disclose that we have spoken, when she learns of it, she may feel that I have betrayed her."

"I understand your dilemma. Truly, I do. But I don't believe we have a choice, knowing that Sarah tends to take flight when she is frightened. What say you to keeping our conversation from Sarah until I have informed Mr. Swyndhurst that I have confirmed her whereabouts, as well as the news about the child?" inquired James.

"Perhaps that is best, though I dislike keeping anything from her. She is only now beginning to recover from what happened to her. I pray that breaking her trust in this way doesn't cause her to revert back to the fearful woman she once was. It took her some time to even dare step out of doors. As determined as she is, she managed it, but it frightened her half to death the first few times."

"Let us hope and pray that everything turns out for the best and that, in the end, she understands why you had to keep the information from her."

Daniel nodded.

Even though the news of Sarah's condition was troubling, James felt relieved he had finally found Mr. Swyndhurst's wife. Given Sarah's condition, however, he believed this kind of news needed to be given in person, not by a missive, and said as much to Daniel. "I know his heart shall break even more for Sarah when he hears about the baby, but he needs to be aware of the situation in advance of seeing her."

"When do you think your employer shall turn up at my home?" inquired the physician with some trepidation. He felt that he had done the right thing in disclosing all to Mr. Haddon; however, he dreaded Sarah's reaction at seeing her husband on his doorstep.

"Even though it is my intention to deliver the news in person, it should be no more than a fortnight for me to travel to Amesbury and back again with Mr. Swyndhurst," the hired man replied. "I am quite certain Mr. Swyndhurst will wish to set off without delay."

"Very well," Daniel responded. Though he knew they were doing the right thing, he was still ill at ease about the whole matter.

When everything was settled, the two men parted company. James was relieved at finally finding Sarah, but Daniel left with a heavy heart. As he thought about the fact that he would soon be seeing Sarah, he wondered how he was going to keep her from detecting that something was wrong. He had never been very good at hiding his feelings. He decided to pray that God would help him rein in his emotions before he arrived back at home.

Chapter 27

As Daniel walked in the door to his home, he had an odd feeling in the pit of his stomach. Though he felt convinced that he had done the right thing, he knew Sarah might feel differently. He hoped that, ultimately, it would all work out for her good. All the same, it concerned him greatly that, after this, Sarah might never trust him again. To settle his mind that he had indeed done the only thing he could, he went in search of Joanna. If she agreed that he had not been afforded any other option, he knew it would calm his anxious nerves.

As he entered the house, Mr. Hoyt approached. Aware of his son-in-law's concerns that one of his patients might be in town to find Sarah, taking Daniel aside, he asked if he might have a private word. Daniel directed him toward his examination room. Once the elderly gentleman was certain they would not be overheard, he inquired whether Daniel had learned any additional information about the man in question.

If not his wife, he knew his father-in-law was the next best person to ask about what he had discussed with James Haddon; therefore, after shutting the door, the two gentlemen made themselves comfortable. Daniel then explained all that had transpired between himself and Mr. Haddon.

While observing his father-in-law for a reaction, he anxiously inquired, "What is your opinion? Did I do right by Sarah?"

As he scratched his head, the elderly gentleman answered, "Yes...considering all that you have told me about Mr. Swyndhurst and his search for his wife, it sounds as though he deserves to know where she is. Sarah may see it quite differently, I'm afraid."

"She may indeed. That is why I assured Mr. Haddon that I would not disclose our conversation to her. I fear she might make a run for it if she were to learn that her husband shall soon be here. I am also quite concerned that the friendship we have forged with Sarah shall be harmed by all of this."

"That is understandable. But in my judgment, you are making the right decision about keeping such news from her, for the time being, anyway. And you should not feel too badly about telling everything to this James Haddon. It appears that you had no choice. And, my boy, is this not what we have been praying for? An answer to Sarah's dilemma?"

"To be sure. I just hope that I have not rushed things. What if I am wrong and this is not what's best for Sarah?" inquired Daniel.

Knowing his son-in-law's heart, Joseph responded, "You mustn't question yourself. As Sarah's husband shall not arrive for several days, we have time to pray for Sarah that she shall be prepared to see him when he comes."

Later that night, while Daniel and Joanna were alone in their bedchamber, he informed her of his conversation with James Haddon. Astonished, she quietly listened while he explained his feelings regarding his part in what had transpired. Joanna sensed that it was no little matter for her husband that he had revealed everything to a man who would be reporting back to Sarah's husband. Daniel had always been a protector, and she loved him for it. But just now she could see how much that side of his nature was causing him pain.

After sitting there for a moment to collect her thoughts, Joanna finally responded. "Daniel, after what the man told you about Mr. Swyndhurst's relentless search for Sarah, what else could you have done? The man clearly wants his wife at home, even knowing what has happened to her, which, I might add, is exactly as it should be."

"Yes, it would seem that he does. And as you say, it is only right that he should want her home. The difficulty for all of us, now, shall be in keeping Mr. Swyndhurst's forthcoming visit to ourselves. If Sarah were to learn of it, I fear what she may do. Your father and Mr. Haddon agree that there is indeed reason for concern."

Joanna concurred with the possibility of Sarah running off again if she were made aware of what was to come. All the same, similar to her husband, she disliked keeping such a thing from her friend and hoped when all was said and done, Sarah would understand.

◊◊◊

The next morning, Joanna avoided eye contact with Sarah as much as possible. As she was overwhelmed by guilt for keeping her friend in the dark about Daniel's conversation with Mr. Haddon, she felt that Sarah might suspect that something was wrong by her countenance or her odd behavior.

Before too long, however, as Sarah often did, she gathered up her Bible and made for the backyard. She liked her private time with God to be out of doors. Stepping out onto the somewhat thawed ground—which with winter all but coming to an end had only sparse areas of snow—she quickly moved in the direction of the old, wooden bench near the little stream at the far boundary line of the Thompsons' property.

Arriving at the bench, she sat down and placed her Bible upon her lap. Feeling the sun's warmth on her back, she thought about the beautiful oak tree towering over her. With a chill still in the air, she was grateful its branches were bare, for she had no need for shade just now. As she began to pray to the Lord, she expressed to Him how grateful she was for the Thompsons and Mr. Hoyt. She counted them amongst her greatest blessings. They had been there for her during a very difficult time, and she dreaded the day she would have to leave the comfort they daily offered her.

Joanna glanced out the kitchen window toward the backyard. In the distance, she spotted Sarah sitting on the bench by the tree with her head bent low. She knew her friend was likely reading her Bible and praying. Watching Sarah spending time with the Lord reminded Joanna to pray that He would give her young friend strength for whatever was to come, for she knew it wouldn't be long before the little peace Sarah had known since she had arrived would be a thing of the past. And the guilt she had been feeling at keeping secrets from Sarah prompted her to also pray that Sarah would forgive her, and Daniel, when she learned that they had aided her husband in finding her.

Chapter 28

Back at the Swyndhurst estate, Alexander was waiting for word of Sarah from his hired man. Having recently received the missive concerning James Haddon's fall, which had left the man injured, he had been praying his friend's leg would heal quickly. He felt awful that James had been hurt, for having an injured leg would certainly be burdensome for anyone, but the mishap had also delayed the search for Sarah.

Knowing how long it takes to receive correspondence from Boston, Alexander surmised that, by now, it could have been up to two weeks since James had injured himself. All this waiting was getting on Alexander's nerves. In addition, from the time that James had set off for Boston, Alexander had been too distracted to accomplish much of anything. He finally decided that if he didn't learn something soon, he would go to Boston himself to learn how James was faring, as well as what his hired man had learned regarding Sarah.

The children had settled in and seemed to be adjusting well to their new surroundings. In Martha and Mr. Swyndhurst's opinion, that they were having regular meals as well as clean clothes to wear, might have had something to do with how well they were getting on.

Jonathan and Hannah Bleasdell had told Alexander that they were prepared for the children to come whenever he had need of them, which he hoped would be very soon. With Alexander's father living in England, Jonathan had not only been a good friend, but in some ways a surrogate father to him. And Hannah seemed as concerned for Alexander's well-being as any mother or older sister might have been. In fact, it was Jonathan who had spoken to Alexander concerning his eternal destination. Alexander had observed his devout father over the years and had grown up going to church, where he had heard the gospel message time and time again. But before Jonathan had spoken to him, Alexander had not received Christ as his Savior. He had been attempting to earn his way to heaven—thinking that works were enough. After talking with Jonathan, however, Alexander had learned that the only way to obtain heaven and a right relationship with God was to receive the sacrifice of God's Son on his behalf. Jonathan had explained that none of us could ever be good enough to deserve heaven. For Alexander, when Jonathan had read Ephesians 2:8-9, "For by grace are ye saved through faith; and that not of yourselves: it is the gift of God: Not of works, lest any man should boast," he had gained a better understanding of salvation. In some ways, Alexander had felt relief at hearing that no one had ever been good enough, for deep down he knew he had also failed in this regard.

After Alexander had received Christ's sacrifice and repented of his sins, he had allowed God preeminence in his life. It was then that he realized the reason all of his previous efforts at living a worthy life had been extremely difficult—if not impossible—was that it had all been done in his own strength. Now that he had allowed the Lord to have control, his endeavors at living faithfully, which had seemed such a struggle before, had been made possible through the power of the Holy Spirit, for God had begun to conform Alexander's will to His own. He had finally learned how to have a true relationship with a loving and merciful God.

While Alexander paced around in the house, unable to handle even the smallest of tasks, someone knocked at the door. Hoping it might be news of Sarah, Alexander hurried to the door. After thrusting it open, as he had hoped, James Haddon was standing there, smiling.

While practically pulling James off his feet, Alexander ushered his friend toward his study. Not wanting to wait another moment to hear what James had to say, Alexander eagerly said, "By your smile, I take it you have good news."

After taking a seat to rest his throbbing leg, James responded, "Indeed! I have found Sarah! As we had hoped, she is staying with Mr. Hoyt's daughter. Though I felt my injured leg would have hindered my search, I could not have been more wrong. The very man I had been looking for—Daniel Thompson, Mr. Hoyt's son-in-law—was the physician who came to look after my leg.

"Mr. Harvey, at the hat company, had explained the physician's possible connection to Mr. Hoyt—who had been with Sarah the day they met together. After the mishap with my leg, I finally gained an audience with the gentleman; however, each time he paid me a visit, and I attempted to gain information regarding where he lived and whether he had a houseguest, he would change the subject. It turns out that he suspected my reason for coming to town had something to do with Sarah. That is why, at first, he had not been forthcoming."

Though he had been informed of some of this by James in his last correspondence, not wanting to miss a word of what had transpired since, Alexander quietly listened. He would not have interrupted the man for the world, for he knew that very soon James would get to the part about where to find Sarah.

The hired man continued, "At last, my leg had mended. I knew Mr. Thompson had come for the last time. Though on his previous visits I had been hesitant to reveal too much, this time I felt I had no choice but to tell the man everything. I hoped he would understand and be willing to tell me if Sarah had been lodging with his family. Thankfully, the man had sympathy for your plight. After learning that you had never given up the search for your wife, he explained that he had simply been protecting her.

After discussing the matter with me, he could see that keeping you from her would not be for the best."

Thinking about the fact that it was to the home of a physician that Sarah had gone, Alexander said in a strained voice, "James, God must have truly been watching over my poor wife. She most likely was in need of a physician after what happened to her. I am glad that, since I could not be, Mr. Thompson was there."

Knowing it was out of concern rather than jealousy that Alexander spoke, James quickly responded, "Just as you would have been, had you been afforded the opportunity."

"James, you must take me to her straight away," insisted Alexander almost breathless.

"Of course. Whenever you wish," James replied. "However, there is one other matter." James had been hesitant to tell his employer of Sarah's condition, so he had dragged the story out longer than necessary as he attempted to gain the courage.

Looking intently at his friend, Alexander knew whatever James had to disclose could not be good news, or he would not have held the information until the last. "James, whatever it is…I am prepared to hear."

"It is just that…well, Sarah is with child," he responded in almost a whisper.

Suddenly, Alexander came to his feet. Unable to contain his anger, he nearly shouted, "If I ever get my hands on her attacker! My poor wife! How she has suffered. If she had ever thought to return home, she wouldn't have even considered it once she had learned about the child." As he began to calm down, he stated, "This is just one more reason I am happy that she has been under a physician's care."

While indicating his agreement with a nod, as he watched his friend pace about the room, James remained quiet to allow the distraught husband time to process the news. James was also mulling over what raising another man's child would mean for Alexander. *He would have to be a strong man, indeed,* thought James. *Every time he looks at the child, he shall remember what happened to his wife.*

Before long, focusing on the task at hand, Alexander made his way over to the door and said, "Let us go to the kitchen. I must speak with Martha. I shall ask her to prepare you something to eat while I gather up the things I shall need for the trip. I should like to set off within the hour."

After rising to his feet, James followed after Mr. Swyndhurst. When Martha caught sight of the men approaching, she was eager to hear why Mr. Haddon had come. After learning that her employer and Mr. Haddon would soon be setting off for Boston to fetch Sarah, Martha broke down in tears.

Mr. Swyndhurst had not shared all with his servant. He knew she would find out about the child soon enough.

Wiping her eyes, Martha—filled with joy—said with a tremor in her voice, "Not only shall I prepare something for Mr. Haddon, but I shall also pack some food for your journey."

Glancing back over his shoulder as he was leaving the room, Mr. Swyndhurst responded to the elderly woman whom he dearly loved. "Very good! I am much obliged to you, Martha." With that, he headed for the stairs, taking them two at a time. In no time at all he had returned to the kitchen, ready to set off.

"Martha, would you have Peter take the children over to the Bleasdells' home? I wish I had the time to take them myself, but we really need to be going. Send my apologies, won't you?"

"Not to worry. We shall see to the children. You just go and get our girl," she responded, scarcely able to contain her excitement.

Mr. Swyndhurst and James set off soon after. They were unaware that Matthew Raymond had spotted Mr. Swyndhurst's hired man hastening by on his way to the estate. Within moments, as he had been prepared ever since Sarah had left town, Matthew loaded up his wagon. He wanted to be ready in the case that Sarah's husband and hired man took leave of Amesbury, and he felt certain that, this time, they would.

Allowing Mr. Swyndhurst time to be some distance ahead, Matthew Raymond waited atop his wagon. When he felt the two men were far enough away, he set off after them. It was going to be a little tricky keeping well enough behind, but close enough to not lose sight of the two men.

He wasn't sure just how he intended to get Sarah ahead of her husband, once they arrived at their destination, but he hoped an opportunity would present itself. As he rode along, he rehearsed his plans for what he would do once he had recaptured Sarah. He knew just where he would take her.

Chapter 29

It had been almost two days since Alexander and James had set off for Boston. Matthew Raymond, knowing Mr. Swyndhurst would certainly recognize him, had stayed well out of sight until the other two men had gained their lodgings each night. Additionally, he had risen before sunup each morning to keep an eye out for their departure. He hadn't been exactly sure where their final destination would be, but he was beginning to have his suspicions as to where they were headed.

By noon, as Matthew had suspected, they arrived in Boston. He was more confident than ever that Sarah was somewhere close. And as this was the town to which he had planned to take her, Matthew could not have been more pleased. After the recent death of his brother, he had inherited a modest dwelling on a secluded road far from the center of town. Even though he had visited his brother but rarely, with what he remembered of the home, he was certain Sarah would not be seen by anyone. The nearest house was several miles away. Additionally, he intended to tell her that if she ever attempted to flee, he would harm those she loved. He was certain that tactic would work well in keeping her under control. All that was left to do was to get his hands on the woman so he could whisk her away.

As Alexander and James approached Daniel Thompson's home, James directed his employer's attention toward the structure. "That is the place...there...up ahead. Along with the directions provided for me by Mr. Thompson, he also furnished a description of the house."

With his emotions all a jumble, Mr. Swyndhurst merely nodded. He could scarcely believe he would be seeing his wife in a matter of minutes. "I have not the words to describe my deep gratitude to you for finding Sarah, James."

"That is what you pay me for," he said with a chuckle. "But truth be told, I would have assisted in the search, regardless."

The two men had been friends long before Sarah's disappearance. They were all the more so now; therefore, Alexander knew what James had said was true—he would have helped him search no matter what.

As Joanna had been anxious on Sarah's behalf about what was to come, she had been glancing out the window so often over the past couple of weeks that she was surprised Sarah had not questioned her about it. Just now, she was taking another peek. Her heart jumped in her chest as she saw a wagon approaching. Knowing it was probably Sarah's husband and his hired man, as she didn't recognize either man, Joanna moved toward the door and waited for them to knock.

Joanna then looked up and thanked the Lord that Sarah was in her usual place at the far end of the backyard—sitting on the bench—studying her Bible. And the timing for her father's outing with her sons could not have come at a better time. They had gone into town to do a bit of shopping, for her father had been promising her boys that before he set off for Amesbury he would, within reason, purchase whatever they desired at the general store.

After opening the door and quickly greeting the gentlemen, Joanna directed them toward the parlor. While motioning for them to be seated, she indicated that she would go and fetch her husband. Not many words were exchanged, but no one seemed to notice. They were all too anxious about how Sarah was going to react when she learned her husband had arrived.

Nervously, Joanna hastened toward Daniel's examining room. She was grateful he had not had any patients that morning. Opening the door, she said in a whisper, "Mr. Swyndhurst and his hired man have arrived."

Nodding, Daniel asked his wife where Sarah was. When she explained that Sarah was out in the yard reading her Bible, he was grateful the road approaching their home could not be seen from her location. As he followed after his wife, he prayed that all would go well between Sarah and her husband. He also prayed that Sarah would not feel he had betrayed her and would understand his reasons for having revealed where she had been staying to her husband's hired man.

Coming into the parlor, Daniel greeted the two gentlemen. He then said, "God has seen fit to give us a few moments alone. Sarah is in her usual place at the far end of the yard. There is a little bench there that she likes to sit on while reading her Bible. Mr. Swyndhurst, allow me to say how sorry I am that you and Sarah have gone through this terrible ordeal."

With tears in his eyes, Alexander responded, "I am most grateful to you for looking after my wife and for letting me know where to find her. I have been frantically searching for her over the many months she has been gone. If it is all right with everyone, I cannot wait any longer. I must go to her."

Daniel escorted the anxious husband from the room. He then directed him to where he would find his wife. Joanna remained with Mr. Haddon in the parlor. Once Daniel had returned, while the gentlemen conversed, she went to the kitchen to prepare tea and something to eat. She assumed the two gentlemen would be famished after their long journey.

Not suspecting a thing, Sarah was quietly sitting in her usual spot, reading. All at once, she heard footsteps. As she glanced over her shoulder, she expected to see one of the boys. With the sun in her eyes, she couldn't make out who it was, but she noted that the figure was too tall to be one of the Thompsons' sons. Assuming it was Daniel, she began gathering up her things, for she thought he must need her for something or he would not have come looking for her.

However, before she had a chance to stand, Alexander had come around to the front of the bench. As she raised her eyes to question Daniel about what he needed, she was alarmed by what she saw. "Alexander! How...did you—"

Breaking in, Alexander moved closer and softly responded, "Sarah, thank the Lord I have finally found you." After taking a seat beside her, he reached over and grasped her hand.

With hands shaking, she dropped her eyes. Taking note of how little there was of her lap, with her rather large midriff resting upon it, with her free hand she endeavored to pull the quilt—which was presently draped over her shoulders—around to conceal the fact that she was with child.

By now, Alexander had guessed what she was attempting to do—hide her swollen middle; therefore, after letting go of her hand, he slid one arm under her legs and the other around her back and lifted her onto his lap. Her entire body was shaking at this point. While turning her head away, she wondered how she was going to hide her midriff now.

Pulling his wife against his chest, Alexander whispered, "I know everything, Sarah. There is no need to try and conceal anything from me. I love you, and nothing shall ever change that. I am ashamed you know so little of me that you felt the need to run away. Had I not gone away after we were wed, perhaps none of this would have happened. At the very least, had you been afforded the opportunity to know me better, you would have known you could have come to me."

Sarah buried her face against his chest and wept. Alexander remained silent for a time, allowing his wife to cry. Finally, he spoke words of comfort. "Sarah, you must not believe for one moment that after what has happened, I would thrust you aside."

Through her tears, she responded in no more than a whisper, "How can you want me now? I am carrying another man's child!"

Resting his chin atop her head, he wrapped his arms around her even tighter. "Sarah, the man forced himself upon you." Placing his hand on her round middle, he continued. "You and this child are completely innocent in all of this. I want you and the baby more than anything in the world."

Astounded, she responded, "How can you say that about a child who has been fathered by someone else? What is more, why would you want me after another man has—?"

While gently patting her round middle, he responded, "He may have fathered this child, but he shall never be the child's father. In taking another man's wife, he gave up that right. You and I belong to each other;

237

therefore, as I see it, this child is as much mine as it is yours. Moreover, the child is a part of you—the person I love most in the world. How can I not want him, or her? What has happened to you is terrible, but this child's life is precious to God, so it shall be to me as well."

Alexander was grateful he had been afforded time to process the news about the baby as he traveled from Amesbury to Boston. When he prayed about what he might say to Sarah, it was as though God had given him the words. In his heart he had heard, "All life is precious to the Creator of all life. The life within Sarah is no different, no matter *his* origin. Remember, to Me this child is fearfully and wonderfully made."

"You keep saying *our* child. Can you really take this child as your own?" she inquired, amazed by all that her husband had said and that he was actually sitting there holding her. *Perhaps I am asleep and this is really just a dream—a wonderful dream!*

"I most certainly can. As far as I am concerned, the child need never know the truth of his or her parentage."

Sarah fell silent. When she had first come to the realization that she was with child, she could not bring herself to care or even think about the child growing within her; however, as the infant began to make its presence known—by moving about within her womb—she had begun to feel a great affection for the child. She then recalled when she had first realized that she couldn't fathom ever being parted from the child, which, at present, was kicking up a storm. She was, in fact, surprised that Alexander hadn't felt the kicks beneath his hand.

Breaking into her thoughts, Alexander questioned, "Sarah, after you went away I began to suspect that it was Matthew Raymond who attacked you. Tell me, was he the man?"

All at once, memories of that night came flooding back, causing Sarah to shake violently. With a tremor in her voice, she answered, "Yes. I never told anyone about this, but he followed me to Amesbury from Cambridge."

"Your father mentioned that he had chased off a man who had been bothering you. Was he the man?"

"Yes. I was hoping if I just kept my distance from him, he would leave me alone, and most of the time he did."

"If I had been with you right from the start of our marriage, you might have told me and none of this would have happened," Alexander responded with sincere regret.

Glancing up at her husband, Sarah assured him, "Alexander, it is not your fault. We both agreed to the sort of marriage we have."

"Had! As I said before, I no longer want that kind of marriage." After a few moments, he said, "Well...we do not have to speak about this right now. I just needed to know for sure who the man was in order to make the constable aware. Like me, he suspected that it was Matthew Raymond. I shall send James over to alert the constable here in Boston that he might send word to have the man locked up. That way, by the time we return to Amesbury, he shall already be put away where he cannot hurt you again."

Suddenly, Sarah came to the realization that she would soon be going home. She had mixed emotions at the prospect. Owing to her nightmares, as well as the memories of that terrible night, for her, Amesbury had become a rather dark place; however, that Alexander wanted her and the baby did more for her heart than she could say.

The husband and wife fell silent for a time. Alexander was so grateful to finally be holding his wife that he just wanted to remain where he was for a while. Sarah, though she still felt ill at ease about her round middle being seen by her husband, simply continued to lean against his chest, sobbing silently. All the emotions she had been suppressing for months had finally let loose.

After a while, sensing that his wife had at last calmed, Alexander spoke. "Let us go in so that I might talk with the physician about whether you should travel, in your condition. If he gives his consent, I should like to set off for home tomorrow. As I said, I also need to send James off to see the constable, now that we know for certain that it was Matthew Raymond."

Still stunned by all that was happening, and also not quite certain she wasn't dreaming, Sarah responded, "Alexander, if it is all right with you, I shall follow shortly. I need to tend to this face."

"You are not trying to rid yourself of my company to run off again, are you?" he questioned with a wink to hide his genuine concern.

"I promise, I shall be in straight away," she said with a smile.

After kissing the top of her head, Alexander placed her back on the bench and rose to his feet. He then went in the direction of the house. Besides making sure that Matthew Raymond was no longer a threat when they returned to Amesbury, he also wanted to get his wife home as soon as possible. He had to be certain it was all right for her to travel.

Sarah sighed as she watched her husband go. She was still unable to fully believe she had married so wonderful a man. After drying her face on her sleeve, she began gathering her things.

Chapter 30

Matthew Raymond had pulled his wagon off the road in the cover of woods. Following that, he crept along the tree line to the house at which Mr. Swyndhurst's wagon had stopped. While moving toward the backyard to keep out of sight, unexpectedly, he caught a glimpse of Mr. Swyndhurst and Sarah at the far end of the yard.

As chance would have it, while he waited and watched, the woman was soon left alone when her husband returned to the house. From what Matthew had seen, they had been quite cozy with each other, so he assumed she would soon follow after her husband. He had to seize her now, or it would be too late. He may not have another opportunity before the pair set off for Amesbury, which, to Matthew Raymond's way of thinking, to wait for that would be too risky. If he was unsuccessful at capturing her along the way, everyone in the town of Amesbury would hear about what he had done. If that happened, he could never show his face again. And once word got out about his crime, wherever he went, he would risk being caught and thrown in jail.

Creeping up behind the bench on which Sarah was presently sitting, collecting her things, reaching around,

Matthew covered her mouth with his hand. He felt certain she was far enough away from the house that no one would hear her should she scream, but he didn't want to take any chances.

He was correct in thinking she might cry out, for though the sound was muffled by his hand, she was doing just that. Sliding his other arm around her upper body, he pulled her over the bench and into his arms. He hadn't missed the fact that she was obviously with child. With the young woman kicking and biting while attempting to escape his grasp, he hastened over to the edge of the yard along the tree line.

Back at the house, the Thompson boys and their grandfather had just returned home. Mr. Hoyt went straight into the house, while the boys started for the backyard to play. All at once, the brothers caught sight of a strange man carrying Sarah off. From where they stood they could see that she was trying to get away.

The eldest of the Thompsons' sons, with his brother close behind, ran as quickly as his legs would carry him toward the house. Once indoors, while gasping for air, Daniel, Jr., blurted out, "A man is carrying Sarah off!"

Alexander jumped to his feet, as did everyone else in the room. "What? Where?"

The boy grabbed the stranger by the hand and ran for the door. As they made their way to the backyard, while the two were yet running, the boy pointed in the direction he had seen Sarah and the man.

Alarmed that his wife and a man, he assumed to be Matthew Raymond, were nowhere to be seen, Alexander ran for his wagon. The boys' father and James were right behind him. After the men had climbed onto the wagon, they raced out of the yard in the direction they had observed dust, which had obviously been stirred up by another wagon. Daniel then said a prayer that they would find Sarah, and quickly. The boys stood with their mother, watching as the wagon hastened down the road.

Seeing that Alexander was clearly too distraught to manage, James had taken hold of the reins. *The poor fellow. After all he has been through, and now this. We must get Sarah back!*

With tears in his eyes, Alexander stated that it was entirely his fault; he must have led the man straight to his wife. Daniel then insisted it would do no good to place blame and that they needed to focus on finding Sarah.

Nodding, Alexander stared straight ahead. "Can you not go any faster, James? We have to catch them!" The fearful husband hated to think what would happen to Sarah if they didn't.

Within a few moments, pointing, Alexander yelled out, "There they are!" Grabbing his musket, Alexander braced himself for what was sure to be a battle. Daniel had taken hold of his muzzle loader on his way out of the house. James, while clutching the reins in one hand, reached under the seat for his firearm. At this moment, he was glad that he never traveled without a weapon.

As they were closing in on Matthew Raymond, Alexander could hear Sarah screaming for the man to let her go. The distraught husband's heart was racing as he thought about the terror his wife was experiencing with the knowledge that she was, once again, in her attacker's hands.

The men could hear Matthew Raymond raising his voice at Sarah. "That is my child you are carrying! I am sure of it. You are coming with me, so stop moving about!"

Sarah, angry now, yelled right back at him, "You have no right to take me! And the child is mine, not yours!"

For an instant Matthew lost his grip on the tiny woman. Seizing the opportunity, she quickly climbed over the seat to the rear of the wagon. While trembling all over, she made her way to the far edge. That she could see Alexander and the others gave her some hope that she might yet escape her wicked captor.

As the chase had gone on for some twenty minutes, Matthew Raymond finally spotted the turn off for his brother's house, the home to which he had been intending to take Sarah. He decided that if he could just get himself and Sarah within its walls, he might just fend off the men who were pursuing them. As he abruptly turned onto the road leading to his desired destination, Sarah tumbled out of the back of his wagon.

Whirling around, Matthew Raymond saw Sarah sprawled out on the ground. He then noted that the other wagon was rapidly approaching. Coming to a halt, he secured his reins, grabbed his firearm and turned, ready to fire. He had no intention of allowing Sarah to slip away from him now. Moreover, he could not allow the men to reclaim Sarah and then make a getaway, or they were sure to go directly for the constable.

As soon as their wagon had come to a stop, Alexander and Daniel jumped down and started running toward Sarah. Seeing that Mrs. Swyndhurst's abductor had lifted his weapon—pointing it at Mr. Swyndhurst and Mr. Thompson as they were approaching Sarah—James raised his musket, ready to fire.

Alexander knelt down on the ground beside Sarah. Then, hearing two loud blasts, his eyes flew in Matthew Raymond's direction. To his relief, the man was slumped down on the seat in the front of his wagon. Glancing back at James to ascertain whether he had been injured in the gun fight, Alexander observed that James was well, for he had already climbed down from the wagon and was now moving in their direction. Relieved that everyone—except Matthew Raymond—was safe, Alexander directed his attention back to Sarah.

While moving out of the way so the physician could assess Sarah's injuries, Alexander prayed she hadn't been severely hurt. Daniel gently checked her over for broken bones. He then felt the back of her head, for she had landed hard and was presently unconscious.

"It is essential that we get her back to my house as quickly as possible. But she must not be jarred any more than necessary. Mr. Haddon, while Mr. Swyndhurst and I see to Sarah, would you, with all caution, go over and assess Sarah's abductor's condition?"

Alexander then revealed the evil man's name to the physician while James strode over to the man's wagon. As Alexander lifted Sarah, James called over that the man was dead. Although he felt a bit uncomfortable that he was glad to hear the news that a man was dead—since it was this particular man—Alexander sighed with relief. The wicked man would never again endanger his wife.

James hastened back to Alexander's wagon and climbed up—prepared to set off the moment Sarah was situated. Alexander and Daniel sat in the rear of the wagon with Sarah. As the wagon began to move, Sarah opened her eyes.

"What has happened?" she inquired, still a bit dazed. Before Alexander could answer, she remembered Matthew Raymond. "Where is—"

Seeing the fear in Sarah's eyes, Alexander interrupted, "He is dead, Sarah. You are safe."

Suddenly, Daniel observed a wetness seeping out from under Sarah's clothing. Fearing the worst, that her water had broken and she was quite possibly losing the baby, he glanced over at Alexander.

Staring at the physician, for he had also noticed the wetness, Alexander began praying for his wife. He then grasped Sarah's hand and held onto it until they arrived back at the Thompsons'.

Once the wagon had pulled up close to the front door, Sarah was lifted out. James was then sent to find the constable in order to inform him of Matthew Raymond's crime, as well as where to find the man's body. Alexander carried Sarah into the house and directly to the physician's examining room, at which point she was placed on the table for Daniel to assess her. From the loss of blood, evidenced by her stained clothing, and the earlier flow of water, besides the risk to her life, he was certain she was losing her child.

Speaking softly so Sarah wouldn't hear, the physician said, "Mr. Swyndhurst, I believe we should take her to her bedchamber where she might be more comfortable. This table is no place to deliver a child."

Alexander was saddened to hear the physician confirm his fears; Sarah was losing the baby. Obeying Mr. Thompson's orders, the worried husband gathered up his wife and followed the physician to Sarah's room.

Once there, Alexander placed his wife on the bed. He then went in search of a chair. After returning to his wife's room, he placed the chair over next to the bed and took hold of her hand. When Sarah glanced over at him, he could see there were tears in her eyes. *I wonder if she knows what is happening. Perhaps she heard Mr. Thompson.* To console her, he said, "Sarah, there is no need to fear. The physician shall look after you."

Closing her eyes, she nodded. Besides fearing for the baby, she was ill at ease at having the two men in the room with her. As she had no choice, she pushed such thoughts aside and silently prayed that the baby would survive. She had only just begun to accept the fact that she was with child—had even begun to feel love for the child, and now she knew, even though Daniel hadn't said as much to her, she was losing the baby. She had felt the wetness, and there had been constant pain since the ride back to the Thompsons' home.

Daniel and Alexander sensed, though she had not cried aloud, she was in great agony. They had seen her shudder every few minutes. Before long, the pains became so intense that Sarah gripped Alexander's hand.

When Joanna had come to check on Sarah soon after they had arrived, Daniel had sent her for clean toweling and hot water. Hearing a knock on the door, Daniel called for Joanna to come in. As his wife entered, Daniel sent Alexander away, for husbands were rarely permitted in the room when their wives were giving birth and the physician didn't think Alexander could take much more of seeing his wife in pain. After Alexander had gone, Joanna took up vigil beside Sarah's bed. She was also on hand to assist her husband in whatever capacity he required.

Quite often, though the town had a midwife, Joanna had assisted her physician husband in bringing babies into the world. The circumstances were often those in which the midwife felt the presence of a physician might be necessary—cases where the mother had previously had a difficult time or the child appeared to be arriving ahead of schedule.

A short time later, Sarah gave birth to a tiny baby boy. As it was still too early for the child to arrive, given that he was not expected for another couple of months and he had clearly been injured in the fall, the child was certain to die within a few minutes of entering the world.

After calling Alexander back into the room, Daniel, knowing it wouldn't be long, had placed the child alongside Sarah. The husband and wife caressed the tiny baby boy as he lay dying. Once the child's heart stopped beating, Alexander, with tears in his eyes, wrapped him in a blanket and took him from the room. Joanna remained behind with Sarah while Daniel solemnly looked after the grieving young woman.

Before long, the doctor and his wife had tucked an exhausted Sarah into a clean bed. They then went in search of her husband. Finding him in the parlor with the lifeless child, they decided it was best to leave him to himself, for, to their astonishment, he was clearly grieving over the loss. Not that they thought he would take the child's death lightly, but under such circumstances many a man might have been a little relieved.

A short time later, James Haddon returned. He soon learned that Sarah had lost the baby. Saddened by the news, he scarcely touched the meal Joanna had prepared for him. Joanna soon showed him to one of the guest bedchambers, where he settled in for the night.

Chapter 31

While Sarah slept, Alexander remained in the parlor, holding the lifeless infant. At first light, he and Mr. Thompson set off to bury the child. Alexander knew it would be some time before his wife would be strong enough to be out of bed. This was a task that could not wait. Moreover, he had no desire for Sarah to have to endure the tiny boy's burial.

As they approached the burying ground, Alexander stated that he wished to name the little lad after himself and his father before him. "My son, never to be forgotten, is to be called Alexander Swyndhurst III."

Though he had only known the man for a few days, at that moment Daniel felt immense admiration for Alexander Swyndhurst. As he continued to observe Mr. Swyndhurst holding another man's son—a son born of an attack upon his beloved wife, whom he had now named after himself—Daniel knew he was standing in the presence of a decidedly honorable man.

As the ground had softened a little with the presence of spring, Alexander had been able to break up the earth where he was to lay his son. Before long, the dirt was shoveled back over the small grave. With tears streaming down, Alexander spoke words over the child. He then prayed that Sarah's heart would mend from all that she had been through.

As they made their way back to the Thompsons', Daniel patted Alexander's shoulder and expressed how proud he was of him for looking upon the child as his own. He then assured him that Sarah would recover physically, but warned that her emotions were altogether another matter. Sarah had, in fact, only just begun to heal over the dreadful event that had taken place a few months before. With the loss of the baby, as well as having, again, faced her attacker, Daniel believed it may be some time before she was herself. He warned that she may need a great deal of time to herself, to work through everything that had occurred.

Upon their arrival back at the house, Joanna greeted them at the door. "Sarah has been asking for you, Mr. Swyndhurst."

With haste, he went to his wife's bedside. As he approached, he asked, "Sarah, how are you feeling?" He hoped she would not ask about the child.

Without answering his question, she inquired as to where he had gone. Joanna had explained that he and Daniel had gone off together, but she had not said where.

Not wanting to upset her, he evaded the question by fluffing her pillow and asking yet again how she was feeling and whether she had rested at all.

A bit frustrated, Sarah again asked where Alexander had gone. She assumed it had to do with making arrangements for burying her son, or perhaps speaking with the constable about Matthew Raymond. As she thought about the infant, she didn't believe she could bear to see him again. It was simply too painful.

With a sigh, Alexander sat down on the edge of her bed, after which he reluctantly began explaining where he had been. "Sarah, Mr. Thompson and I took little Alexander to the burying ground in town. I am sorry not to have told you, but I felt it was for the best. To see him again might have caused you additional agony. I could not bear that. You have been through so much already."

As she listened, she thought she heard him say "little Alexander" when referring to the baby. Stunned, she questioned him about it. "Alexander, did I hear you correctly? Did you say 'little Alexander' in relation to the baby?"

While brushing her hair away from her face, he responded, "Yes, it has always been my intention to name my first son after my father, and myself; so, naturally, that is to be his name, that is, if you are all right with it."

With tears spilling from her eyes, she looked fixedly at her husband, wondering how she could have ever deserved him. "Alexander, you are too wonderful for words. How could I have ever believed you wouldn't want me...or the baby? What man has ever done so much for his wife—naming a son that isn't even his after himself? Even loving the child—as evidenced by the tears I saw in your eyes when he—"

Leaning down, Alexander kissed Sarah's forehead and then insisted that she rest. When she had finally fallen asleep, he quietly slipped out of the room. Mr. Hoyt, James, and the Thompsons had remained in the parlor, conversing over everything that had happened. The boys were out in the barn feeding the horses—out of audible range. While Alexander was yet in with Sarah, Daniel had shared with the others what had happened at the burial.

Mr. Hoyt had thought about going along but had decided against it, believing the grieving man needed his privacy. Upon hearing all that had taken place, the elderly man was glad he had left the two younger gentlemen to themselves to bury the child, for he was certain it had been easier on Alexander that way, not having too many along on such a solemn occasion.

Making his way to the parlor, Alexander found Mr. Hoyt, James, and the Thompsons. After he had taken a seat, all those in the room, in turn, expressed their belief that he had done a very good thing in naming the child after himself. They all agreed that the gesture was sure to go a long way in mending Sarah's broken heart. Mr. Hoyt went on to say that, for Sarah, knowing the child would be recognized as the couple's first son would also make it easier for her to feel at liberty to speak of him, rather than hide away the fact that he had ever existed, like some terrible secret.

Alexander was grateful for their comforting words but felt they were undeserved, for he believed that had he been more attentive to his wife, none of what she had been through would have even occurred. "I am much obliged to you all; however, I feel that I am unworthy of such praise." While the conversation continued, the others became aware of what James had sensed all along; not only would Sarah need a time of healing, but Alexander would as well. It was now clear to all that he had placed the blame for all that had happened squarely upon his own shoulders. Although over the next hour they all attempted to convince him otherwise, he would not let go of his guilt.

Chapter 32

Sometime during the night, Alexander had gone to check on his wife. After lighting a candle, he noticed that she was awake. Seeing him, his wife requested his assistance. After helping her to her feet so she could see to her needs, he noticed blood on her nightgown as well as on the bed. He assumed that some blood was to be expected, but the amount he saw seemed excessive. To his surprise, however, as lethargic as she was at that moment, she hadn't even noticed—which only served to add to his fears. When his wife was ready to return to her bed, he gently placed one arm around her and the other under her elbow to assist her. Once she was settled, he pushed the blood-smeared chamber pot aside. With great concern, he went immediately to wake the physician.

After hearing what Alexander had observed, Daniel—lantern in hand—rushed to Sarah's bedchamber. From the amount of blood on her clothing and bed, he surmised that she had been hemorrhaging for some time. As he observed her, he noted that her face was also extremely pale. At this point, he sent Alexander from the room. A few moments later, Joanna came in to help her husband tend to Sarah.

Alexander had been pacing out in the hallway for some time when Daniel finally opened the door. Coming out of the room, the physician directed Alexander toward the parlor. After motioning the anxious husband over to a chair, Daniel began, "It seems Sarah suffered more from the fall than I had previously thought. In fact, it appears as though her injuries were so great that it is highly unlikely she shall ever bear another child."

"But what of Sarah? Is she going to be all right?" Alexander inquired with great concern.

"I do believe she shall recover, as the bleeding seems to have subsided; however, she has lost a great deal of blood and shall need bed rest for some time yet. You and James are welcome to stay on until she is well enough to travel."

With gratitude, Alexander responded, "I am much obliged to you for all that you have done for my wife, and now for me. I don't know how I shall ever repay such a debt."

"Nonsense! Having Sarah with us has been a pleasure. Besides," he said with a smile, "she has more than earned her keep. I should be getting back in there. Joanna is getting Sarah cleaned up and into a fresh nightgown. Between the two of us, we shall see that her bedding is changed as well." As Daniel rose to his feet, he suggested that Alexander get some rest, explaining that Sarah would probably be sleeping soundly for the remainder of the night. He then assured the concerned husband that he would be checking on Sarah every couple of hours to see that the bleeding had ceased for good.

Aware that the news of never bearing another child would be devastating to Sarah, after returning to his room Alexander prayed for his wife. For him, though, that his wife would survive the ordeal was all that concerned him. He then thought about the Strout children. They were for all intents and purposes his and Sarah's children now. His wife might never have another child of her own, but having three that she dearly loved living with them might just be enough for her. At least that was Alexander's hope.

The following morning, after checking on Sarah, Alexander went to speak with James. Once he had explained the situation, that the duration of their stay had been prolonged because of his wife's injuries, he inquired whether the man wished to be on his way. They had all known that the premature delivery had added days to their stay, but now there was no telling how long it might be before they could leave.

After listening to all that his friend had to say, James insisted he had no desire to set off alone. He then assured Alexander that he would stay on as long as necessary to see the couple safely home.

Later that afternoon, apart from Sarah, all of the adults had gathered in the parlor. As Daniel had expected, with the loss of blood, Sarah had scarcely stirred for hours. While they were conversing, Alexander found it an opportune time to disclose that he had taken in three children. He went on to describe Sarah's relationship with the family. He explained that she had always taken great care to see to the children's needs, even to her own detriment.

The Thompsons and Mr. Hoyt were not at all surprised to hear about Sarah having regularly cared for her neighbor's children. Mr. Hoyt had already shared with his daughter and son-in-law what Sarah had told him of the situation with the Strout children, including the fact that it was from there that she had been returning when Matthew Raymond captured her. Daniel and Joanna had also seen for themselves how it was with Sarah; of her own accord, she had spent many hours looking after their sons.

While Mr. Swyndhurst spoke with the Thompsons and Mr. Hoyt, James quietly listened. He had already been privy to much of what his friend was presently sharing with the others.

When Alexander had concluded with his news concerning the Strout children, he asked that everyone keep the information to themselves. When the time was right, he would inform Sarah of the new additions to their household. He felt that after suffering the loss of little Alexander, now was not the time. And he had already determined before ever taking leave of Amesbury that he would not tell Sarah until he felt she had sufficiently recovered from all that she had been through.

The conversation shifted when Alexander inquired, "Mr. Thompson, have you informed Sarah she might never have another child?"

Looking thoughtful, the physician responded, "No, I have not. She was not well enough to hear such news last night, and she has scarcely moved all day; consequently, I have not had an opportunity. And please, call me Daniel. With all that we have been through together, in so short a time, I feel that we have a connection beyond merely newly formed acquaintances."

Nodding, Alexander then asked if Daniel thought it a good time to tell Sarah such dreadful news, with her yet recovering. "Might it not be better to put off telling her for a time?

With everyone now on a first name basis, Daniel responded. "Alexander, I have always found it best to be honest from the start, for in my experience, there is never really a good time for such news. And if put off for a later time, it often becomes more and more difficult to bring the subject up; nevertheless, as you are her husband, I shall leave the decision to you."

"If you think it best to tell her sooner rather than later, I have no objection. Though I dread having to do so, we shall tell her before we set off for home."

While the gentlemen conversed, Joanna thought about the Strout children. She felt certain that, considering the situation, having the children in the Swyndhursts' home would be good for Sarah and might ease her pain over never having another child of her own.

Soon, the boys came into the parlor asking after Sarah. It was clear to all that the Thompsons' sons had formed a strong attachment to Mrs. Swyndhurst over the months she had been living with them.

"Boys, Sarah is resting. I would appreciate it if you would talk softly whenever you are near her bedchamber," Joanna said in a low tone. The boys had not been privy to the goings on over the past couple of days, other than what they had observed when Matthew Raymond had carried Sarah off. Once Sarah had safely returned to the Thompsons' home, the boys were extremely relieved. Though they were told very little, they hadn't inquired further. Both boys began to comprehend that, though Sarah had been rescued, she was not well.

Although they wished to see their friend, the boys agreed to keep quiet so Sarah could rest.

Sensing his sons' confusion, Daniel decided right then that it was time to inform them that Sarah had lost the baby, or they might continue seeking her out. "Daniel...Joseph...Sarah's baby has died; therefore, she shall not be up and about for several days. When she is well enough to be out of bed, she and Alexander shall be setting off for home."

The boys, saddened by the news about the baby, seemed to comprehend what the loss meant for Sarah's husband as well, for they both approached Mr. Swyndhurst to offer their condolences. Joanna and Daniel couldn't have been more proud of their boys.

Sometime late in the night, when Alexander had come to her room, Sarah inquired whether Daniel had said anything about her ability to have more children. She had been tossing and turning as she thought about what her injuries might mean for future children. She couldn't rest until she knew.

Though Alexander hesitated to answer, she suspected the truth. "He doesn't believe that I shall, am I right?"

As he sat down next to Sarah on the bed, Alexander caressed her brow. "Sarah, though he cannot say for certain, Daniel suspects that your injuries were too severe—the damage too great." That she had even asked signified one thing to Alexander: his wife was at least considering the idea of having a traditional marriage. He thought she had been moving in that direction before she fled town. He now felt certain he had been right. With that knowledge, he wished more than anything that he could tell her they would have more children.

While silently nodding, she turned her head away. She felt tears flooding her eyes and didn't want Alexander to notice. He had been so good to her about having another man's baby. Now she may never be able to give him a son of his own.

Chapter 33

It had been nearly three weeks since Sarah's baby had died. The time was rapidly approaching for the Swyndhursts and James Haddon to take leave of Boston. Joanna and Sarah had grown very close in the months they had been together. Although Sarah's departure had not yet happened, the ladies were already saddened at the knowledge that they would soon be parted.

Even though theirs had been a short acquaintance, Daniel and Alexander had also formed a brotherly bond from their shared, albeit difficult, experiences. They had each swiftly developed a deep respect for, and confidence in, the other.

Joseph Hoyt suggested that when it came time for the couple and James to take their leave, he follow after the trio in his own wagon. Alexander and James were happy to comply with the elderly man's wishes.

Daniel spoke with Sarah that morning concerning his desire to have another look at her. He wanted to be certain that she was indeed well enough to travel. As they made their way to his examination room, she felt it was time to broach the subject of whether she could have more children. She was sure Alexander had been relaying Daniel's thoughts on the matter, but she wished to hear it firsthand.

Once she had been thoroughly examined, taking a deep breath, she asked, "Daniel, was Alexander correct? You believe me incapable of carrying another child, do you not?"

His countenance one of sadness, he responded, "I am afraid so, Sarah. Your injuries were rather extensive. I could be wrong; however, I do not believe that I am. I am truly sorry."

With a heavy heart, she responded, "Daniel, I am grateful to you for your honesty. It is rather unexpected that I would concern myself with such things, given that when I married it was for expediency's sake, not for...well, Alexander and I simply did not care for each other in that way."

"And now?" Daniel inquired, though he knew the answer. It was obvious to him from the moment he met Alexander that the man adored his wife. And from what he had seen of Sarah's actions and glowing face whenever her husband was present, he was certain she felt much the same.

"Presently, I believe he is the dearest man alive. But you are a close second, Daniel," she said with a smile.

Daniel smiled warmly at Sarah's comment about his being a close second. He had grown to love Sarah as one would love a little sister. His heart, at that moment, was heavy at the thought that he would greatly miss his petite friend.

Sarah continued, "My heart swells when I think of him." All at once, her countenance fell. "Daniel, how would you have felt if Joanna had been unable to have children?"

This, Daniel knew he could answer with all sincerity. "Sarah, I would not have loved her any less. Though I am glad we have our sons, I did not marry her for her ability to provide children for me. I married her because I adored her and wanted to spend the rest of my life with her, regardless of any obstacles that might have arisen, or may yet."

"Since Alexander didn't plan on having a traditional marriage when you were wed, he certainly won't be too disappointed that there may never be any children from your union. In fact, Sarah, he has said as much to me. At some point, your husband's feelings for you changed from indifference to adoration. I have never seen a man more concerned for his wife. Just having you, shall be enough. Take my word for it."

She had to agree; Alexander had come home from England a different man. At first she had feared the change, but now she was delighted with the transformation in their relationship.

"Daniel, you and Joanna have become the dearest people in the whole world to me. How shall I ever do without you both, and the boys, of course?"

"When you return home, you shall be so happy with Alexander, you shall scarcely think of us," he said with a warm smile. "Well, let us go and find that husband of yours. I believe if you take it slow while traveling, you can manage the journey. But the moment you are home, you must take to your bed for a few days of rest."

With a twinkle in her eye, she responded, "I shall allow you to tell him the first part—that I am well enough to travel—if you omit the 'bed rest' directive."

Chuckling, he placed his hand against her back to shepherd her from the room. As they made their way to find Alexander, he countered, "You can depend on me," pausing for effect, "to give him the entire directive."

As Sarah was now well enough to travel, the following day the Swyndhursts, Mr. Hoyt, and James Haddon, after a tearful farewell, set off for home.

As Daniel had suggested, Alexander took it slow as they traveled, for he had no wish to tire his fragile wife.

After four days of stopping off several times along the way for food and rest, the couple and their traveling companions finally arrived in Amesbury. As they neared his home, Mr. Hoyt called out a farewell from his wagon. Alexander and James called back a sendoff to their friend. As Sarah waved farewell to Mr. Hoyt, she felt immeasurable gratitude toward him for all that he had done for her.

As James plodded along, Alexander and Sarah snuggled close together. When Sarah spotted Matthew

Raymond's house, she turned her face toward Alexander and pressed in tight to his arm. Glancing down, Alexander surmised, by her countenance, that his wife was ill at ease at seeing her attacker's home. Placing his arm around her, he pulled her close and whispered, "He is gone and can never harm you again."

Hearing Sarah sigh, Alexander was reminded of how blessed he was to have found his wife and that she was now safely in his arms. He was also grateful the journey from Boston, as it brought them into town from the opposite direction, hadn't carried them by way of Alice Strout's home, for he had no desire to divulge that bit of information just yet.

When they arrived home, after a grateful Alexander had thanked him over and over again for finding Sarah, James parted company with the couple.

Just after Alexander and Sarah had descended the wagon, having heard them approaching, Martha came running out to greet the Swyndhursts, primarily Sarah. Pulling the young woman into her arms, she exclaimed, "Sarah, I have missed you so! You must never leave us again. Do you hear?"

"I have no intention of doing so, Martha."

"Good! Now let us go in. Everyone is anxious to see you." While keeping her arm around the young woman as they walked, Martha, with Sarah in tow, made her way to the house.

Alexander smiled at his servant-friend escorting his wife. He felt certain she would not allow Sarah out of her sight for some time to come. Knowing this brought peace to his heart. Not that he believed Sarah would ever go away again, but he did not want to take any chances.

Chapter 34

After the trio had entered the house, with delight in seeing the Swyndhursts safely at home, Peter approached. While smiling widely at the young woman for whom he had been praying, Peter awaited instructions from her husband. After warmly greeting Peter, Mr. Swyndhurst directed him to fetch his, and Mrs. Swyndhurst's belongings from the wagon. Peter was more than happy to do so. When the servant had returned shortly after, he was instructed to carry Sarah's things up to 'her' bedchamber.

Sarah listened as her husband directed Peter toward her bedchamber, *not his*, with her satchel. After thinking about this for a moment, she began to suspect the reason must be that he no longer wished to have a marriage in the traditional sense. Not that she blamed him. Although he accepted the baby as his, it was, after all, another man's child. She thought about how good he had been to her since learning the truth. If all that could ever be between them now was a special sort of friendship, she was grateful at least for that. Besides, she felt undeserving of even that, for had she listened to him in the first place and not gone to the Strouts' home that day, none of the trouble that had befallen them would have even occurred.

And yet, while we were in Boston did he not say that he wanted a real marriage? With time to think about everything, he must have changed his mind, she thought.

Once Alexander had seen to getting Sarah settled, he asked his head servant to prepare Mrs. Swyndhurst something to eat and have it sent to her bedchamber. He then spoke to his wife. "Sarah, Daniel insisted that you rest for a few days once we arrived back at home. Come with me. I shall escort you to your room."

As Sarah thought about how different things were going to be than they had been before she left, she felt a sense of sadness. She never would have believed she would yearn to share her husband's room, but that was exactly how she was feeling just now. Not that she was prepared for anything more than merely sharing a room, but to have him near, she believed, would have been comforting somehow. Being back in the town where the terrible incident had taken place, for Sarah, was exceedingly disconcerting. Pushing it from her mind had been hard enough while she was in Boston; now that she was home, she wondered how she could think of anything else.

Glancing up at her husband, she replied, "Alexander, I wish to wash first. I shall not be able to rest comfortably until I have done so."

"Very well. I shall have Peter fetch the tub from the laundry. When you are through, come and find me so that I might see you to your bedchamber," he said with a smile. He then added, "It would be best if you put on a nightgown rather than a day dress after you have bathed, as you are to remain in bed for a few days."

Nodding, she turned to go. Slowly taking the stairs, she made her way to her room. Once she had gathered up fresh clothes, she went back down to the kitchen. While she waited for the water to heat, she and Martha had a cup of tea at the table. As Martha observed her young friend, she could scarcely believe her eyes. Sarah was actually home. Though the elderly servant desired to discuss what had happened the night Sarah went away, she knew now was not the time. Then, glancing across the table at her mistress, she wondered if Sarah would ever wish to talk about that terrible night. If she had to guess, she was fairly certain the answer would be no, she would not.

A short time later, behind the closed door to the buttery, Sarah stood in the wooden tub and reached down to wet her cloth in the warm water. As much as she wanted to sink down in the tub, after having lost a child not all that long ago, she knew she shouldn't just yet. Soon, she began to grow weary as she stood there, and decided to quickly finish up with her sponge bath. She then dried herself off and donned her nightgown. She really could have washed up in her bedchamber but hadn't wanted to say as much to Alexander. *He doesn't understand that women don't usually bathe so soon after—* She hastily turned her thoughts back to Alexander, for it was still too painful to think about the child. *As it is, I bathe more often than most, so it was understandable that he assumed I needed Peter to fetch the tub. All I really needed to do was wait for the water to heat to carry up to my room, enough for the washbasin.*

After draping a small quilt around her shoulders, she gathered up her soiled clothing from the floor. Upon leaving the buttery, as he had requested, Sarah went in search of her husband. Finding him in his study, she stated that she was ready to go to her bedchamber. Once he had risen from his chair, smiling in her direction, he came close and took her by the arm. He then led her from the room.

As they mounted the stairs together, Sarah felt ill at ease. She wondered what it was going to be like living under the same roof with her husband now that things had changed between them. *Before I went away, we had started to become a real husband and wife. And he searched for me all of those months. But most astonishing was that he was so wonderful about my child, even naming the boy after himself; nevertheless, as I suspected might be the case if I ever returned, he clearly no longer wants me for a wife—in the traditional sense, anyway. And yet he does seem happy to have me home again. This is all so confusing.*

By the time the couple had reached Sarah's bedchamber, Alexander had begun to wonder what was on his wife's mind. She hadn't said a word as they had made their way up the stairs. After opening the door to her room, he escorted her in. He then ushered her over to the bed. Once she was seated on the edge, he pulled a chair up alongside her. As she climbed under the bedcovers, she kept her eyes averted from his.

Sensing that something was wrong, reaching over, he took her hand in his. "Are you all right, Sarah? It must be difficult being back here."

Not wanting to share what she had been thinking about, she simply said, "I am fine, Alexander. Just a bit tired. I believe I shall rest now. I do not wish to keep you from whatever you were doing before I came to find you."

Believing his wife that she was merely tired and ready to sleep, he rose to his feet. Leaning down, he placed a kiss upon her cheek. After making his way quietly from the room, he gently closed the door behind him. Standing there on the other side of the door, he prayed for his wife that her mind and body would fully mend. He then went to find Martha to inform her that Sarah wished to rest for a while and that she would eat something later. He also took the opportunity to disclose all that had happened to his wife, including that she had been with child, but because of the fall had delivered too early and lost the child.

When Martha learned that Matthew Raymond had followed Alexander to where Sarah had been staying and had abducted her again, she was horrified. For the elderly woman, who dearly loved Sarah, it was going to take a good deal of time to come to terms with all that her beloved mistress had been through. In all the months

Sarah had been gone, what Martha had already known of the situation had constantly plagued her, and now she would have more of the atrocities her mistress had suffered weighing upon her.

In her bedchamber, Sarah lay staring at the ceiling. After a time, her eyes finally closed in sleep. Not long after she had nodded off, however, she had a dreadful nightmare. Trapped within her sleep state, the face of Matthew Raymond filled her slumbering mind with terror.

About this time, Martha decided to check on her mistress. If the young woman had awakened, the elderly servant worried she might be in need of something. Additionally, she wanted to look at her once again. She couldn't quite believe Sarah was actually home. As she approached the door to the young woman's bedchamber, she heard crying coming from within. She quickly opened the door and found Sarah, sound asleep, tossing about on her bed. Martha surmised that her mistress was having a nightmare, thus she took hold of Sarah's shoulders and gave her a little shake.

All at once, Sarah opened her eyes. Still trembling, she grasped Martha's hand. "His face...I could not get away."

As she sat down on the bed next to the frightened young woman, Martha whispered, "It was just a bad dream. You are safe now." *It isn't a wonder she is having bad dreams after all that has happened.* It nearly broke Martha's heart that Sarah had been so mistreated. Seeing her terrified face, just now, merely added to the pain she was feeling with regard to Sarah.

As the young woman came fully awake, she realized she was indeed safe in her own bedchamber and that Matthew Raymond was truly dead, never to hurt her again. "Martha, I will be all right now. I believe I shall come down to the parlor for a while."

Though Martha knew that Mr. Swyndhurst intended for his wife to remain in bed for a few days, she thought it might be best to go along with Sarah's wish. She believed Mr. Swyndhurst would agree once he learned of Sarah's nightmare.

After making her mistress comfortable in the parlor, Martha went to find Mr. Swyndhurst. While glancing out the kitchen window, she spotted him in the yard and went out to speak with him.

Seeing the elderly woman approaching, with concern, Mr. Swyndhurst met her halfway. "What is it, Martha? Is Sarah all right?"

"Yes, she is presently reclining in the parlor. I need to speak with you while she—"

Interrupting, he inquired, "Why is she out of her bed? She was instructed to rest for a few days. When we set off for home, she had not fully recovered from her injuries, as well as birthing a child; the journey only added to her fragile state. "

To calm him, Martha continued with her explanation. "I was certain you would agree with her decision to rest in the parlor, rather than in her bedchamber, once you knew what had happened. You see, Sarah had a terrible nightmare about that devil of a man, Matthew Raymond; therefore, we both thought it best that she come down to the parlor. She needed a distraction from thinking of that horrible man."

Nodding, he replied, "Yes, if that be the case, perhaps it is best that she rest where there are others around. I shall go in and speak with her."

While placing her hand on Mr. Swyndhurst's arm, Martha advised, "It might be better if you did not let on that I told you. I would not want her to think I came running to you to inform on her."

Seeing that his servant-friend had been greatly disturbed at seeing Sarah in such a state, Mr. Swyndhurst decided to try and make light of the situation. So, with a smile he replied. "I shall not speak of our conversation—the one in which you 'came running' to inform on my wife."

"Oh, you do like to tease," she replied with a chuckle. "I had to tell you, or you might have chastised her for not keeping to her bed."

"I am happy you told me, Martha. You are correct—I surely would have scolded her for coming out of her room when it is essential that she rest. I had already planned on being firm on this point, if necessary. We both know how she can be."

After Martha returned to the house, Alexander waited a short while before going in. He wouldn't let on that he knew about the nightmare, but he wanted to be close in order to soothe his wife. In all of the months she had been away, he wanted nothing more than to have her home where he could comfort her. She was home now, and he had every intention of making up for lost time.

Chapter 35

The next day, hoping to find the Swyndhursts at home and doing well, Susanna and William Pressey came to call. A few weeks prior, Jonathan Bleasdell had informed them that Alexander had found Sarah and that he was expected to return with her within a fortnight. He had also warned them not to say a word regarding the Strout children, as Alexander wished to wait until Sarah had fully recovered before sharing the news. Not wanting to descend on them too soon, the Presseys had waited much longer than the predicted time of the Swyndhurst's return.

After Martha had escorted the Presseys into the parlor, she went to inform Sarah that she had guests. Alexander was not at home, for he had gone to speak with Jonathan. He had yet to disclose all that Sarah had been through. Though he knew that his wife was with child before taking leave of Amesbury to fetch her, he had not disclosed the news to the Bleasdells. As it was now, he had more to tell than he had before he left. He also hoped to check on the children. He hated having to leave them with the Bleasdells now that he and Sarah had returned; however, he knew Sarah was not in any shape to take care of them, and take care of them she would—of that he was certain.

Upon his arrival, Jonathan shepherded Alexander to the stable so they might speak privately. As they entered the impressive structure, the two men took a seat on a bench by the door. Jonathan, a lover of animals, had a fine stable with enough stalls to board his own animals, as well as a few horses for folks who were unable to provide shelter for their own animals. Quite often, he had taken his pay in the form of food; thus, the Bleasdells' kitchen was frequently stocked with plenty of breads, cakes, and the like.

Looking intently at Alexander, Jonathan remained quiet so as to allow his friend to speak uninterrupted. Alexander clearly had a lot on his mind. When the younger man sighed, but had still not spoken a word, it became obvious to Jonathan that Alexander had no idea where to begin. Jonathan then prodded him along by suggesting that he start at the point when they found Sarah.

"Very well, Jonathan. When we arrived at the home where Sarah had been staying, I found that she had been well cared for. In fact, the man was a physician who had trained in England. We have not his like in most, if not all, of the colonies, as there is not a medical school here as yet. As you know, most of our medical men have merely apprenticed as surgeons or apothecaries under men with no formal schooling. It had to have been God's handiwork that Sarah had been taken to this particular home."

"Quite so; God was surely looking out for your wife, for it is very true that we don't often see men with his training in the colonies. Some might question where God was when Sarah was put upon. For myself, I have no need for an answer to that sort of question. In this world there are trials, many of which are brought about by evil men— men who use their God-given freewill for selfish and wicked acts. The man who attacked Sarah is a prime example of just such a man. Even in all of this, God is with us through every trial, when we allow Him to be. In fact, I have observed that you have drawn your strength from Him over the many months you have been searching for Sarah."

"Indeed, Jonathan. I never would have made it through, if not for Him."

"Thanks be to God that you have found her and she is home now. You mentioned having been grateful that Sarah was being looked after by a physician. Were there extensive injuries from the attack, requiring the care of a physician?" Jonathan asked with concern.

While staring at his hands, Alexander said almost inaudibly, "Sarah was with child as a result of the violence perpetrated against her."

Jonathan was stunned by the news. After allowing what Alexander had said to sink in a moment, he solemnly inquired, "Did you say that she 'was' with child? Has she had the baby, then?"

"Yes, but the child died soon after his birth. It was just too early for him to arrive. The worst of it was that she would not have delivered so early, if not for Matthew Raymond."

"I don't understand. What has he to do with it?"

Wringing his hands, Alexander replied, "Unbeknownst to James and me, he followed us from Amesbury to Boston. He must have kept back just far enough that we never caught sight of him. I spotted another wagon a time or two, but never suspected it was Matthew Raymond. Soon after our arrival, I went out in the Thompsons' backyard to speak with Sarah, after which I left her alone so that I might go in and speak with Daniel about whether it was safe for her to travel. She wanted a moment to tend to her face. She had been crying, you see. She was to follow soon after. Seeing his opportunity, with Sarah alone, Matthew Raymond seized her."

"How dreadful! How did she escape?" Jonathan questioned, dumbfounded by all that he had heard so far.

"As Daniel, James, and I were racing after them in my wagon, Sarah fell out of the rear of Raymond's wagon. There was a gun-fight following that, which left the despicable man quite dead! I am sorry to say that I was, and still am, extremely relieved the man is no longer amongst the living."

"Sarah must have been terrified! So, I assume the injuries she suffered from the fall were the cause of her premature delivery?"

"They were indeed. We almost lost her, along with the baby."

"You have all been through a great deal. I insist that you leave the children here with us for as long as you deem necessary for Sarah to recover—and you, for that matter."

"I am much obliged to you, Jonathan. I have not yet informed Sarah that the children had been living at the estate. As she has just lost a child, and may never have another, I am uncertain how she shall feel about raising someone else's children."

"I understand your hesitation, but I have to say— with what I know of Sarah—she shall most assuredly be overjoyed by the news."

"I share your opinion, but I cannot be certain. Regardless, until her body has fully healed, I intend to wait. She shouldn't care for the children until she is well. I know she would try; therefore, for her own good, I must impose on you both a bit longer."

"As I have said, they are welcome to stay as long as you like. Sarah would indeed put it upon herself to see to their every need...despite the fact that there are servants to assist her," Jonathan said with a grin. Though he didn't know the tiny woman well, from what the children had told him, he knew that much about her.

Following their conversation, Alexander went in to visit with the children. He knew he couldn't stay long, for a lengthy absence from his home would require an explanation. Having business with Jonathan would be an acceptable excuse, he reasoned; that is, unless he tarried too long.

Without revealing too much, Alexander explained as best he could to the two older children the reason he could not yet fetch them home at this time. Clearly content with the Bleasdells, the children didn't put up much of a fuss about staying on a while longer. Alexander was quite certain that Hannah and Jonathan had given the children their undivided attention while they had been staying with them. Conversely, he had been so consumed with finding Sarah that he had paid little heed to them while they were at his estate.

Later, after Alexander had returned home, he found his wife in the parlor with the Presseys. He hoped their visit had not been too tiring for her. He also wondered what she had shared with them, if anything, concerning what had happened to her.

After taking a seat beside his wife, Alexander explained that he had been to see Jonathan. Without giving much detail, he told his wife, and guests, that he and Jonathan had some things they needed to discuss. Though his explanation was vague, Sarah seemed to accept it without hesitation. As the Presseys had already been informed about the children, they did not press for details. Then, surveying his wife, Alexander felt certain that her lack of interest in where he had been was simply due to exhaustion. She looked to him as if she might collapse right where she sat.

The Presseys seemed to notice her fatigue as well, thus they soon took their leave. While walking them out, so as not to be overheard, Alexander spoke softly. He assured them that he would fill them in on everything later. William patted his friend on the shoulder as an indication that he understood that now was not the time to go into it.

Upon his return to the parlor, Alexander noted that Sarah had taken leave of the room. He surmised that she had gone up to her bedchamber to rest. After quickly mounting the stairs, he went directly to her room. As he knocked, he heard her softly call for him to come in. Once he had entered, making his way over to her, he took a seat on the bed.

"You must be completely done in. Having visitors so soon was simply too much for you."

As Sarah was already half-asleep, she didn't argue. Alexander remained just long enough to see that she had indeed fallen asleep before taking himself off to his room to rest as well. It had been a long day. Explaining to Jonathan about all that had happened in Boston had completely exhausted him. After stretching out on his bed, he thanked God for sparing him yet another loss. Losing one wife had been difficult enough, but Sarah was safely home now, and he was exceedingly grateful.

Sometime during the night, as Martha had left her door ajar to listen for Sarah, the servant heard noises coming from the young woman's bedchamber. Supposing her mistress was, yet again, having a bad dream, she hurried to her room. As she approached the bed, she knew it was exactly as she had suspected; Sarah was thrashing about from fright.

As she attempted to wake her mistress, she prayed God would help Sarah to put all thoughts of Matthew Raymond behind her. After Sarah came fully awake, she and Martha talked for some time. While they were conversing, the young woman asked Martha not to reveal to her husband that she had regularly been having nightmares since arriving home. She explained that she had had them before, when she had first arrived in Boston, but they had almost completely ceased in the months she had been staying with the Thompsons. Nevertheless, owing to the latest incident with Matthew Raymond, to her dismay, they had begun again.

Considering that he had felt the need to distance himself from me by returning me to my own bedchamber, I do not want to trouble him. And I should not wish for him to be pressured into having things the way they were before, she thought. But what she said aloud was, "It is just that I have no wish to be a bother to him with this."

Martha wanted to say to Sarah that she highly doubted Mr. Swyndhurst would see his wife as a bother, but she refrained. "Very well, Sarah, if that is your wish."

After the elderly servant had gone, Sarah was reminded of what a faithful friend she had in Martha, and until that moment she hadn't realized just how much she had missed the dear woman.

As Martha made her way back to her room, she wondered why Alexander had returned his wife to her own bedchamber. *Surely she would fare much better with someone there to comfort her. And though she hasn't said as much, I believe Sarah wonders about it, too. As much as I am tempted to stick my nose in, I shall not. For the time being, I will leave it for the two of them to work out.*

Chapter 36

The next morning, Sarah made her way out of doors to take in the fresh air. Spring was well on its way. Sarah could hardly wait for her favorite season to fully arrive. Just now, however, she bundled up for the chilly weather before going out.

As she strolled around the backyard, she thought about Alice Strout and her children. Though she longed to call upon them, there were two obstacles in her way: Alexander and her own fears. Alexander had expressed his desire that she remain at the estate until she had completely recovered, and knowing that she would have to pass by the place where Matthew Raymond had grabbed her was yet too frightening to consider. Though the man was dead, the memory of that night was still too fresh.

As she continued to walk about, she chided herself for being so weak. After all, what had she to fear from a dead man? But try as she might to rid herself of the terrible emotions she had been experiencing, connected to the man, she could not push them away.

Before long, Alexander joined his wife, who had by now alighted on a bench in the yard. From there, she had been enjoying the warmth of the sunshine as well as observing the first robins to return after the long, cold winter. Seeing them somehow brought hope to her heart that in the face of all the dreadful things that had occurred, God was still there looking after even the smallest of creatures. She then recalled what the Scriptures had to say: "Behold the fowls of the air: for they sow not, neither do they reap, nor gather into barns; yet your heavenly Father feedeth them. Are ye not much better than they?"

All at once, Sarah realized that Alexander had taken a seat beside her. She wondered why she hadn't noticed him. "Good morning, Alexander."

As he looked closely at his wife, Alexander sensed that she seemed at peace. "How are you feeling today?" Had he known the battle she had been fighting against her fears just moments before, he may not have believed her so tranquil.

"I believe I am getting a little stronger every day. Sitting here in the warm sun does more for me than just about anything else. God's creation is so magnificent! I cannot help but be overwhelmed by its splendor."

Smiling at his wife's words, Alexander responded, "Yes, God's handiwork is truly grand." Reaching over, he took hold of her hand. He dared not discuss anything regarding the baby or Matthew Raymond with her, for he believed she wasn't yet ready. Though they had talked over such things while they were in Boston, they had not spoken along those lines since returning home. All he could do for now was to simply make certain that Sarah had everything she needed, and wait. He hoped that, in time, she would reveal all that was on her mind. He longed for things to move forward between them, as they seemed to have been before they had been separated for so many months.

As she felt the large hand enveloping her own, she understood that God had truly given her a protector in Alexander Swyndhurst. She could not fault the man's care of her commencing with his return from England. As she thought about it, even if they never move beyond what they have now, she was most grateful for the man now sitting beside her. She hoped, however, that in time they could talk about things of a personal nature, not just the trivial conversations they had grown accustomed to since returning from Boston. Oh, she knew they had their faith in common, but as far as normal conversations between a husband and wife, she was left wanting.

From the window overlooking the backyard, Martha had been observing the couple. Though she had promised Sarah she wouldn't say anything, she wondered whether she should inform Mr. Swyndhurst that his wife was still experiencing nightmares. When the young woman had come into the kitchen that morning, she appeared, to Martha, as though she had not slept much after suffering the bad dream the night before. Even though she had talked with Sarah until the young woman was ready to go back to sleep, Sarah must have remained awake long after the two had parted company, Martha had reasoned.

Martha decided to give the matter over to God in prayer. "Lord, Sarah needs Your touch. She has been through so much for her young years." Suddenly, Martha noticed Sarah coming to her feet, thus she quickly moved away from the window. She didn't want to be caught spying.

Sarah had begun to feel cold, so she decided it was best that she return to the house. Seeing her red nose, Alexander wasn't at all surprised when she was ready to go in.

"It is still a bit chilly. In a few more weeks, the weather shall be warm enough for you to be out of doors for longer periods," smiled Alexander as he escorted his shivering wife to the house.

"Yes, the cold weather is almost behind us."

By now, the couple had reached the door to the house. As they entered, Sarah moved in the direction of the parlor, with Alexander close behind. He hoped she would spend the remainder of the day resting, but he had decided not to impose his desires upon her. He then observed that she had stretched out on one of the settees and wondered whether he should stay or leave her to herself; for things had seemed overly formal between them while they were in the yard. Though they were cordial with each other since they had arrived home, he felt that there was not the warmth they had previously shared while in Boston, and he wondered at the reason for the change.

Sarah had felt the stilted exchange as well. The difference was that she believed she knew the reason; things had changed between them from the time when Matthew Raymond had forced his way into their lives. She didn't blame Alexander. She was just grateful he had wanted her to come home at all; otherwise, she would have been looking for a place of her own in Boston, far away from those she loved—those she had come to realize she had greatly missed while she was away.

She hadn't even, as yet, had a lengthy conversation with Esther, which was not at all what she desired. All she wanted was for things to return to normal with everyone in the household, but it seemed they all thought her too fragile to treat her as they had before. Esther in particular had been keeping away from her. She wondered if it was because her friend felt guilty for having told her secret.

After seeing to it that his wife had everything she needed, Alexander excused himself. Shortly thereafter, because she had not rested much the night before, Sarah had fallen asleep. Before long, Martha came to check on the young woman. Finding her asleep, she covered her with a quilt and then quietly left the room.

After making her way to the kitchen, Martha found Mr. Swyndhurst seated at the table. When she had sat down across from him, she said, "Mr. Swyndhurst, Sarah has fallen asleep in the parlor." Without divulging the reason, she went on to say that she didn't believe his wife was resting well at night.

Mr. Swyndhurst agreed, for he had seen the dark shadows beneath Sarah's eyes. "Give her time, Martha."

Martha decided to broach the subject of the separate bedchambers. "Is there some reason you and Sarah are sleeping in separate bedchambers?"

Though he knew it was really none of Martha's affair, he answered anyway, for he was aware that she only asked out of concern. "It is just that I had all but forced sharing a bedchamber on her before she went away. Given what has happened with Matthew Raymond, twice, taking her against her will, I thought it best that she have her own room. Though she seemed to adjust to sharing my bedchamber before she went away, this time I intend to allow her to make the decision. Moreover, Daniel Thompson, the physician with whom she had been staying, suggested that she might require time to herself."

In understanding, Martha nodded. "The physician may be right. Perhaps that is best, then, having separate rooms for now. And as you say, it seems Sarah hasn't been afforded the opportunity to make many of her own decisions, what with her father choosing a husband for her and then what happened because of that awful man. Oh...I didn't mean that her father had made a bad decision where you are concerned."

"Not to worry, Martha. I understood your meaning. That was exactly my thinking on the matter."

What her employer had said made a great deal of sense to Martha; however, she still wished she hadn't promised not to tell him of his wife's terrifying dreams. The elderly servant hadn't let on—since mentioning the one that had occurred just after they arrived home from Boston—that the nightmares had continued. With the couple in separate bedrooms, she reasoned, there wouldn't be much he could do about it anyway.

Chapter 37

It had been nearly a month since Alexander and Sarah had returned home from Boston. Though she had been plagued with nightmares, the young woman was feeling much stronger. Alexander, without being heavy-handed, had been very attentive. It had taken much patience on his part—not speaking up every time he felt his wife was overexerting herself.

On numerous occasions from the time of Sarah's return, Martha had noticed the young woman stepping out the front door as if she were about to set off somewhere; however, every time, within minutes she had returned. Suspecting her mistress had been attempting to go for a walk, most likely in the direction of the Strouts' home, she hadn't bothered to inquire about it.

On this particular morning, Martha was staring out the window when Mr. Swyndhurst entered the room. "What has you so captivated, Martha?"

Turning toward him, she responded, "It is Sarah. I believe she is attempting, as she often does, to venture out of the yard."

With curiosity, Mr. Swyndhurst approached the window. As he watched, he noticed that Sarah appeared to hesitate at the edge of the yard. Turning toward Martha, who was standing beside him watching as well, he said, "She seems uncertain about going any farther."

Nodding, Martha informed, "She is doing admirably. She usually doesn't make it much beyond the front door."

Eyes wide, Alexander glanced at the elderly woman. "Is this a regular occurrence, then?"

"To be sure. I believe she misses the children but is too afraid to venture out of the yard. I have often wondered if we ought to have told her where the children are—that they are not even at their old home."

"If her love for the children motivates her to move beyond her fears, then I believe we should leave off from telling her, for the time being anyway. Who knows, if she keeps making the attempt, she may yet succeed. But if she allows her fears to get the best of her, she may be held prisoner by them. Let us keep watch over her for now. If she does indeed make it to Alice's former home, we shall have to explain where the children have gone. And if she is still so fearful, she may not be ready for the children to return. Besides, you know as well as I do, the moment she learns where they are and that they are to return here when she is well, she shall insist they come home immediately."

Hearing the door, Mr. Swyndhurst and Martha turned. They hadn't noticed that Sarah had given up and returned to the house. As she entered the kitchen, she observed her husband and Martha standing by the window. Surmising they had witnessed her failure, she shrugged and left the room.

"She must feel so defeated," sighed Martha. "Perhaps one of us could accompany her. With one of us by her side, she might actually do it."

Shaking his head, Mr. Swyndhurst countered, "No, Martha. She must wish to do this on her own, or she would have already asked one of us to go with her."

"Or she may simply be too embarrassed to have anyone else see her fail. If we explain that we understand how difficult this is for her, she may not be so concerned with what we shall think of her if she fails, and she might just ask one of us to go with her."

"Nonetheless, I say we ought to allow her to do this on her own. I think it best, Martha. Please abide by my wishes."

Nodding, the elderly woman moved toward the counter and began preparing the afternoon meal.

Alexander disliked having to speak in this fashion to his servant-friend, but he knew that with her heart breaking as a result of watching Sarah so encumbered by fear, unless he spoke firmly to her, she might go against his wishes and offer to walk with his wife.

Up in Sarah's bedchamber, she lay across her bed, angry with herself that she was so terrified of leaving the estate. *What is the matter with me? The man is dead! He has no power over me.* "Lord, help me to put the dreadful memories of Matthew Raymond behind me. I miss the children so. I have been home nearly a month and have yet to see them."

After a time of prayer, Sarah rested peacefully until Esther came to fetch her—stating that Martha had prepared something for her to eat. "If you would rather take your meal up here, I shall inform Martha."

"No...no, that is quite all right, Esther. Please tell Martha that I shall be down directly." Nodding, Esther went to speak with the head servant to inform her that Sarah would be coming to the kitchen. After Esther had gone, Sarah decided that very soon she needed to speak with her friend to let her know that she was not angry with her for revealing her secret.

After rising to her feet, Sarah ran her hands down over her gown to smooth out the wrinkles. She then pulled the pins from her hair and combed through it. After refastening the pins, she started on her way. As she made her way out of her room, she began to feel a bit flustered at having been seen by Martha and Alexander when she had unsuccessfully attempted to leave the yard. She hoped there would be no mention of it. It was at times like these she wished Esther was taking her meals with them, as Martha had always done. Having her there might distract her husband and Martha from what they had seen.

Alexander met Sarah at the foot of the stairs to escort her to the kitchen. During the meal, Martha and

Alexander had conversed with Sarah as though nothing out of the ordinary had even happened. As she had hoped, there was no mention of the event in the yard. She even began to wonder if they had actually seen her failure. *Perhaps they were caught up in a conversation, and the fact that it took place near the window was just a coincidence,* she thought.

Chapter 38

It was Worship day. As usual, Alexander had gone to church alone. Besides the fact that Sarah hadn't been well enough since their return from Boston, now that she was much stronger, she had been reluctant to go, for she feared everyone's questions. After the service, Alexander approached Reverend March to inquire whether the busy pastor had time to meet with him during the week.

"Certainly, Alexander. Or perhaps as soon as everyone has gone, we might talk now."

While Alexander was waiting, Jonathan, Hannah, and little Mary greeted him. The Bleasdells had sent the older Strout children out to the wagon ahead of them. Once Alexander had given them a brief synopsis of how things were going at home, they assured him they were still prepared to keep the children for as long as he needed.

When they had finished discussing the children, Alexander walked them out to their wagon. The older Strout children seemed delighted to see him. But as was the case the last time he had visited them at the Bleasdells' home, they were unmistakably quite content with Hannah and Jonathan. Before long, the wagon pulled away and Alexander returned to the church.

Then, when the building had cleared, the two men approached the front of the room. As soon as they had each taken a seat, the reverend inquired as to the reason for the meeting. Alexander began by explaining all that had taken place since he and Sarah had returned from Boston— including that he had not told her of the Strout children and where they would be living when she was well. He had already, on a previous occasion, filled him in on all that had occurred in Boston.

Looking thoughtful, the pastor asked the reason Alexander had not informed his wife that he had taken the children in.

"Reverend, Sarah has not yet recovered from all that has happened to her. I fear if she were to learn that Alice left the children in our care, she would press for me to fetch them back. Furthermore, given what has happened, she has been fearful of even venturing out of our yard. Most days she makes an attempt, only to return a few moments later. I believe her love for the Strout children shall drive her to finally do it. In the past, when calling on the Strouts, she often walked there. I am certain that when she attempts to leave, it is to their former home she is endeavoring to go."

Looking confused, the pastor questioned, "Why not simply ask you to convey her there?"

As he rubbed his chin, Alexander responded, "I cannot be sure, but I believe she understands that until she is successful at conquering her fears, she shall be held captive by them. You wouldn't know it to look at her, but she can, at times, be quite determined, especially when it is something she wishes to do on her own."

The two men chuckled a bit at Alexander's comment, for they both had seen that side of Sarah. They were also both fully aware that, even to her own detriment, her stubborn streak had almost always been in relation to her service for others.

Alexander then became serious. "What is your opinion? Am I doing the right thing in not telling her?"

"It is hard to say. I do appreciate the complexity of the situation. I suppose if she hasn't inquired about the children, it may be acceptable. If at some point she does wish to know, however, I believe it is best that you are forthright."

"Of course. If she had inquired, I certainly would have told her. To do otherwise would clearly have been dishonest. But even though she hasn't asked outright, I wasn't exactly certain that I was doing the right thing, no matter my motives. That is why I thought to ask your opinion on the matter."

"Well, as I said, Alexander, I am not exactly certain how best to answer you; therefore, let us pray that she shall prevail over her fears, and that you shall know the correct time to inform her of all concerning the children," smiled Reverend March. The two friends then devoted some time to prayer. When they had concluded, Alexander went on his way feeling more at peace.

As soon as he had entered the house, Alexander went in search of Sarah. Finding her in the parlor, he inquired about her day. He then offered to give her an account of the sermon, to which a delighted Sarah readily agreed. She had so missed hearing Reverend March expounding on the Word. In fact, each Sunday, after Alexander had gone, she had felt quite downcast at remaining behind, but she simply was not prepared to face anyone. She wondered what the folks at church knew of what had happened to her. In any case, because she had been away so long, there would surely be questions that she was not at all ready to answer.

Taking a seat next to her on the settee, Alexander began. "Today the reverend talked again of our Savior's death and resurrection, reading from the pertinent passages in Matthew." Opening his Bible, Alexander began reading about the night that Jesus was arrested, "'Then cometh Jesus with them unto a place called Gethsemane, and saith unto the disciples, sit ye here, while I go and pray yonder. And he took with him Peter and the two sons of Zebedee, and began to be sorrowful and very heavy. Then saith he unto them, my soul is exceeding sorrowful, even unto death: tarry ye here, and watch with me.'"

After pausing a moment, Alexander asked, "Do you recall how, each time, after Jesus had gone off to pray, when He returned to where the disciples were waiting, He found them asleep?"

Listening closely, Sarah nodded.

Alexander continued, "In verse forty, it states: 'And he cometh unto the disciples, and findeth them asleep, and saith unto Peter, What, could ye not watch with me one hour?' And then in verse forty-one: 'Watch and pray, that ye enter not into temptation: the spirit indeed is willing, but the flesh is weak.' How many times I have felt that I too have failed the Lord. Before Jonathan explained the way of salvation, and that it was not by works but through Christ's sacrifice on the cross that we are saved, I had endeavored to earn my salvation. I knew that I had failed miserably, but until I learned differently, I felt helpless to change things."

Sarah then conveyed her agreement with what her husband had said. "Indeed, Christ's sacrifice—paid at a heavy price—was an amazing gift. Alexander, do you think if the disciples had understood that Jesus was about to be arrested that very night, they would have remained awake to pray?"

"It is difficult to say. It does seem that even though Jesus had stated what was going to happen, they had not fully understood—as evidenced by their doubt when the women later came to tell them that the tomb was empty. They didn't seem to comprehend that Christ had actually risen. Two of them had to run and see for themselves. As I said, I could not judge them for it, for I have failed the Lord many times."

Dropping her eyes to her lap, she responded, "As have I."

Hearing Sarah's somber tone, Alexander looked over at his wife and responded, "Remember, Sarah, you need only give an account to the Lord for your own sins, not for those perpetrated against you. We can pray for those who misuse us, but we are not guilty of their sins."

With her eyes still lowered, Sarah whispered, "But sometimes things we have done opened the way for others to harm us, such as when you asked me to promise not to go to Alice's when you were away. Had I listened to you and not gone—"

"That is precisely what I am talking about. What Matthew did to you was not your fault." Seeing that the conversation was upsetting Sarah, Alexander changed the subject. "Why don't we go out to the backyard? The sun is shining. It is a beautiful day." Taking hold of Sarah's hand, Alexander stood to his feet, pulling her up with him. As soon as they had left the parlor, they donned their warm outer clothing and went out the rear door, where they spent a considerable amount of time taking in the fresh air.

Chapter 39

The following day, in keeping with her routine, Sarah quietly made her way out the front door. Having seen her mistress leaving, Esther went to inform Martha. Unbeknownst to Sarah's husband and head servant, Sarah had confided in her friend about what she had been attempting to do, which was to make her way over to the Strouts' home. In fact, the two young women had begun to discuss many things, just as they had done before Sarah had left town. Once Sarah had explained to Esther that she didn't blame her for revealing her secret, the two had hugged and things had returned to normal between them.

Finding Martha in the doorway of Mr. Swyndhurst's study, conversing, Esther stated that Sarah had gone out the front door. Mr. Swyndhurst quickly rose from his chair to follow Martha, who had already moved in the direction of the kitchen. Esther had seen Martha watching Sarah on a few of her previous attempts to leave the yard; thus, she believed the elderly woman would want to know that her mistress was at it again. Just as she had been, the young woman knew Martha had been hoping and praying that

Sarah would finally conquer her fear of leaving the estate on foot.

Looking back over her shoulder, Martha thanked Esther for coming to tell them. As they made their way to the window, Martha and Mr. Swyndhurst each silently prayed that, this time, Sarah would make it. Esther stole a few looks through another window out of sight of the head servant and her employer.

Out at the edge of the yard, looking up, Sarah prayed that God would give her strength to walk along the particular stretch of road—the one that held such terrible memories for her. After stepping out of the yard, Sarah took a deep breath. Then, putting one foot in front of the other, she set off down the road.

Had she seen her husband and Martha watching her from the kitchen window, she would have observed two faces with tears streaming down their cheeks. "She is actually doing it!" exclaimed Martha.

Glancing down at his servant-friend, Alexander smiled, "That she is." Wiping his face on his sleeve, he said, "I better follow at a distance to see that she is all right."

Nodding, Martha responded, "That might be best. She is sure to be upset when she learns the Strouts are not at home. You shall have some explaining to do."

"Yes, that was my thinking." With that, grabbing his coat, Alexander quickly followed after Sarah. As he could see her walking up ahead, he held back a little so as not to be seen.

When Sarah neared the dreaded spot, she picked up her pace to nearly a run. With her heart pounding, she raced by. Once she had cleared the location by several paces, she began to relax.

Alexander observed as his wife hastened by a certain section of the road, and then began to slow to her usual stride. *That must have been where Matthew was lying in wait for her. The worst is over; she made it beyond that point. I am glad that I shall be with her on the return trip, for she is sure to be fatigued from the whole ordeal.* Before long, Alexander noticed that Sarah had turned off toward the former home of Alice and her children. Quickening his step, he caught sight of Sarah standing at the front door to the house, knocking.

As he made his way over to her, he noticed that she had ceased from knocking and was now turning around. He then watched as she took a seat on the step. She suddenly glanced in his direction.

As her husband approached, she peered up at him with a quizzical expression. "No one is at home, and the window dressings have been taken down. It almost seems as if they no longer live here. Where could they have gone?"

When he had taken a seat beside her, he responded, "Sarah, Alice has moved to Ipswich to be with her sister." He quickly decided to answer only what he was asked and not offer up any additional information. He then wondered just how much he was going to have to disclose.

"But why? Why would she leave?" she inquired with tears threatening to fall.

While placing his arm around her shoulders, he replied, "It seems after you went away she felt that the burden of caring for her children, alone, was too much. I believe she finally understood just how much you had been doing for her."

"She must have thought her sister would be of some help to her with the children."

Alexander knew right then that he had to tell her everything; however, just as he was about to inform her that the children had been living at their home and would be returning when she had recovered, he decided not to disclose that last bit of information just yet. He knew she would want them to come back right away. He didn't believe she was quite well enough for that responsibility.

"Actually, Sarah, Alice didn't take the children with her."

Upon hearing this, Sarah's eyes darted in Alexander's direction. "What do you mean, she didn't take the children?"

"Just what I said—she did not take the children with her."

Full of questions, she stared at her husband. She then began to let loose. "How could she do that? She just left them behind, or is it only temporary? She is sure to come back for them when she is settled, is she not? Where are they now?"

Attempting to avoid eye contact, he answered, "No...it isn't temporary. She felt she could leave, given that Ipswich is not that far away. She intends to make regular visits." He had still not answered the question of where the children were now.

As shaky as she had felt before she arrived at Alice's door, with her concern for the children, Sarah had all but forgotten her fears. "Where are they, Alexander? And how are they getting along without their mother? Are they settled with the fact that she has gone off and left them?" She was now beginning to grow angry at Alice. *After all I have done to help that woman care for her children, to have her simply abandon them!*

Surmising that his wife was furious, Alexander started to grin. *This little bit of a woman can be quite fierce when protecting those she loves.* He decided to put her mind at ease. "They are with the Bleasdells and doing quite well. Jonathan and Hannah have enjoyed having them. Remember, not too many years ago the Bleasdells lost a child. Little Mary is nearly the same age as Henry was when he died."

In understanding for what it was like to lose a son, Sarah nodded and said, "Perhaps they are much better off with the Bleasdells. I am sorry for Alice. I should not have been angry with her. She was only doing what she thought best, of that I am certain."

Alexander was beginning to feel the tension in Sarah's shoulders ease. Hoping the conversation might end there without his having to reveal that the children had been living at the Swyndhurst estate with him, and would soon be again, he changed the subject. "Sarah, I am proud of you for conquering your fears."

Surprised by her husband's comment, she inquired, "How did you know?"

"It wasn't too difficult. We knew you were going out in the front yard nearly every day. When Martha told me what was going on, from that point on I have been joining her in watching out the window to see if you would make it," he answered as he pulled her against his chest. "I understand that even though the man is dead, you have frightening memories connected to this town, and that stretch of road."

As it was beginning to sink in that she had actually done it, she began to smile. "I was starting to believe it was hopeless, and that I would never make it beyond our property line. Since I did not see him after he was shot, it is hard for me to believe he is actually dead. In any case, I did it. I really did it!"

"That, you did!" he responded with delight at seeing his wife's eyes light up, owing to her accomplishment.

"Alexander, I wish to see the children. Do you think the Bleasdells would mind very much if I paid them a visit?"

"No, indeed, for I am certain the children would love to see you. Jonathan and Hannah would as well. We shall plan on visiting, very soon."

As he glanced down at his wife, he observed that her countenance was one of joy. And now that her mood had changed—that she was no longer angry at Alice or as fearful of venturing away from the estate—Alexander was relieved he had not had to tell her everything. Then, rising from the steps together, the husband and wife set off for home. Hand in hand they strolled down the road, even a little beyond their own estate; however, as they neared Matthew Raymond's former home, Sarah began to tense.

"I never knew he lived so close until the day the constable and I went to see him, after you had gone away. Just after I had returned from England, the reverend had informed me of Matthew's interest in you. It must have been frightening for you when, after what had happened in Cambridge, he showed up in Amesbury."

Sarah merely nodded. All she wanted to do just now was turn back and start for home. She needed to feel the safety of being within its walls.

Feeling her hand tighten against his, Alexander said, "Sarah, it was a beginning. Do not expect more of yourself than you ought." Pulling her close, he turned her in the opposite direction, away from the home that Matthew Raymond once owned. Alexander continued to talk in an attempt to calm his wife as they walked. When they were almost home, Sarah allowed herself to breathe again.

As they entered the door, Martha quickly approached and pulled Sarah into her arms. As the young woman relaxed against her, Martha felt that Sarah had indeed taken a giant step toward putting the whole Matthew Raymond ordeal behind her.

Chapter 40

Later that night, after Sarah had gone to bed, Martha and Mr. Swyndhurst had tea together in the parlor. They were both elated over the events of the day. While they were conversing, Martha inadvertently gave away Sarah's secret—that she had been troubled with nightmares since returning from Boston. When she realized what she had done, the elderly woman placed her hand over her mouth; however, Alexander had already picked up on the slip of the tongue.

"Did you just say that Sarah has still been having nightmares?" Taking note of the nod of his servant's head, he inquired, "Why did you not tell me?"

Disappointed in herself for making such a blunder, Martha answered, "She asked me not to. What was I to do? Go against her wishes?"

"No; I suppose not. Why did she ask you not to tell me?"

"I believe she said something about not wanting to bother you."

"Martha, now that I am aware of the situation, I wish for you to come to me if it happens again."

"Very well. But it may be late in the night."

"That makes no difference. If necessary, wake me." Wanting to be certain Martha had understood, he stressed the point. "I am quite serious, Martha. No matter what Sarah has said, I wish to know."

She then nodded to demonstrate that she would comply with his wishes. *I guess I am a bit relieved that he finally knows. At any rate, until Sarah finds out what I have done.*

After Martha had gone to bed, with her door partly open as usual, she was again awakened by sounds coming from Sarah's bedchamber. Once she had quietly made her way to Sarah's door, the elderly servant listened for a moment. All was quiet now. But just as she was about to return to her own room, she heard her mistress cry out. Martha then hurried into the room. As had happened on many a night since her return from Boston, Sarah was tucked up at the head of her bed, sobbing. Scooting onto the bed, Martha reached over and gently placed her hand on the young woman's arm. As she had many times before, she reminded Sarah that she had nothing to fear. "Sarah, you are safe. That terrible man is dead." Then, shaking her head, she whispered to no one in particular, "I had hoped that after today she might also have put her nightmares behind her, just as she has her fear of leaving the yard."

Hearing the door opening behind her, Martha turned to see who had entered. Seeing the young woman's husband approaching, she rose to her feet. Surmising that he had come to check on his wife and had heard the sounds, silently, she patted his arm and then left the couple alone.

While taking a seat next to where Sarah was currently balled up weeping, Alexander spoke softly to her. He reassured her she was safe at home in her own bed.

Sarah was beginning to awaken at this point. While wiping her eyes, she caught a glimpse of someone sitting next to her. Hearing her husband speaking to her, she calmed a bit. Then, with an unsteady voice, she whispered, "I am sorry, Alexander. I must have had another bad dream. I did not mean to wake you."

Alexander moved in closer and lifted her chin. "I think it is time you come back to my—that is, *our* bedchamber, where I can comfort you when this happens." Sarah was thinking just then about how it had been upon their return the month before. Her husband had directed the servants to place her things in her private bedchamber. As she was not aware of the real reason he had done so, she didn't want to go along with his suggestion, not until she was certain that it wasn't out of obligation that he had said it, because of her nightmares. "Alexander, there is no need to give up your privacy. I shall be fine now."

Unable to comprehend why she would have said that about his privacy, he inquired, "I don't quite take your meaning? Did you believe it was my desire that we have separate bedchambers, owing to some need for privacy on my part?"

Feeling a little awkward, she forced herself to clarify. "I simply meant that things have changed between us since—"

As it began to fully dawn on Alexander what she had thought had been his reason for the separate rooms, astonished, he asked again, "Sarah, did you believe that I wanted it this way, with us away from each other each night?"

Dejectedly, she nodded. "I didn't blame you. Who would want a wife who had given birth to another man's child?"

Stunned by what he was hearing, Alexander pulled his wife into his arms. "Sarah, first of all, as I have said before, none of what happened was your fault. Secondly, I claimed the child as my own, did I not? And had he lived, I would have been honored for him to call me Father.

"Furthermore, I had your things brought into this bedchamber because I thought that, after what had happened, you might need time to yourself. I didn't want to be as demanding as I had been before by insisting that you share my bedchamber. Sarah, I thought we had settled all of this in Boston."

With relief washing over her, she leaned into his chest, and sighed. After a few moments, he lifted her and carried her to *their* room. Once they were settled in, bedcovers in place, Alexander spoke gently to his wife. "Sarah, I believe that in time, once you have allowed yourself to experience the way God intended it to be

317

between a man and a woman—a husband and wife—you shall have loving, cherished memories to overtake the terrible ones you now have—the very ones that have been frequenting you in the night." After blowing out the candle, he whispered, "Now go to sleep. If you have any more bad dreams, be sure and wake me."

While processing all that her husband had said, Sarah remained contemplative for a little while. *Perhaps he is right. Even though Matthew Raymond is dead, I often feel as if that terrible man still has power over me. He said as much when he proclaimed that I was his. I have never been able to get his words, or what happened, out of my mind.*

Realizing his wife hadn't answered him about waking him if she had another nightmare, Alexander whispered, "Sarah, did you hear what I said about waking me?" He wasn't certain she was even awake.

Hearing her husband's voice, Sarah responded, "Yes, Alexander. I heard you. I was just thinking about what you said with regard to supplanting the bad memories. Alexander...that terrible man, at times, made me feel that I belonged to him—as though I were his property. He even said as much."

"He couldn't make it so by wishing it, Sarah. No matter what he said, it simply isn't true. That is just another example of how mistaken he was in his thinking. God intended for a husband and wife to belong to each other. It was never His intention for any man to own a woman. I belong to you just as much as you belong to me.

What is more, it is never acceptable to take another man's wife, or for that matter, any woman against her will."

Once again, Sarah was quiet. Alexander allowed the silence, knowing his wife was thinking over what he had said. After a few moments, he felt her move closer to him.

"I love you, Alexander," she whispered. "I believe I would like to make new memories."

Wrapping his arms around his wife, Alexander asked, "Are you certain?"

"Yes, I want to feel as though I belong to you and that you belong to me—that we belong to each other. I want that man out of my thoughts."

"I truly believe that if we come together in this way, it shall help you put him, and the memories, behind you. Be that as it may, it is also going to take time and prayer to fully heal emotionally."

"I understand, Alexander."

When morning came, the couple had entered into a different kind of marriage. It was no longer an expedient marriage between strangers. It had now become a marriage in which each person felt loved and treasured. What is more, Sarah finally understood God's plan for how it should be between a husband and wife. She now felt safe in the arms of her loving husband, rather than terrified in the grasp of a man who had no right to claim her as his own.

Chapter 41

Two days later, Sarah awoke to her husband sitting next to her, waiting for her eyes to open. He had a surprise for her that couldn't wait. All he would say was that after she dressed, there was somewhere he needed to take her. A short time later, anxious to find out where they were going, Sarah was standing by the wagon, eagerly awaiting her husband.

Pleased at the sight of his wife's excitement regarding his surprise, Alexander approached and helped her onto the wagon. While attempting to hide a smile about the delight he knew he would see upon Sarah's face the moment she learned the truth, Alexander climbed up beside her.

Before long, they arrived at the Bleasdells' home. As they neared the front door, though Sarah was overjoyed that she would finally be seeing the children, she silently questioned why Alexander had said it was a surprise. *Has he forgotten that he already informed me that the children have been staying with the Bleasdells?*

Just then, Jonathan opened the door. As soon as Sarah entered the house, Elizabeth and Samuel Strout came running over to her. With tears in her eyes, she wrapped her arms around them. Hannah soon approached with a now three-year-old Mary in her arms. It had been some time since the little girl had seen Sarah, so she timidly observed her siblings' elation at seeing the somewhat familiar woman.

Samuel, full of excitement, was eager to share with the Swyndhursts all that he had been doing with Jonathan's son, David, who lived on the property as well. The young man explained that the Bleasdells' son had a little shop close to the house in which he made clocks and that David Bleasdell had been good enough to take him under his wing by showing him a thing or two about the clock-making business. Samuel had decided that he, too, would be a clockmaker when he grew up, and he said as much to the Swyndhursts, who were listening attentively. All of this was explained with Samuel scarcely taking a breath.

Sarah and Alexander, both attempting to hide a smile, had glanced at each other several times while the young man enlightened them on what he had been doing. It was clear to the couple that Samuel found David Bleasdell's work extraordinary. Elizabeth stood silently by, holding Sarah's hand while her brother chattered on.

Jonathan said quietly for Alexander's ears only that his son had been courting a young lady by the name of Abigail Colby and that having an extra set of hands around afforded David additional free time to spend with his lady. Alexander smiled at Jonathan's commentary on the matter.

After Jonathan and Hannah had escorted the couple into the parlor, they directed them to be seated. The older children had gone out of doors to play, while little Mary joined the adults in the parlor. As they all conversed, Alexander explained, mostly for his wife's benefit, that when Alice Strout had approached him with an unusual request, he had seen for himself the lack in Alice's abilities. Looking directly at his wife now, he further explained that it had been Alice's desire that he take the children so she might remove to Ipswich to be with her sister. Taking his wife's hand, he stated that without her there to help out, Alice had felt completely overwhelmed, and that after some prayer concerning the situation, he had agreed to take the children. He knew he had said some of this before, the day Sarah first made it all the way to the Strouts' former home, but he wanted to explain everything, to her, in context.

It was Hannah's turn to explain how the children had come to be with them. Gaining Sarah's attention, she began, "When Alexander learned of your whereabouts, he asked that we take care of the children so he might go and fetch you. Peter brought the children to us the day Alexander set off to collect you."

It still hadn't fully occurred to Sarah what all of this meant, that the children would be living at the Swyndhurst estate *with her*. All she could think about, just now, was her admiration for the Bleasdells and Alexander for looking after the children.

At last, Alexander lightly squeezed his wife's hand. Aware that she still had not taken his meaning concerning the children, he inquired, "Sarah, do you still not understand?"

Staring blankly at her husband, Sarah remained thoughtful, but silent. All at once, it came to her what they had all been trying to explain. Turning to the Bleasdells, and then back to her husband, she smiled widely.

Seeing that she had finally comprehended what he had been trying to say, with a chuckle, Alexander stated for the record, "The children are ours now, Sarah. Though they have been here for a time with the Bleasdells, when we set off for home in a little while, they will be accompanying us."

Astonished by all that she had heard, Sarah stood up, reached over and wrapped her arms around her husband and kissed him. "I cannot believe it! The children will be living with us?" she said with more of a question than a statement.

Chuckling, the amused husband then responded to her reaction to the news. "Now, that is more like it." Still grinning, he continued, "Yes, they shall be residing at our home, just as they had been before I set off for Boston." By now, the Bleasdells were also laughing at Sarah's reaction.

The older children soon returned. With her heart full of joy, Sarah quickly pulled them into her arms. They were her children now. She would no longer have to worry over them, for she would be there every day, from that time forward, to see to their care.

After a short visit, the Swyndhursts and the Strout children went on their way. Though the children had enjoyed their stay at the Bleasdells' home, they were overjoyed that Sarah had returned and they would be living with her. Sarah had always meant the world to them. Not having seen her for so long a time had been difficult for them. Samuel had been reassured that he could return to the Bleasdells' to work alongside David any time he wished. As the children snuggled with Sarah in the rear of the wagon, while riding along, they all felt loved and cherished, which was just as the tiny woman had always made them feel. Alexander, glancing back at his family, had to wipe away a tear or two.

By the time the children were tucked in their own beds that night, little Mary had again warmed to Mrs. Swyndhurst. Sarah kissed her on the head and thanked God for how things had turned out. She also prayed for Alice, knowing that it must have broken her heart to make such a decision. After blowing out the candle, she turned and left the room. Then, closing the door behind her, she noticed her husband standing there waiting for her. They walked arm in arm to their own bedchamber. As they entered, Alexander asked if Sarah believed he had made the right decision in allowing the children to live with them. By way of a response, reaching up, she placed her hands on his cheeks, and then, gently pulling him down to her level, she kissed him.

"Does that answer your question? To me, you are the most wonderful husband in the entire world! Though I married you out of obedience to my Father's wishes, I am now so glad that I did."

His countenance one of pure happiness, Alexander responded, "Thank you for allowing me in your life, Sarah. God has truly blessed me with the best *little* wife possible."

"Little! I'll give you little," Sarah responded teasingly, while pretending to poke her husband in the stomach.

Lifting her to his level, Alexander wrapped his arms tightly around her and said, "I love you my dearest...*little* wife."

Chapter 42

A month after the Strout children had returned to the Swyndhurst estate, the senior Mr. Swyndhurst arrived from England, for Alexander had sent word to his father months before that Sarah had gone missing. Alexander had also explained what had happened to cause her to flee. The elder Swyndhurst had set off for Amesbury the moment he was able to make the arrangements.

Upon entering the house, the father embraced his son. He was yet unaware that Sarah had been found and was safely at home where she belonged. "Alexander, tell me, has Sarah been found?" After so many weeks at sea, he couldn't wait a moment longer to know if the young woman was safe.

After Alexander had directed Peter to see to his father's things, he escorted his father to the kitchen. As they were making their way there, the son responded to his father's question. "Yes, Father, she has. There is much to tell. Let us get you something to eat while we talk."

Martha was presently in the kitchen when the father and son entered. "Mr. Swyndhurst! It is wonderful to see you. Your son mentioned that he thought it possible you would come once he sent word of what happened to Sarah."

"Yes, I had to come." Turning then to his son, he said, "Son, you had been through so much already, I simply couldn't leave you to manage the situation with Sarah, alone." He then turned to the elderly servant and said, "Martha, apart from you, of course."

Nodding, Alexander replied, "I fully expected that you would come. You may have noticed, I was not at all astonished to find that it was you at the door."

"Where is Sarah now?" the older man inquired.

"At the moment, she is out in the backyard with the children," responded Alexander.

"What children?" the father asked with a furrowed brow.

Martha and Alexander chortled at the strange expression upon the elder Swyndhurst's face. Glancing at each other, Martha and her employer were each thinking the same thing; there was much to explain.

"Father, while you eat I will tell you everything." Alexander then spent the next hour filling his father in on all that had happened. The elder Mr. Swyndhurst had only known about the attack and that Sarah had fled town. Now that he was aware of all that his daughter-in-law had been through, his heart felt heavy. He then thought of Sarah's father, his old friend Mr. Goodwin. *It would have broken the man's heart to learn that his daughter had suffered so. It had been his dying wish to see his daughter safely married. The very man from whom he had attempted to protect Sarah has now done his worst to the young woman.* Thinking about all of this, the older man believed it was a good thing that his friend had not lived to see what his precious daughter had suffered.

"Oh, Alexander! The poor girl! To think you may never have found her. And after all of this, the two of you have taken on someone else's children."

Alexander's father had yet to learn that his son and daughter-in-law had come to love each other deeply; thus, he thought that taking care of the Strout children, with the kind of arrangement his son and daughter-in-law had, might prove difficult for them.

Seeing the questioning expression on his father's face, Alexander informed him, "Father, my relationship with Sarah has greatly changed. Ours is no longer...well, as they say, 'a marriage of convenience'. We have come to love each other very much."

The older gentleman's eyes filled with tears upon hearing his son's words. "Alexander, Sarah's father and I had hoped and prayed that one day the two of you would come to love each other."

Beaming, Alexander responded, "Father, you have done a marvelous job of concealing your wishes. You must have known that neither Sarah nor I were prepared for a traditional marriage at the time everything was arranged."

"Precisely! Had we shared that we wanted more for the two of you, you may not have agreed to marry. In fact,

Sarah's father left me a written message to give his daughter, should the time ever come that the two of you found love."

"Father, do you have it with you? I am certain that Sarah would wish to see it."

"As a matter of fact, I do. I keep it with me always, kind of a reminder to pray for the two of you. After Sarah and I have had an opportunity to discuss the matter, I shall retrieve it from my belongings."

A few moments later, Sarah and the children, parched, entered the kitchen. "Mr. Swyndhurst! I had no idea that you were coming!" Sarah exclaimed with astonishment.

Taking her in his arms, the elderly gentleman replied, "Sarah, my dear girl, I had to come. My son sent word that you were missing. I set off almost immediately, not knowing what I would learn when I arrived. Thank the Lord it was good news."

Sarah felt great comfort within the arms of her father-in-law—much the same as she had always felt in the embrace of her own beloved father. Lingering there a moment, she responded, "Yes, we have all been through a great deal, but all of that is over now." Feeling a kiss atop her head, Sarah's eyes filled with tears. Without warning, the children began fighting with each other. Turning, Sarah motioned them over to her so as to introduce them to her father-in-law. "Children, this is Mr. Swyndhurst. Mr. Swyndhurst, this is Samuel," she said while moving the young man forward to greet the gentleman. As Elizabeth approached, Sarah placed her hand on the girl's arm. "This is Elizabeth, and over there by the door is Mary."

Appearing apprehensive, Mary remained where she was until Alexander made his way over to her. After lifting her in his arms, he turned and strolled over to his father. "Mary, this gentleman is my father, which, I believe, makes him your grandfather."

With her eyebrows lifting in surprise, Mary answered, "He...he is my grandfather?" Some of her friends at church had grandfathers. As she had watched them interacting, of a Sunday, the little girl had often thought grandfathers seemed rather nice.

The elderly gentleman approached and took the little girl from his son. "Yes, Mary, I am your grandfather now. What do you say to that?"

Wrapping her arms around his neck, she replied, "I...th...think it is very nice." Her two older siblings smiled at the young girl's reaction to their new acquaintance and family member.

By now, Alexander had come over beside his wife. Pulling her close, he leaned down and whispered, "I think she is going to like having my father around."

Smiling up at her husband, Sarah responded, "I believe I shall as well."

Later that night, after the children had gone to bed, Mr. Swyndhurst went up to fetch the note Mr. Goodwin had intended for his daughter. A few moments later, the senior Swyndhurst came strolling into the parlor. A little apprehensive about how to broach the subject of the note—for he didn't want to cause Sarah pain at the remembrance of her beloved father—he decided to come right out with it, for he knew no other way. "Sarah, I have something for you."

"What is it, Mr. Swyndhurst?" she asked, curious.

"Sarah, I would be delighted if you would address me as Alexander, or Father. In fact, to keep things straight around here, I think Father would be best. We wouldn't wish for two men by the name of Alexander to come running whenever you call," he said with a chuckle.

The idea of having someone to call Father pleased Sarah. "I believe I should dearly love calling you Father. If you are certain it is acceptable."

"Most assuredly," he said with a smile and a wink. He then took a seat next to his daughter-in-law. Reaching over, he placed the parchment in her hands. "Sarah, your father gave this to me. It was his intention that, when the time was right, I deliver it to you. I believe the time has come for you to know what your father had been praying for, regarding your marriage to my son."

Sarah's hands began to shake as she carefully held the missive from her father. Flanked on both sides by Swyndhurst men, Sarah felt their reassuring strength.

Seeing that his wife was struggling, Alexander reached over and placed his hand over hers.

"Sarah, would you rather have some privacy? If you wish, we shall leave you to yourself."

Turning toward her husband, Sarah softly replied, "No. I would rather that you both remain here with me." She then began to read in no more than a whisper.

"*My darling Sarah. If you are reading this, I have passed on and am now in the presence of our Lord. I couldn't go without letting you know that my greatest hope, other than that you share my faith in our Lord—which I know you do, is that you and Alexander may one day have the kind of relationship your mother and I had shared. One in which there is a strong commitment, love, understanding, and appreciation between you and your husband. I realize that the circumstances with Mr. Raymond have caused you to believe you would never want such a marriage.*"

Stopping there, she said, "If he only knew...but I am glad he never did." She then continued:

"*But, my dear girl, it is my honest belief that you shall be missing out on one of God's greatest gifts, next to His son, of course, if you do not allow yourself to have that kind of marriage. Having someone to love is a marvelous thing. Just as being loved by someone is also quite wondrous. Seeing as I have asked my good friend, Mr. Swyndhurst, not to give you this note until he felt the time was right, I have to believe that you and Alexander have found love, or it is simply that Mr. Swyndhurst believes a message from me might prompt you to do so. I love you my sweet daughter. If you haven't already done so, please open your heart and allow your husband in.*

"Your loving father"

With his daughter-in-law's head still bent over the missive, seeing the tears drop upon her lap, the elder Mr. Swyndhurst glanced at his son. As his son looked intently back at him, neither man felt sure of what to do for the petite woman sitting between them.

Finally, Sarah's husband spoke, "Sarah, are you all right?"

Wiping at her eyes, she responded in a shaky voice, "I just miss him so. He was such a wonderful father. This missive is further proof of his love for me." Glancing then at her father-in-law, she smiled and said, "I am much obliged to you for giving this to me. I assume you felt the same as Father, did you not?"

Extending his arms toward her, the elderly gentleman pulled Sarah over to him. After wrapping her in a tight embrace, he responded, "Indeed I did, and how could I have felt otherwise? I knew my son was marrying a marvelous young woman. Alexander's heart was so broken, I was not at liberty to share my feelings, similar to your father with you. It seems that God has made a way for the two of you to find each other, and without our assistance, no less," the elderly gentleman said, smiling warmly. "It would have pleased your father to know that our prayers for our children were answered. At least in that—our prayers—we can say that we helped the process along," he said with a chuckle.

At that moment, with her father-in-law and husband sitting there with love for her in their every expression, Sarah felt warm all over. Her father had seen fit to place her in a family where she would be loved, and her heavenly Father had moved on her heart that she would allow herself the love of her new family. Moreover, though she had never expected to, she loved them as well.

Postscript

Jonathan, Hannah, and their son, David Bleasdell/Blaisdell, are part of the authors' lineage. David was a clockmaker who resided in Amesbury, Massachusetts. Jonathan's father and grandparents arrived in the "new land" in 1635 on a ship called the *Angel Gabriel*, which wrecked not far off shore.

Susanna and William Pressey, part of the authors' lineage and main characters in book #2 of the *Unshakable Faith* series, lived and died in Massachusetts Bay Colony.

Susanna Pressey and Hannah Bleasdell were sisters, originally of the Jameson family. Their grandmother, Susanna North Martin, though a devout Christian, was hung as a witch in 1692.

David Bleasdell married Abigail Colby.

Genealogical outline provided by:
http://www.blaisdell.org/

Epilogue

In less than two years' time, everything had changed for Sarah. Distraught and in need of comfort, once again, she accompanies Mr. Hoyt on a visit to his daughter, Joanna's, house. Read book four of the Unshakable Faith series to find out what happens next for Sarah Anne Swyndhurst.

Other Books by Bryant and Dorman

Lost Love and Shipwrecked
Madeline Pike Finds Hope in the New Land

Grandmother's Namesake

Coming Soon

Sarah Anne's Faithful Friends

17379718R00191

Made in the USA
Middletown, DE
22 January 2015